A CO...
OF
DREAMS

Complimentary Copy
NOT FOR SALE
eLectio Publishing
eLectioPublishing.com

A COLLISION OF DREAMS

George Dalton

ELECTIO PUBLISHING
LITTLE ELM, TX
WWW.ELECTIOPUBLISHING.COM

A Collision of Dreams

By George Dalton

Copyright 2014 by George Dalton

Cover Design by eLectio Publishing, LLC

ISBN-13: 978-1-63213-038-9

Published by eLectio Publishing, LLC

Little Elm, Texas

http://www.eLectioPublishing.com

Printed in the United States of America

Without limiting the rights under copyright reserved above, no part of this publication may be reproduced, stored in or introduced into a retrieval system, or transmitted, in any form, or by any means (electronic, mechanical, photocopying, recording, or otherwise), without the prior written permission of both the copyright owner and the above publisher of this book.

If you purchased this book without a cover, you should be aware that this book is stolen property. It was reported as "unsold and destroyed" to the publisher and neither the author nor the publisher has received any payment for the "stripped book."

The scanning, uploading, and distribution of this book via the Internet or via any other means without the permission of the publisher is illegal and punishable by law. Please purchase only authorized electronic editions, and do not participate in or encourage electronic piracy of copyrighted materials. Your support of the author's rights is appreciated.

Publisher's Note

This is a work of fiction. Names, characters, places, and incidents either are the product of the author's imagination or are used fictitiously, and any resemblance to actual persons, living or dead, business establishments, events, or locales is entirely coincidental.

The publisher does not have any control over and does not assume any responsibility for author or third-party websites or their content.

This book is dedicated to

My beautiful wife Jean.

Each woman in the story reflects some of her.

CONTENTS

CHAPTER ONE The Girl in His Dreams 1
CHAPTER TWO The Man in the Mirror 5
CHAPTER THREE Sam Rides Away 11
CHAPTER FOUR Looking for a Horse 17
CHAPTER FIVE Collecting Some Money 23
CHAPTER SIX Going Back 29
CHAPTER SEVEN Mattie Ann Lives in Town 33
CHAPTER EIGHT Aunt Millie Encourages Mattie Ann 39
CHAPTER NINE Guys Get a Bath 41
CHAPTER TEN Indian Attack 45
CHAPTER ELEVEN Sam Takes the Body Home 55
CHAPTER TWELVE Searching for Sam 61
CHAPTER THIRTEEN Sam Found Something Special 63
CHAPTER FOURTEEN Waiting to Hear Something 67
CHAPTER FIFTEEN Taggert Family 73
CHAPTER SIXTEEN Somebody New Making Whiskey 77
CHAPTER SEVENTEEN Mattie Ann's letter 81
CHAPTER EIGHTEEN Building the Fence 85
CHAPTER NINETEEN Mattie Ann Talks to Rosa 91
CHAPTER TWENTY Sam Talks to Mr. Carville 93
CHAPTER TWENTY-ONE Outlaws Can't Find Sam 97
CHAPTER TWENTY-TWO Sam Hires Juan 99
CHAPTER TWENTY-THREE The Horses 101
CHAPTER TWENTY-FOUR Mattie Ann Gets Sick 103
CHAPTER TWENTY-FIVE Training the Horses 107
CHAPTER TWENTY-SIX What Will the Future Hold? 111
CHAPTER TWENTY-SEVEN The Dead Cougar 117
CHAPTER TWENTY-EIGHT Sam Meets a Girl on the Train 123
CHAPTER TWENTY-NINE The Kiss 129
CHAPTER THIRTY The Letter 131
CHAPTER THIRTY-ONE The Prettiest Girl in Town 133
CHAPTER THIRTY-TWO Getting the New Bull into the Bowl 135
CHAPTER THIRTY-THREE The Bull 139

Chapter	Title	Page
CHAPTER THIRTY-FOUR	Surprise Behind the Waterfall	145
CHAPTER THIRTY-FIVE	The Storm	153
CHAPTER THIRTY-SIX	Kidnapping Mattie Ann and Rosa	157
CHAPTER THIRTY-SEVEN	The Meeting in the Chief's Lodge	163
CHAPTER THIRTY-EIGHT	Searching for Mattie Ann	165
CHAPTER THIRTY-NINE	Sam Tries to Trade for the Women	169
CHAPTER FORTY	The Fight	173
CHAPTER FORTY-ONE	Coming Home	181
CHAPTER FORTY-TWO	Taggert's Arrest	183
CHAPTER FORTY-THREE	Mattie's Worry	189
CHAPTER FORTY-FOUR	Rescuing the Women and Kids	193
CHAPTER FORTY-FIVE	Naming the Ranch	199
CHAPTER FORTY-SIX	Encounter with a Rattlesnake	201
CHAPTER FORTY-SEVEN	Searching for Sam	207
CHAPTER FORTY-EIGHT	The Rescue	213
CHAPTER FORTY-NINE	Going for the Herd	215
CHAPTER FIFTY	A Scary Sound	221
CHAPTER FIFTY-ONE	Juan's First Train Ride	225
CHAPTER FIFTY-TWO	Sally Jo's Stepfather	231
CHAPTER FIFTY-THREE	The Shoot-Out	237
CHAPTER FIFTY-FOUR	Revenge is Sweet	243
ACKNOWLEDGMENTS		249

CHAPTER ONE
The Girl in His Dreams

"Get your hands off the lady." Sam stared at the thug's gun. Better keep an eye on his hands in case he tries to go for it.

Who was this jasper? Sam couldn't stand there and let some drunken fool assault a lady, in broad daylight on Main Street. Especially one as pretty as she was.

The young lady jerked away from her attacker and pressed her back against the splintery old wood on the front of the building.

The thug hunched his shoulders and froze, then turned his head and glared over his shoulder. "Aw, we're just funnin'." He moved his right foot back and whirled toward Sam. His pistol came up as he turned. Flame shot from the barrel of his gun. The bullet missed and splintered the boards at Sam's feet.

Sam jumped back and slapped his palm down on his gun. It slipped leather like lightning and fired twice, so fast it sounded like one loud blast rattling the glass in the storefront windows. People peered through open doorways like rabbits peeking out of their holes, curious, but safe. One wore a plaid shirt, another a tan vest, and a third was in a faded blue denim shirt. One by one the curious eased out onto the street and gawked at the body lying on the boardwalk.

Sam glanced at the young woman, who held her hand over her mouth, her eyes wide with fear. *WOW, she looks like the kind of girl I'd like to marry someday. This is probably not a good way for me to meet her.*

A big swarthy man wearing a badge ran toward him. His boots echoed on the boards as he thundered down the boardwalk. His presence dominated the scene, like an actor rushing onto a theater stage. "What's going on here? What happened?"

One man said, "Marshal, it was a fair shooting."

"One of them Taggerts came busting out of the Boot Strap Saloon and almost knocked this lady down," one woman said.

Another man stepped out from the crowd and pointed to the man lying on the boardwalk and said, "He tried to get ugly with this young lady and the young feller spoke up for her. Taggert drew first and shot at this fella and missed."

The first man pointed at Sam, "This'n didn't miss."

The marshal turned to Sam and asked, "Is that the way it happened?"

Sam stood there feeding two new shells into his six-gun. "Why don't you ask the lady? She's standing right there."

"Mattie Ann, what happened?"

Mattie Ann took a deep breath and said, "Yes, sir." She pointed to the man lying on the ground. "That man grabbed me and tried to kiss me. It was awful." She then nodded toward Sam. "When he told the man to leave me alone, the man started shooting."

Her whole body shook as she started to cry.

Several women rushed to her. One put her arm around the girl's shoulder. Another picked up her shopping basket and gathered the contents scattered across the ground.

The marshal took a silver dollar out of his pocket and placed it on the dead man's chest. He turned to Sam. "You goin' to be in town long?"

Sam cut his eyes back to Mattie Ann. "I'm not sure. It depends if I can find work."

The marshal turned to a bystander and said, "Get Big Ed to take care of the body."

Turning back to Sam, he said, "Come over to the office. I've got some papers we'll need to fill out. Everybody says it was an honest killing, so I don't have no complaint with you."

As they walked to his office, the marshal said, "Well, son, you haven't been in town an hour and you've bought yourself a pack of trouble. The fellow you shot was Billy Wayne Taggert."

"I never heard of him."

"You will. You'll hear from his gang. The Taggerts are a tight-knit bunch. They came out of the mountains of Tennessee a few years back. They live up around Lone Tree Canyon. The army thinks they've been making moonshine whiskey and sellin' it to the Indians, ever since they got here. We've also had some stage holdups and cattle rustlin' that never happened before they came. Ain't nobody ever caught 'em doing it. Everybody thinks they're the gang that's doing it though. I'd bet a month's pay that what everybody thinks is right."

"Why don't somebody go up there and arrest 'em?"

"A couple of US Marshals came in here one time and went up the canyon to serve a warrant on one of 'em. The marshals never came back. We searched, but couldn't find hide nor hair of 'em anywhere. You keep alert with your eyes lookin' around ya, young fella. Those Taggerts are a bad bunch." The marshal opened his office door and motioned for Sam to take a seat. "Where'd ya learn to shoot like that?"

"It comes natural. You just point your gun like pointing your finger at something and you shoot. Plus, last summer I worked in a traveling carnival show with an old man who was a trick shooter and he taught me some stuff."

"Son, why are you here?"

"I'm looking for a job right now and, as soon as I can save up some money, I want to homestead some land and start a ranch of my own."

"Are you married?"

"No, not yet. I was hoping to meet a gal in these parts and get married. After I get my ranch going."

"Well, you make enemies mighty quick, but you may be in luck. Joe Carville owns the biggest spread this side of El Paso. He has only one daughter. The pretty girl you took up for is Mattie Ann Carville. Her daddy puts a lot of stock in her. More than he does his land holdings. Especially since his wife died a couple of years back. Now, I don't fault you for shootin' ole Billy Wayne. He was rotten to the bone."

The marshal's chair squeaked as he shifted his weight, "I cotton to you, son. However, I can't have any more shootin' in my town. We're peaceful folks. Here's what I want ya to do. Get on your horse first thing in the mornin' and ride south about three miles. Take the trail west about six miles and you'll find a big ranch house sittin' way back off the road on your left side. That's the Carville place. You talk to Joe. I'm sure Mattie Ann will have already told him what happened. You tell 'im you're looking for work. He'll probably hire ya. Don't come back to town for a while. Now, if he doesn't hire ya, get back on that horse of yours and ride out of here as fast as you can."

The marshal picked up the blackened coffee pot off the iron stove and refilled his cup, then said, "The Taggert gang is gonna be riled up. Now, you be careful because those people are mean folks and you killed one of' em."

"But he drew on me first."

"Won't make no never-mind to them. Now go on over to the saloon and get yourself a drink and tell Stella I said you need a room. Then, in the mornin', you get out of town. You do have some money, don'tcha?"

"Yes sir, but I ain't no coward."

"Son, I never said you were a coward, but if you try to go against that whole gang, you're a dang fool. Now go on over there and get a good night's sleep, then straddle that bronc of yours and ride out of here at first light."

Standing up and putting on his hat, Sam said, "Thank you, marshal."

Sam's spurs jingled as he walked back and untied his buckskin. He stepped into the saddle and trotted to the livery stable. After stripping off the saddle and bridle, he grabbed a handful of dry hay and brushed the horse down. Not until after his horse was cared for would he check on a room for himself.

Sam thought, *I'll ride on, but surely the marshal is overreacting.*

CHAPTER TWO
The Man in the Mirror

Standing in the door of the livery stable, Sam glanced up the street: just a few people going about their business like nothing had happened. Sam decided he needed a beer to wash the trail dust out of his throat. As he walked to the saloon, he glanced at the sun. *Must be two more hours till sundown.* An old brown hound dog lay sleeping in the street next to the boardwalk. The dog opened his eyes and looked up as he approached. Sam reached down and rubbed the old fellow's ears. "How are you doing, old one?"

The old dog's tail thumped against the hard-packed ground as if to say, "Well old boy, I won't bother you if you don't bother me."

Sam walked up and looked over the bat wing doors. The saloon looked like every saloon he'd seen—a long wooden bar ran along the back of the room, with tables scattered around. *I can't believe that just a few minutes ago I had to shoot a man, right where I'm standing. I could be the one lying dead right now.* He felt a cold chill start under his hat and go clear down to his boots. *I don't want to keep thinking like this. All I want to think about is a beautiful girl in a blue dress.*

Pushing the bat wing doors open with his left hand, he stepped into the sawdust on the floor. In one quick glance, he saw a dozen dusty cowhands lounged about, trying to wash down the trail dust with cheap whiskey. Nobody paid him any mind. Sam walked to the end of the polished mahogany bar and stood where he could watch the whole room as he ordered a beer. When it came, he noticed his hands tremble a little as he lifted the mug.

A sudden noise caused him to glance up into the mirror on the back wall. A droop shouldered, whiskered old man of about fifty stomped in through the doors, followed by a younger man.

The old man's eyes locked on Sam. "Hey you! They're saying over at the bank my boy got shot. Are you the one who done it?"

A COLLISION OF DREAMS

The man stood with his feet spread apart, his hands on the butt of his gun. All sound in the room came to an abrupt hush. Even the piano player quit without finishing the ragtime tune he had been playing.

Sam knew he had never seen the man before, but he recognized trouble when he saw it. He swallowed the last of his beer in one gulp. With a slow, deliberate motion, placed his mug back on the bar. People scrambled to get out of the line of fire. Sam threw some money down. He deliberately turned around and walked with even purposeful steps toward the angry old man. Sam stopped right in front of him. Beads of sweat popped out on the older man's upper lip. He obviously didn't expect someone to close the distance. Everybody knows that in a gunfight you don't want your opponent too close, because, when the shooting starts, you're both liable to end up full of holes like a leaky washtub.

The challenger took a step back.

Sam's fist slammed into his chin with a crack heard around the room.

The old man flew backward and sprawled on the sawdust floor. He blinked several times and shook his head, struggled to get up off the floor. As he tried to get up, he fumbled for his holstered gun. Sam's gun sprang into his hand. Rather than pull the trigger, he tried to bend the barrel of his six-shooter over the man's skull. Blood splattered on the sawdust from a six-inch gash in the man's head. His eyes rolled back in their sockets. He was out cold.

Sam turned the pistol until the muzzle pointed straight at the younger man, who blocked the doorway. "Get him out of here, unless you want to challenge this gun."

Reaching down, the man by the door grabbed the old man off the floor and lifted him by the shoulders, backing out through the bat wing doors. The old man's boot heels dragged through the sawdust. The younger man looked at Sam and said, "This ain't over, we'll see you in hell."

Sam walked back to the bar and ordered another beer. The piano player started to play "The Buffalo Gal Rag." Conversation resumed as if nothing had happened. Again, Sam's hands shook as he lifted his glass. He stared into the mirror. *What am I going to do? This looks like a good place to settle down and that has to be the prettiest gal I've ever seen. Things have started going downhill pretty fast. According to the marshal, I guess I have made a bad enemy.*

The woman behind the bar came back and leaned her elbows on the countertop. "Man, you've bought a pack of trouble. Do you know who that was?"

"I guess he's the daddy of the drunk who attacks ladies doing their shopping, since he asked, 'Who shot my boy?'"

"He's head of the Taggert gang. Now you're going to have the entire murdering bunch after you. You should've killed him."

"Why? He was grieving over his boy. Are you Stella? The marshal said to ask you if you had a room for tonight."

"We have rooms. We're not full yet."

"How much?"

"Depends. Do you want to sleep by yourself or with somebody?"

Sam stared at her, a mischievous grin starting to spread across his face.

Her cheeks flamed. "I mean do you want a room by yourself, or to share one with another cowhand?"

A big grin spread across his face.

"You're getting a double. Cost you fifty cents, cash in advance, smart aleck," she said, laughing as she held out her palm for the money.

As he stowed his duffle in the room, he thought, *What should I do now? Should I turn tail and run or should I stay around and put up a fight?*

* * *

Randolph Taggert was wide-awake and fighting mad by the time he got to the shack he called home. He stormed into the house, grabbed a jug of whiskey off the shelf, plopped down at the kitchen table, and bellowed, "You boys get in here."

He watched as the whole gang shuffled in around the table. Everybody knew something bad had happened.

Ma Taggert asked, "Pa, what's the matter?"

"Some jaybird done killed Billy Wayne, that's what's the matter."

"Oh my goodness." Then she stopped and looked at Pa. "What happened to your head? You're bleedin'. Let me get a coal-oil rag and stop the bleedin'."

"Get away from me, woman. The no-account that shot Billy Wayne is still there in town. Y'all hear me? I want that son of a gun killed. I want him dead. Jess, you and Mort wait until daylight. I want you to ride into town and find out who that hombre is. Now don't go gettin' yourself kilt. You just find out his name and where we can find 'im. Turn around and hurry back here. We have some plannin' to do. He's fast with them six-shooters, so we need to figger out somethin'. Boys, I want that jaybird kilt. Ain't nobody gonna kill one of my boys and live to tell about it."

* * *

"Oh, Aunt Millie, I have never been so scared and thrilled at the same time in my life. Thing happened so fast. First a smelly brute crashed into me." She shuddered and said, "Then, to make things worse, he tried to kiss me."

Frowning, she said, "His clothes were dirty, and he even had tobacco juice on his beard. I really felt like I was going to get sick and throw up."

"Then what happened?"

"A handsome cowboy yelled at him to take his hands off of me. Then I couldn't believe it—the brute whipped out a gun and tried to shoot him for taking up for me."

"Sweetheart, were you hurt?"

"I'm alright. When he turned to shoot the cowboy, I jerked my arm away from him. Everything happened so fast. That gun was loud. My ears hurt. Aunt Millie, I've never been so scared in my life.

"The next thing I knew the big brute fell on the boardwalk. I was really confused. Part of me was glad when I realized the cowboy had shot him, and part of me was sad that a man had died. Does that make sense?"

"Mattie Ann, maybe you should get to know this knight. It is not every day you get to meet a real man of gallantry."

"What if he was just passing through and he's already gone? If I do meet him, I will thank him for taking up for me. But there is no way I will be interested in any man who is not a Christian."

CHAPTER THREE
Sam Rides Away

Sam climbed into the saddle and rode out when the first rays of morning sun crept slowly over the horizon. The town was still sleeping. It looked so peaceful. He heard the screen door slam and a rooster start to crow, and off in the distance he heard the creak of a pump handle as somebody drew water. A silver morning light cast shadows in hues of blue and grey. He felt a melancholy settle over him. Would it always be this way? Then anger started to set in.

I hate it when people look down on me, like I'm a drifter and a beggar. It goes against the grain to tuck tail and run. However, if I want to find some land and build a home for a wife and kids, I don't need to get into a gang war.

At the edge of town, instead of turning south toward the Carville ranch, he took the trail west. "Buck, I guess that's not the town we've been looking for. Whaddaya say we mosey west? Who knows what we'll come to."

The rest of the morning Sam rode easy in the saddle with the warm sun on his face. Along about evening, he was feeling tired and lonely. He said, "Buck, we need to find a place to camp. I need something I can cook for supper. With all this game around, I see no reason to go to bed hungry."

He lifted his rifle out of the scabbard, then pushed it back into the saddle boot and said, "Buck, I don't want to advertise that I'm a man alone passing through this country. There are still Indians around. I think I'll dig out the old slingshot my grandpa gave me before he died, and kill one of those prairie chickens."

Sam reached back to his right-hand saddlebag and dug around until he found the slingshot. He dug deeper in the bag and found a small sack of carefully chosen rocks. He loaded a rock into the slingshot and waited. Soon a big fat prairie chicken flew up out of the grass. His mouth watered when he thought about the flavor of roasted chicken. SNAP! He let the rock fly.

What? He thought his eyes had deceived him. The bird kept flying. It was a clean miss.

"Well, Buck, it's been a while since I shot this thing. I guess I need some practice."

He notched another rock in the slingshot. Three more times he shot at prairie chickens. Three times, he missed. *I could kill one quick with my pistol. No, you don't want everyone within a mile or so to hear the shot.*

"Buck, I'm going to have to chance a gunshot or go hungry. Indians are a good enough reason a man riding alone shouldn't advertise where he is. There is another reason. You never knew when outlaws might be around."

All at once, a rabbit hopped up. When he did, Sam started to whistle a low tune. The curious rabbit ran a short distance and stopped, then raised his ears to listen to the strange sound. As soon as the rabbit stopped, Sam was ready. He let fly another rock.

Yeehaw! "Buck, now I've got something I can cook for supper."

The sun was painting the western horizon with beautiful shades of purple and orange when he heard the sound of trickling water. Reining the horse off the trail toward the sound, he found a creek with fresh water flowing and plenty of grass to picket Buck on. "This is a good place. Buck, you can eat and drink all you want." He patted the buckskin's neck as he stripped the heavy saddle off and let the mustang have a playful roll in the grass.

In only a few minutes, Sam had gathered dry wood and built a small fire. He chose wood that would not give off much smoke. He did not want to advertise his camp to a group of passing Indian bucks. Soon the smell of coffee brewed on an open fire filled the evening air as Sam skinned the rabbit he had killed with his slingshot. His stomach growled when he smelled the aroma of roasting rabbit.

His mouth watered—he had not eaten anything since breakfast, but some hard tack chewed while in the saddle.

"Buck, you know, this ain't a bad life—we've got plenty to eat and freedom to roam where we want. I don't know why I've got such a hankering to settle down in one place, but that feeling is powerful strong in me."

The sun faded behind the trees and the night air grew colder. Darkness descended upon the valley, like a curtain in a theater. A sip of the strong black coffee helped keep the chill away. The rabbit tasted good and relieved the hunger pains eating on him. The croak of frogs by the creek, crickets in the grass, and a coyote serenading the moon played a symphony as he ate. He loved this part of being on the trail. But there existed one major problem—this life sure got lonely.

Although he loved the freedom of the trail, it did nothing to quince the longing deep inside to have some land, a wife, and family. Sam thought of the girl with the blue eyes and blonde hair, back in Cactus Tree. She sure was pretty. *Too bad I didn't have a chance to stay around and get to know her. She looked like she would have made a great wife and a mother for strong sons.*

"I shouldn't even think about a lady like her, Buck. Her daddy owns a big ranch and all I've got is you, a saddle, and twenty-seven dollars in my pocket. She sure is the prettiest thing I've ever seen though. When I close my eyes, I can still see her wearing a beautiful blue dress, with a mountain of blonde curls piled on top of her head. I see the deepest blue eyes I've ever seen."

He sat enjoying the quiet of the evening, when suddenly the buckskin snorted. Sam glanced at the horse. It had been a wild mustang until a year ago. Horses like Buck made the best watchdogs. Nothing was going to sneak up on one of them. The horse stood facing the trail with his ears pointing forward. Sam grabbed his rifle, easing back into the shadows. Looking over the brush, he could see his bed gear rolled up near the fire. From a distance, it would appear that someone lay sleeping.

A COLLISION OF DREAMS

Quietly, he waited in the brush. He glanced back at Buck, his ears still pointed forward. All was quiet. Sam reached down and wiped the sweat off his palms on his pants leg. Firelight created a light show as it danced on the leaves around the small clearing. He forced his breathing to slow down. Straining his ears, he heard the sound of muffled steps as a horse walked toward him.

Sam thought, *He's probably got socks on that horse's hooves to keep down the noise.*

Sam held his breath and raised his rifle.

That dude didn't stop and call to the camp like most people do. Sam thought, *He is either up to no good or a dang fool. To sneak up to a campfire at night is a good way for a man to get his head blowed off.*

Even though the night air was cool, Sam wiped the sweat from his palms on his pants leg again and gripped the rifle a little tighter. Against the starlit sky, Sam recognized the silhouette of a man on a horse. The rider appeared to look all around as he came. Sam felt sweat trickle down his nose, re-tightened his grip on his rifle, and waited as the rider got closer. He heard the soft swish of the grass as the horse moved toward the campfire.

He's probably trying to see if anybody else is around.

Soon the nightrider rode close enough for the light from the fire to illuminate his features. A man in a plaid shirt sat on the horse with a rifle in his hands. Sam wondered, *Am I asleep and dreaming this?*

The stillness and quiet shattered when the night erupted with gunfire. Echoes of three blasts bounced off the hills. The stranger shot into Sam's bedroll. Sam pointed his rifle at the flash and fired. The body of the man flew off the back end of the horse and landed with a thud in the dust. Sam's ears still rang from the sound of gunfire. His ears picked up another sound. Horse's hooves pounded the hard-packed dirt as someone raced away.

A dove called to its mate from the brush, and a coyote serenaded the moon. Sam held his breath. He waited to make sure the other rider didn't come back. When he felt it was safe, he carefully walked into the light from the fire. With his rifle in his right hand, he reached down and wrapped a rag around a stick. He stuck the rag-wrapped stick into the campfire to use as a torch.

He did not recognize the man lying on the ground. He felt a chill go through him when he realized that two men had come in with the intention of killing him. Were they looking for someone to rob or were they part of the gang from Cactus Tree? Could the Taggerts have tracked him? He was sure of one thing: The buckskin had saved his life.

If I had gotten into that bedroll, I'd be buzzard meat right now.

The dead man wore a fine-tooled pistol belt, and a nearly new six-gun lay on the ground next to him. Sam went through the man's pockets, where he found four dollars and some smoking tobacco.

The man's horse shied away when Sam reached for it. Sam spoke to the gelding in soothing tones. He held out his hand. Hesitantly, the horse came to him. He petted the roan's neck and talked softy as he stripped off the saddle and let it drop, then took the horse to the creek and picketed it with Buck.

He pulled the man's body down near the creek, covered it with sand, and piled rocks and brush over it.

Sam did not want to be surprised again. He moved his bedroll away from the fire. For hours, he lay rolled up in his blanket, with the dead man's pistol clutched in his hand. He listened to the sound of a coyote's howl in the distance. The first time he heard the sound of a small animal moving in the trees, he reached over and pulled his rifle under the bedroll with him. Each time he closed his eyes, he saw the muzzle flashes over again. Eventually, exhaustion took over and he fell asleep, clutching the six-shooter in one hand, his rifle lying next to him on the other side.

In the morning light, he found that a brand new Winchester 73 repeating rifle was in the scabbard attached to the saddle he had taken off the horse. A search of the dead man's saddlebags found a slab of bacon wrapped in brown paper. In another pocket, he found about 100 rounds of .44 shells, but nothing revealing the man's name. Bacon sizzled over the fire and coffee brewed while he led both horses to the stream and let them drink. Then he picketed them near the fire. Squatting on his heels near the fire, he chewed the bacon and sipped horseshoe coffee (cowhands said coffee had to be strong enough to float a horseshoe in to be considered real coffee). As he listened to the two horses munching grass and the crackle of a wood fire, he considered what to do.

It seemed the farther west he went, the more trouble he found. He cheered himself with the notion that he now had two horses, two saddles, two pistols, two rifles—one a new Winchester 73—plus a slab of bacon.

It sure tasted good. Just the smell made him feel better.

He chuckled and said aloud, "Buck, at this rate we'll be rich in a month. We'll have enough to settle down, find a wife, and raise a family like I always swore I would.

"I wonder who the other rider was that rode away. You don't suppose he doubled back to jump me when I ride out of camp, do you?"

CHAPTER FOUR
Looking for a Horse

When Sam walked back to the trail, he found two sets of tracks. He squatted down and looked closely at the tracks, as he wanted to memorize them. The signs on the ground told him that one horse and rider rode into his camp while the other one stayed back and waited. When he shot the first guy, the lookout took off at a dead run.

As he continued to search for more signs, he found steel gray hair stuck to the bark of a tree where a steel gray horse had rubbed against it.

"This horse was a gray steel dust." He looked closer and saw that the right front shoe had a crack in it.

Sam pushed his hat back and stared at the tracks. He thought to himself, *Look for a steel gray-colored mustang with a cracked right front shoe—if the horse does not throw the shoe before he gets to town. It should be easy to locate the horse.*

The fear of the night dissolved into anger in the morning. He hurriedly packed up his gear, wasting no time in getting on the trail of the steel gray horse and its rider.

As Sam rode into the next town, he eyed every horse he passed as he looked for a steel gray-colored mustang. He went straight to the livery stable, put the horses in a stall, and stowed one rifle, the dead man's saddle, and the extra gun belt in the tack room. He checked every horse in the barn. No steel dust was in there.

As he stepped out into the bright sunlit street, everything appeared to be peaceful. He saw a couple of men smoking in front of the barbershop. A lady came out and swept the boardwalk in front of a shop. A lazy old hound dog lay in the street. Sam smiled as he walked by. The dog thumped his tail on the hard-packed ground.

He slowly walked along checking the horses tied to the hitching rail. He found a steel dust horse in front of the saloon. Sam stopped, reached down, and lifted the horse's right front leg. His stomach did a summersault when he spied the cracked shoe. He held the horse's hoof in his left hand and a Winchester in his right.

A giant unshaven man came out of the saloon and bellowed, "Get away from my horse."

Sam stood up and looked over the horse's back and found a six-foot, two-hundred-and-forty-pound monster of a man glaring at him.

The man sneered at Sam, "You ain't nothin' but a kid. I'll whoop the tar out of you for messin' with my horse."

Sam stood at the right front shoulder of the horse. He stared at the big man on the other side. The man had not noticed that Sam held a Winchester under the horse's neck—the end of the barrel six inches from the man's belt buckle.

Surprise registered on the big man's face at the sound of a hammer being cocked. Blood washed from his face and his eyes grew wide when he looked down at the end of a barrel that appeared to be the size of a cannon, only six inches from his belly button.

People up and down the street heard the loud talk. A crowd started to gather.

Sam spoke loud enough for everyone to hear. "This dry gulcher and his partner tried to kill me on the trail last night. They shot right into my bedroll that was lying by the fire. I wasn't in it because my horse warned me we had company. When his partner shot holes in my bedroll, I shot back. I buried his partner out there by the trail. In fact, the horse that used to be his horse is in the livery stable, right now. The rifle I am holding belonged to the dead man. One dry gulcher got away riding a steel dust with a cracked shoe on the right front hoof. This steel dust here has a cracked shoe on the right front and this hombre just admitted it's his."

Beads of sweat appeared on the man's face. "Now see here, this kid don't know what he's talking about. I ain't never shot no bedroll."

The men in the crowd scowled at the owner of the steel dust and women murmured to each other, "Who are we supposed to believe?"

Sam jerked the rifle out from under the horse's neck and stepped around the horse. "Mister, you shuck that gun belt. I'll give you a chance to see if you can whoop the tar out of me." Sam gritted his teeth and glared at the man, daring him to make a move.

The stranger spit in the dirt and, with a smirk, unbuckled his gun belt and handed it to a nearby spectator. He snorted and bobbed his head as if he'd already won. Sam dropped the hammer on the Winchester and handed it along with his gun belt to a man standing near the horse. The bushwhacker had about fifty pounds on him, but Sam didn't care. He was mad.

He'd been fighting since his head was barely tall enough to reach a stirrup. When your ma is a widow and you're dirt poor, every bully in town thinks you're fair game. Those 100-pound sacks of feed he had lifted last summer, when he'd worked in a feed mill, had put iron-hard muscles on his arms and shoulders.

Sam stepped around the horse's tail. Before he squared away to face the man, the big man rushed forward and slammed a giant fist into the side of Sam's head. Lights flashed in his head. It felt like he had been struck with an axe handle. That big dude's fist was rock hard. The blow knocked Sam into the hitching rail.

Had he made a mistake and let his youthful anger get him in trouble?

The bushwhacker moved in for a quick finish.

Sam was ready. He planted both feet and started swinging. He hit the man in the belly with his right fist. The punch was perfectly timed and caught the man coming in. The bushwhacker dropped his fist down to protect his midsection, leaving him wide-open for a left jab. Sam smashed a left into the bushwhacker's face. Blood gushed from a gash the size of a small canyon in the bushwhacker's right cheek just below his eye.

The big man went berserk. He started swinging with both hands. Sam followed up with a left to the chin. The man grabbed Sam, one hand on his collar and the other one grabbing his belt buckle. Lifting him up, he threw Sam over the hitching rail. Dust flew up from the boards when Sam landed with a thud. The crowd heard a whoosh as the wind was knocked out of him.

The big man vaulted over the rail and landed on his feet like a two-hundred-forty-pound cat. His intent was to cave in Sam's ribs with vicious kicks. He drew back his right foot for a bone-breaking kick. Sam flipped over and dived into the leg the man was standing on. He tumbled and fell back into the street.

Sam was the first one on his feet. It took a moment to get his breath back. When the big man got up, Sam swung a work-hardened right fist that shattered the man's nose. Blood splattered. The man's head snapped back, leaving his body wide open. Sam slammed a solid right to the belly.

Sam shook his right hand. *Oh, that hurts. I must have hit his belt buckle. My hand really hurts.* This time the big man staggered back. When he did, Sam slammed a teeth-crunching right to his mouth, again drawing blood. Adrenalin pounded through Sam's veins and the lust to fight was now upon him. He looked like he was warmed up now and actually enjoyed the combat.

The big man charged, swinging with both fists. His fists thudded and thumped.

Sam wobbled and staggered under the power of the big man's blows. He shook his head as if to clear out the cobwebs, then ducked inside the big dudes blow's and battered his body with a vicious attack to his midsection again. The man's mouth hung open and he gasped for air.

All at once, Sam appeared to know he was going to win. He stepped back and feinted with a left then whipped up an uppercut that caught the big man under the chin. The big head flew back, and his knees buckled. His big body went down in the dusty street.

Sam stepped back for a few seconds to allow the man a chance to get up. As soon as he was up, Sam stepped in again. He missed connecting with a left to the anger-contorted face because the bushwhacker suddenly turned his head to the side.

Sam tasted blood when a wicked right caught him on the jaw, making him stagger back. They stood toe-to-toe, throwing punches. Both fighters were bloody, sweating and heaving for air. Sam waded in and slammed a left to the jaw and a solid right that cut another gash over the man's eye. Now blood seeped into both eyes. Punch-drunk, the big man swayed like the deck was pitching under him.

Suddenly the bushwhacker reached inside his shirt and whipped out a gun.

Sam froze. *That's the hard thing I hit.*

The man who held Sam's Winchester tossed him the gun. Sam's reflexes were quick. He swung the rifle like a baseball bat. The butt of the gun struck the man on the forehead. The blow knocked him out cold.

The crowd protested the bushwhacker's foul play. "He tried to pull a sneak gun on the kid."

"Did you see that?"

"He got what he deserved."

"The kid would-ah whopped him anyway if he hadn't done that."

Sam slowly, painfully walked to the horse trough and washed the blood and dirt off, sluicing water over his head. His whole body hurt something fierce and his ear was sore. He was alive. Men walked up to him and slapped his back, shaking their heads in disgust over the bushwhacker. Every clap on the back brought more pain, but he nodded and thanked them.

He was glad it was over. He thought, *I think he broke one of my ribs.*

"Kid, do you want us to hold him till the sheriff gets back to town?"

"No, when he wakes up, put him on his horse, and tell him if I see him again, next time I'll shoot him. I don't want to fight that big dude again."

Sam's head still rang liked a school bell as he walked to the café. He needed a good meal.

The Oak Tree Diner was the only place in town to eat. A saucy little waitress with freckles on her nose and red hair drawn up in a ponytail brought him a cup of coffee.

CHAPTER FIVE
Collecting Some Money

"Morning, stranger, are you just passing through and got hungry?" She had a perky little nose and her flirty grin was contagious.

"I was, but if all the women in La Grange are as pretty as you, I may decide to stay a while."

She wrinkled her nose and smiled at him. "You see the big fellow back there cooking? He's my pa, and he shot the last two drifters who thought I was pretty. You better go ahead, eat up, and move on, cowboy."

"In that case, you better bring me some bacon and eggs before he looks up. He's sure going to use up a lot of ammunition before he finds a cowhand who doesn't think you're pretty. I guarantee you don't get too many blind cowboys in here."

She bopped him on the head with her pad she was writing orders on and swished her hips as she walked away.

Sam thought, *Yeah, her daddy sure has his work cut out for him.* While he ate, the man who ran the livery stable came in and sat down at Sam's table.

"Son, do you want to sell that extra horse and saddle? It's a good looking outfit."

"Yes sir, I can't ride two and the other rig slows me down."

"Fine, when you get through with breakfast, come on over to the livery."

Feeling better after a hot meal, Sam got up, walked to the livery, and completed the sale of the extra horse and gear. He climbed onto Buck's back with sixty-six dollars in his jeans—the most cash money he'd ever seen at one time.

"Buck, I don't know where we're going." He looked in the direction of Cactus Tree and remembered the patch of blue sashaying down the boardwalk. But danger lay back there.

She was pretty and her daddy is rich. I'd better move on, but boy would I like to go back. Just before dark, he spotted some cottonwood trees, which indicated water would be found. Reining the buckskin into the trees, he rode up to a small stream and made camp.

The air had a chill to it the next morning as Sam huddled over the fire and drank black coffee. *I still don't know where I'm going. I just know I want to find a place of my own and have a family. I can't change the way Ma and I had to grow up, but I want my kids to have a good life.*

He put out the fire and scattered dirt over the coals. He gasped in pain from the broken rib when he mounted up. "Buck, let's see where this trail takes us."

As day slowly faded into evening, Sam saw a ranch house sitting back in the fold of the hills. Buck trotted into the yard as a man came out of the barn and walked toward him.

"Howdy." He was leather-tan, like a man who knew the business end of hard work. "Something I can do for you?"

"Right now, I'd be much obliged for some hot grub. I can pay, but I've been on the trail all day and not come to a town. As he stepped down, he grimaced because his legs were stiff from hours in the saddle. His canteen was empty and his mouth tasted like trail dust.

"My wife's putting supper on the table. We don't charge folks for our hospitality. Come in and let's eat."

The man headed for the house and Sam followed. "You got a name you go by?"

"The name's Samuel McClanton, but everybody calls me Sam."

"Sam, I need a man who can break wild horses. You had any experience with that?"

"Yeah, I've had some."

"I'm Fred Burgess. Come on in and you get your belly full. Then let's talk about you staying awhile." He held the door open and Sam walked into the kitchen where lanterns were already lighted on the table, and delicious smells came from the stove. His mouth watered. A woman stood at the stove and piled pork chops on a platter.

"This's my wife, Julie. These are two of the best cowhands in Texas, Tom and Dan. This here is Sam. He's riding hungry and, since we don't turn anybody away with an empty stomach, I invited him to eat with us. Then we're gonna talk about him training those mustangs if he's willing and able."

Each one of the men nodded and Sam said, "Howdy."

Julie said, "Sam, pull up a chair. There's plenty." She motioned to a chair. Sam walked around the table and sat next to Tom.

When everyone was seated at the table, Fred bowed his head. "Dear Lord, we thank you for all your bountiful blessings, we thank you for the rain, and the sunshine that makes the grass grow. Amen."

After supper, the men went outside on the porch to smoke. Sam didn't like the taste of tobacco, so he sat and talked with Fred about the mustangs. Since he didn't know where he was going, he figured he might as well stay a few weeks and help him out. Miz Julie sure set a good table, which was an added incentive.

Fred said, "Here is the deal. I'll pay thirty dollars a month and furnish you a place to sleep, and three meals a day. However, me and the boys are busy getting cattle ready for round up and don't have time to train these mustangs. I can use you to train, but I've got my own way of training horses. You'll have to agree to do it my way."

"What is your way?"

"I don't break horses. I train them like you would a dog."

"I've never trained that way, but if you say it works, I'll give it a try."

"Fair enough. You can start in the morning. Let's go over to the bunkhouse and I'll show you where to stow your gear. Bunkhouse is big enough for six, but you make three. As you can see, we've got plenty of room."

The next morning, Fred showed Sam the pen where he kept the horses.

"We got 'em up on Lonesome Ridge. They're a wild bunch. Like I said, I don't cotton to breaking a horse's spirit. Here's how I want you to train 'em. I want you to take one horse at a time and gentle him by getting his confidence. That way he will learn to trust you. If the horse trusts you, you can teach him to take a saddle and then the rider. It takes a little longer to train a horse than it does to break a horse. But when you get through, you've got a horse you can trust, because he trusts you. There'll come a time when a man needs to trust his horse. God gave us animals to use, but he never intended for us to mistreat 'em."

Fred and the boys went to the cattle. Sam went to work with the horses. The work was hard and hot. When Sam climbed through the rail with the horses, they ran to the opposite side of the corral. He talked softly to them as they edge away from him around the corral. After a few minutes, they sensed that he meant them no harm so they settled down.

Sam shook out a loop in his rope and with a flick of his wrist, dropped a loop onto the neck of a horse. The horse squealed and started to buck, trying to throw off the rope. The rest of the horses broke for the other end of the arena. Sam sang quietly to the frightened horse. After a few minutes, the animal quieted down and Sam walked up to the horse singing quietly, winning the horse over little by little. Two days later he was putting on the saddle.

He repeated this process with each horse.

Fred paid him a dollar a day to train the horses, and, with some of the wild ones, Sam was confident that he earned his money.

All the time he was working he kept thinking about the beautiful girl in the blue dress. *What if I go back and find out she is married or engaged? Well then if she is, I can just move on. Right now I can't stand not knowing. I've got to find out.*

Fred's wife was a great cook, and training horses Fred's way turned out to be fun. Sam decided though that he had to go back to Cactus Tree. *Maybe he could get a job on her daddy's ranch*, he thought. But he knew the chance he was taking.

Sam found Fred in the tack room. "I've got some good horses trained for you, and before I eat you out of house and home, I guess I should be moving on."

"You've done a good job, Sam, and I hate to lose you. I know a young man has dreams, and breaking horses ain't enough. We really appreciate what you've done. Come round-up time we'd be pleased to have you back if you're a mind to. You're always welcome."

Somehow having Fred call him "son" seemed more special than the marshal back in Cactus Tree saying it. He rode away singing. He was heading back to Cactus Tree and a blue-eyed girl. He was not thinking about the Taggerts.

CHAPTER SIX
Going Back

Old man Taggert had been drinking all afternoon. He was fighting mad when he slammed a bottle down on the table. "I don't understand why you can't find one dude. He ain't got no wings. Do you think he flew out of here? It's been two months since he kilt Billy Wayne. Then the smart aleck liked to have kilt me when he gave me a crack on my head. I want him dead."

"Pa, we've looked ever-where and he ain't nowhere around here. He must-a rode on out of the country."

"I want you boys out ridin', checkin' on every ranch around here. He's gotta be somewhere. We're gonna find 'im. Then we're gonna kill 'im."

* * *

When night fell Sam camped by a stream about five miles west of Cactus Tree, and in the fading light of sundown a young buck came to get a drink of water. *Am I far enough away from town to chance a shot?* He decided he was hungry enough to chance it.

Sam brought the deer down with one shot, skinned it out, and cut the meat into big chunks to roast on a spit. His stomach growled when the aroma of roasting meat filled the night air. He watered Buck and picketed him on new grass.

After he ate he sat near the comforting fire. Loneliness enveloped him like a fog. Pain the size of Texas welled up in him with the few memories he had of his mama. *I wonder what life would've been like if pa hadn't been killed? How many brothers and sisters would I have? I know Mama tried her best. I remember the touch of Mama's calloused hands on my face. It's been three years since she died of the pneumonia.*

He swallowed the lump in his throat and hardened his resolve to get everything he'd lost when the Comanche came and killed his pa.

He barely remembered his pa. He was only five when his pa had died. Pa wasn't a rancher, he was a dirt farmer. In fact, he had been plowing new ground with a team of mules when the Comanche raced out of the trees and cut him down, an un-armed farmer.

The next morning, Sam saddled up. "Buck, I've got to know if she is spoken for or not. Even if she's not, I know I have no right to talk to a lady like her, me being just a saddle bum. But we're going back to Cactus Tree. The marshal said her daddy would give me a job. I need to make her understand that I don't aim to stay a saddle bum. Buck, let's you and me try to find her daddy's ranch."

Two days later, Sam and Buck cantered along the trail south of town. The warm morning sun felt good on his face. Fragrances from the honeysuckle growing beside the road were intoxicating. As he rode, he listened to a robber jay squawking as it flew from tree to tree, keeping pace with him. The bird acted like he needed company.

A bunch of outlaws was the last things on Sam's mind that morning. As Buck topped the hill, a magnificent sight came into view. Grass was lush and green for a mile or more before him. Sunlight reflected off a metal roof on the barn. Low mountain peaks standing in the distance would shelter a herd from the icy wind from the north in winter. Half a mile below the rise stood a big magnificent log ranch house with a wide porch across the front. Some kind of bright colored flowers hung in hanging baskets off the roof of the porch. There were well-kept barns and corrals, with cow-pens scattered out back. The place looked like someone with a good head for running a ranch had tended it.

Sam turned Buck into the lane leading to the ranch. He stopped Buck at the front gate. Would he get shot if he went on the property? He thought, *Well here goes nothing. I am a saddle bum who owns a horse, my guns, and nothing else. Well, not quite true. I do have the $106.50 I've saved.*

"Buck, do you see this layout? What you see is the kind of place we're going to own one day." The horse shook his head as if he understood what Sam had said.

When he rode into the yard, a cowhand stood leaning on the top rail of the corral watching him. As he got closer, the man opened the gate and walked toward him. "Looking for work?"

"Yes sir. Is this the Carville spread?"

"Yep, I'm Russ, the foreman. What can you do?"

"Sir, I can do about anything needing to be done on a ranch. The marshal told me Mr. Carville might have a job for me."

Russ studied him a moment, and said, "Why would he tell you the Tumbling C would hire ya? Wait a minute. Are you the guy who shot ole Billy Wayne?"

"Yes sir."

"We thought you had left the country. Ain't you scared to stay in these parts? The Taggerts are a mean bunch." Either the foreman had a frown on his face from the sun in his eyes or he was thinking about the Taggerts. Sam wondered which it was.

"I figure they're not going to ride in here to find me. So I won't have to take 'em all on. And I need some work."

"Mattie Ann told us about the fight. She sure was shook up. Joe'll be glad to meetch-ya. Climb down off that Cayuse and I'll take you to the office and introduce ya."

They walked into the back door and the first person Sam saw was a big Mexican woman in the kitchen.

Russ said, "This is Rosa. Don't tell her I said she's the best cook in the territory or she might get uppity and quit." The grin on his weatherworn face gave him the appearance of a boy up to mischief.

"Russ McCracken, you better geet on outta heere with your Irish blarney or I'll put the loco weeed in your chili and make you crazy. Rosa's not givin' you no samples before the lunch." She smiled and dropped a small curtsy to Sam and winked.

He laughed. Rosa was in her middle years, with silver running through her raven-black hair, but she still had a saucy grin, even with her extra pounds of weight. Her blouse was embroidered with colorful flowers, and her black skirt had splashes of color all over it with embroidered flowers as well.

They walked into the office at the back of the house, where Joe Carville sat in front of a large roll-top desk. "Boss, this here's the trail buster who shot ole Billy Wayne for what he did to Miss Mattie Ann."

Carville stood and walked over, and extended his hand. "I've wanted to meet you. Marshal Jackson said he told you I'd have a job for you. I've been expecting you. I sure appreciate you standing up for my little girl. If I'd a been there, I would've killed 'im myself."

"Sir, all I did was tell him to leave her alone. He throwed down on me. At that moment, I was all out of options."

"One of my boys rode in and said you bent a gun barrel over his old man's head later. Why didn't you shoot him?"

"Well, I figured he was upset about losing his son. I didn't think he deserved to be shot."

"I'm beholden to you, but you left you a hornet's nest behind. Those Taggerts don't forget. Sit down. You're here to see me with a purpose. What can I do for you?"

"I need a job. I'm a good hand and I work hard."

The old man shook his head. "Well, now, here's the thing—if you hire on, you can't go to town like the other hands, least not for a while. If you're willing to stay out of sight for a while until they might forget what you look like, I'll consider it." He studied Sam over the top of his reading glasses.

Sam said, "I ain't afraid to go into town, but if those have to be the conditions, I can do that. Not forever, but for now."

CHAPTER SEVEN
Mattie Ann Lives in Town

Carville stood up, walked around the desk and held out his hand. They shook. "Russ here's the foreman so you'll take orders from him. Pay's $30.00 a month and found. In case you don't know that means room and board. Russ'll show you around."

When Sam turned to go, Carville slapped him on the back. "Welcome to the ranch, and I sure appreciate what you did for my daughter. You hear?"

"Let's get your horse put away," Russ said. "Then we can stash your gear in the bunkhouse." After Buck was rubbed down, Russ led Sam across the hard-packed yard into the bunkhouse and showed him where to put his gear. "You'll work with me today. I'm cutting hay down by the creek."

As they rode down into the meadow, the grass was as tall as the bottom of a stirrup and bending gently in the wind. Russ stepped out into the hay field and swung a smooth, even swing with the cutting bar.

Sam watched for a few strokes then stepped in and started swinging. He was thinking, *There is no way I'm going to let him cut more than I do.* After two hours of backbreaking labor, he reached up and wiped the sweat from his hatband. *Whew, Russ is a worker I'll give him that. He's cut and tied a bale for every bale I've tied, and I've been pushing.*

Russ looked up at the sun, which was directly overhead. "Okay, let's stop and see what Rosa packed for our lunch."

Sam went down under the shade of the trees by the creek and spread the lunch Rosa had packed for them. Before setting down to eat, he went to the creek and washed off the dirt and sweat from his arms and shoulders.

While the two men wolfed down the spicy tortillas and beans Rosa had sacked up for them, Sam said, "Can I ask you something?"

"Sure."

"Why would Miss Mattie Ann walk down the street in a town as wild and wooly as Cactus Tree, all by herself? That appears to be a town with the bark still on."

"You've asked a good question. Her aunt owns the millinery store. Joe likes for Mattie Ann to stay with her aunt from time to time—he thinks she needs a woman's influence. She always comes out here on Saturday and Sunday. Mostly she lives in town with her aunt."

Disappointment welled up in Sam. *Oh no, she don't live here. She lives in town. Well, at least she comes to the ranch on the weekends.*

"Why she was walking by herself is another matter. I don't have the answer. I'm sure her daddy does. In his mind, he places her up high and watches over her like a hen with one chick. Since her momma died, she's the only thing he sets store by." He looked Sam in the eye and thought, *Why are you asking all these questions about Mattie Ann?*

Sam kept his own counsel. He wasn't going to tell the foreman that the only reason he came back to Cactus Tree was because he couldn't stop thinking about his new boss's daughter. This was a fine mess. She was the reason he came back to the ranch. Now he found out she lived in town. He wasn't allowed to go into town. What could he do now?

The sun was nestling down below the western hills when they got back to the yard. The aroma of something smelling mighty good drifted out of the kitchen window. Sam stripped the saddle off Buck and turned him into the corral with the other horses. He pulled his sweat-stained, dirt-covered shirt off as he walked to the well pump.

Grasping the hot metal handle he moved it up and down until cold, clear water gushed out. He splashed some in the pan and washed his face, the back of his neck, and shoulders before heading for the bunk to get a clean shirt.

As they walked toward the house, Sam asked, "Russ, what day of the week is this?"

Russ laughed, "It's Monday. Out here in the wild it's real easy to forget because every day is the same—work from sunup to dark, and get up tomorrow and do it again. You know what? I still love it."

When he stepped inside the kitchen, shadows were dancing on the walls from the kerosene lamps burning on the tables, bathing everything in the room in a soft glow. At a glance, Sam saw a long table in the center of the room crowded with cowhands.

As they entered the dining area, Russ said, "This here's Sam. He's a new hand the boss hired." One by one he introduced the men to Sam: "That long-legged galoot is Tex, that's Dean, the young-un is Jessie, and this here's Loco. He's half Piute and half crazy."

The others at the table laughed and chimed in, "Yeah."

Sam acknowledged each one with a nod. Another of Rosa's dishes passed around the table. They had pork chops, refried beans, and hominy with enough hot chili peppers to clear his head. He thought, *Man, I want some of this stuff the next time I catch a bad cold.*

* * *

Aunt Millie said, "Mattie Ann, I wonder what ever happened to the good-looking young cowboy who shot ole Bill Wayne?"

"I don't know. I try not to think about it, the whole thing was awful."

"Well, it's too bad he moved on because he's good looking, and he had grit."

"Yes, but Aunt Millie, I'm sure we'll never lay eyes on him again. If he had stuck around, the rest of the Taggerts would've killed him by now."

"Young lady, I think you liked him a lot more than you're letting on."

"My dear aunt, it's not like I'm having trouble finding a beau. There are several men in town who've asked to escort me to things.

I'll be going out to the ranch Saturday. If he shows and doesn't get shot up, you keep him here until I get back."

* * *

Tuesday morning Russ sent Sam and Jessie Arnold to work cattle on the north range. Jessie and Sam were becoming more than saddle partners—they were friends. Sam looked over at Jessie when he was standing beside his horse; his chin was a little taller than the saddle. That would make him about five foot nine or ten.

Russ had said, "Okay, here's what I want you to do. Find a cow with a cut or scrape caused by a cow horn or sharp limbs. When you find one, rope the critter and throw it on its side. While one of you keeps it down, the other one cauterize the big wounds and put salve on the smaller cuts. That's to keep blowflies from getting to the wounds. Some of those cows weigh close to twelve hundred pounds and they won't like being roped or held down. So y'all be careful."

The first stars coming out every night would find two bone weary cowhands dragging back into camp. They fixed themselves a quick supper, rolled their bedrolls out under the stars, and tried to find a spot with no rocks to sleep.

"Sam, let's knock off early today."

"What'll Russ say?"

"Nothing, it's Saturday."

"What has that got to do with it? It ain't even dark yet."

Jessie said, "I know, but tomorrow's Sunday."

"What's that got to do with anything?" Then he thought, *If today is Saturday, Mattie Ann should be here.*

Jessie interrupted his thinking, "Ole Joe and Mattie Ann go to church every Sunday. So we have the day off."

"Really? Maybe I can get my socks washed. Do the guys ever go to church with 'em?"

"Naw."

"When's the last time you went to the meeting house?"

"Been a long time, what about you?"

"Not since Ma died, three years ago. I don't have much good to say when it comes to all that religious stuff."

"If your ma died three years ago, what about your pa?" Jessie stopped and looked at Sam with a frown on his face.

"Pa was killed by Comanche when the Indians hit him while he was plowing a field."

"How old were you then?"

"About five."

"No kiddin'? Where did you and your ma live after your pa died?"

"We stayed on the farm, just Ma and me trying to make a living on a black land farm."

"Wow, what was that like?"

"It was pretty rough, especially on Ma. She was no farmer and she had a little kid to raise."

"Did she teach you to use a sling shot?"

"Naw, my grandpa taught me before he died. It was a good thing I had it because we couldn't afford to buy powder or shot so most of the game I killed was with a slingshot."

They rode along silently for a little way then Jessie asked, "Sam, have you thought anymore about the outlaw gang?"

CHAPTER EIGHT
Aunt Millie Encourages Mattie Ann

"Mattie Ann, I think that Thompson boy has taken a liking to you."

"He doesn't go to church and you know what 2 Corinthians 6:15 says: 'what has a believer in common with an unbeliever?'"

"Well, if you are going to quote the bible, you should read 1 Corinthians; it says each woman is to have her own husband. You are nineteen. It's high time you started picking one out."

Laughing, Mattie Ann said, "God will send the right one someday. I'll just wait."

"If you wait too long, all the good ones will be gone."

"The Thornton boy did ask me to go to the box supper with him."

"What did you tell 'em?"

"I told him I would think about it."

"Mattie Ann, he is a nice looking boy and he goes to church—what are you waiting for?"

CHAPTER NINE
Guys Get a Bath

Sam said, "If this is Saturday, maybe I can get a bath tonight. It's been awhile since I had one."

"That's sure as the devil obvious. Haven't you noticed I keep ridin' upwind of you?" Jessie threw his head back and laughed.

"Look whose talkin', you pole cat. We'd of caught a lot more of them cow critters except the stink fog comin' off you scared 'em clear into the next county. Didn't you notice the only cows we were able to get a rope on were the ones we came upon from downwind?"

The easy banter made Sam realize he'd made a friend. They rode together into the creek. As they crossed, Sam grabbed Jessie by the shirtsleeve and jerked hard. Jessie flew off his horse and splashed into the water.

He came up sputtering and spitting.

Sam sat on his horse laughing.

Jessie reached over and jerked Sam's right boot out of the stirrup and up-ended him off the other side.

The fight was on. When Sam came up for air Jessie scooped a double handful of water and sloshed it in his face. Sam spun away, whipped around, and grabbed the back of Jessie's shirt, and jerked him backward down into the water. He was laughing so much he got a mouthful of dirty water. The two cowhands shrieked with laughter like schoolboys, each one trying his best to dunk the other.

Their mounts stood on the bank, getting splashed by sprays of water cupped and thrown from calloused hands. Soon the horses tired of the drenching and drifted toward the barn to get away from the fools in the creek.

Jessie looked up and realized the horses had headed for the corral. "Hey, you dumb Cayuses, come back here." When he started to yell, the horses ran faster.

Twenty minutes later, two dripping wet cowhands stumbled into the bunkhouse. Russ took one look at them and said, "I don't know what you two've been up to, but you ain't goin' to eat supper looking like wet squirrels, so get some dry clothes on."

Jessie said, "Fellows, don't ever turn your back on this skunk."

Sam grinned and said, "I couldn't get far enough downwind of him, so I had no choice. He needed a bath. I obliged him. The ungrateful hound took me in with him."

"Look who's talking. We figured out real quick we didn't need a rope to catch cows. All we had to do was get old Sam here upwind in a cow critter's face and she'd faint like she was dead. All I needed to do was walk over and doctor her. Of course, we had to go back and waste a lot of time fanning a bunch of 'em. We had to get 'em up so the buzzards wouldn't think they were dead and start feasting on 'em."

"Now if that ain't the tallest tale I ever heard. Did you know ole Jessie here had a buzzard following him around all week? That thing was some kinda confused. Ole Jessie did get up and move around, but he smelled like he'd been dead for a week."

Tex walked into the room. "What in tarnation is going on? I heard a bunch of laughing all the way out to the corral."

Russ said, "Never mind." He pointed at the entertainers and said, "You two shut up this foolishness and get in some clean clothes so we can eat."

When they walked into the kitchen, the first thing Sam saw was Mattie Ann wearing a pink gingham dress with a full-length white eyelet apron. She hurriedly sat platters and bowls of food on the table. All of the hands treated her like she as a little sister. She smiled and greeted each one. The girl stopped in mid-stride when her eyes met Sam's. She blinked, and looked again. It appeared she had trouble believing what her eyes were seeing. "It's you. You work for my father?"

"Yes ma'am."

GEORGE DALTON

Regaining her composure, she said, "After I realized you had to kill that man or he would've killed you, I wanted to thank you. You were gone by the time the commotion settled down. That must be horrible for you. I'm sorry."

"Yes ma'am." *Do I look like a dunce? Was that all I could say? How do I make her see me as something other than one of her daddy's cowhands?*

All during supper, he kept his head down and stared at his plate, too embarrassed to look at her. But no matter how hard he tried not to look at her, every time he looked up she floated around the room. She looked like an angel, refilling water glasses and talking with the cowhands. His collar started to feel too tight and he had trouble swallowing his supper.

When she reached over to fill his glass, her arm brushed against his. This sent an electric tingle all through him. He had known lots of girls, but never one who brought this kind of reaction out in him—both wonderful and terrifying at the same time.

CHAPTER TEN
Indian Attack

Summer dragged on. Time seemed to crawl along like an old turtle from Monday to Saturday. After two months, Sam thought, *She still doesn't know me. I never get a chance to talk to her by myself. Only time I get to be around her is on Saturday at mealtime. That's with a room full of cowhands. It's driving me crazy. At least she doesn't appear to be interested in anyone else.*

At breakfast, Russ said, "Guys, this is the first of September. Sam, you and Jessie take the big wagon, go up in the hills, and cut firewood. We better stock up. Winter's coming."

Jessie and Sam gathered the tools they'd need and loaded a wagon. The drive to the tree line took about twenty minutes. When they stopped near the trees, Sam looked down across the valley. What a beautiful day. The sun was warm but not hot. He could see a soft haze in the air above the river. The only sound he could hear was the twitter of birds in the trees. A man could live forever like this.

The sound of axes filled the air with a rhythm as the men chopped, and whacked, and sawed down the trees. They used the long two-man crosscut saw with a handle on each end to cut the trunks into lengths that would fit in the fireplace. Sam straightened up and pulled the kink out of his back. He loved the fragrance of fresh-cut wood.

Even though the air temperature felt a little on the cool side at this altitude and he was working without a shirt on, a sheen of perspiration still glistened on Sam's chest. Life was good. He didn't have a worry in the world at this moment.

Thunk—something hit the tree trunk beside his face violently. Sam whipped his head around and was shocked to find an arrow imbedded in the tree beside him. His first thought was, *Hit the ground!* His next thought was, *Oh no, my rifle is in the wagon. At last we've both got our six-shooters.* Flat on his stomach, he faced the direction the arrow had come from.

Six young Comanche bucks charged toward them. Sam fanned his gun, spraying bullets into the charging warriors. Two braves fell. As quickly as they had appeared, the Indians disappeared into the brush and weeds.

"Sam, can you see anything?"

"No, but don't look for 'em where they went down. They'll roll over and come up somewhere else." As he said that, another arrow slashed into the ground right in front of his face, splattering sand in his eyes. Sam rolled to his right.

The braves charged again.

Jessie fired and one Indian fell.

The other three hit the ground again.

Sam's ears were ringing with the concussion of the gunfire.

It was now deathly quiet—there was no sound, no birds singing, nothing. The sun beat down on the back of two scared, lonely cowhands. Sam's lips felt dry. He wished he had a drink of water. Then he realized his canteen was hanging on the side of the wagon, thirty feet away. His mouth was dry, and that canteen was full of water. It occurred to him, *If I can see it, so can the Indians.*

"Sam, you got any water on you?" Jessie's whisper seemed loud on this hill, with no other sound except the rustling of the leaves caused by a light breeze blowing through the trees.

"Yeah, my canteen's hanging on the side of the wagon. Help yourself." Sam glanced at the wagon, and then turned his attention back to scan the area for Indians.

"Sam, if you was the right kinda partner, you'd get that canteen and give me a drink. My mouth's as dry as a toad's fart."

"I don't have any idea how dry a toad's fart is, but I'll give you half of all the water I've got. All you gotta do is walk over to the wagon and get it. Now, shut up and listen for any sound of them moving around."

The shadow of the tree slowly stretched across the ground. Jessie said, "Sam, you think they're gone?"

"I don't know, but I ain't gonna stand up to find out."

All at once, Jessie let out a loud squeal. He jumped up and started dancing around. It looked like he was having a seizure or something, yelping like an Indian.

Sam thought, *Oh my gosh, he's having a conniption or something. He's oblivious to the danger he's in. He's gonna get his head blowed off.* Sam scanned the area, waiting for the charge. Not seeing any Indians, he turned his attention back to Jessie in time to see a little tiny field mouse drop out of the bottom of Jessie's pants leg. Sam watched one terrified little mouse scurry under the pile of branches they'd cut.

Sam laughed like a loon. "Jessie, you dang fool. You might've got your head shot off. If those Indians were still around, you'd have more arrows poking out of you than a pincushion."

Standing there shaking his pants leg, he said, "Pardner, I wasn't worried about what those Indians might shoot off."

Sam stood up and looked around. There were no bodies in sight. Obviously the Indians had disappeared back into the brush, carrying the dead and wounded with them. As Sam and Jessie loaded the wagon, both cowhands kept their Winchesters with them.

"Sam, where do you think they'll be?"

"Your guess is as good as mine, but I don't aim to stay around here and find out. Let's get this wagon loaded and get out of here."

All the way back to the ranch Sam drove the team and Jessie tried to scan all four directions at the same time. He whipped his rifle to his shoulder, and fired...*bang!*

Sam started laughing. "You sure killed that dead cedar tree lying on the ground over there."

"Well, it was brown and it looked like an Indian brave lying on the ground."

"Uh-huh," Sam grunted.

The wagon rolled into the yard. Tex came to meet them. "We thought we heard shootin' over on the ridge. What happened?"

"Why you long-legged stork, we was fightin' off half the Apache Nation," Jessie said. "How come you didn't come and help us?"

Russ walked up about that time. "What's this about?"

"Sam and me got jumped by a whole passel of Apache warriors. We're lucky to still have our hair."

"Jessie, how many Indians did you see?"

"At least half of the Apache Nation, we was surrounded. We're talkin' about fierce fightin."

Russ turned to Sam and asked, "How much of that story is true?"

"Well, we did get in a shoot 'n scrape with some Apache bucks."

"Now let me ask you: How many bucks did you see?"

"I counted six, but it sure seemed like a lot more than that with arrows flyin' everywhere."

"Did you shoot any of 'em?"

"Yeah, we knocked down three. I can't tell you if all them were killed. We won't know because they took the ones we shot with 'em. Of course, the scariest part was that field mouse."

"Aw, Sam, you don't need to tell that."

The other cowhands gathered around the wagon said, "What field mouse?"

"Right in the middle of the fight, old Jessie jumped up and started dancing and yellin'. He scared the devil out of those Indians. They thought he was having some kind of evil spirit or something. So they took off, runnin' down the hill. They were yellin' and throwing down their bows and arrows as they ran like deer. It was something. I tell you it was scary watchin' old Jessie. I was fixing to take off my self. Then I saw that great big old field mouse fall out of his pants leg."

"Sam ain't telling the whole truth. That thing that crawled up inside my pants felt like it was big as a grizzly bear. There wasn't enough room for me and him both inside these britches. One of us had to get out of there. I forgot all about a few little old Indians."

Sam jumped up and started shaking his leg and dancing all around the ranch yard. Several of the men were holding their sides and gasping for breath, they were laughing so hard at Sam's demonstration of Jessie with a mouse up his pants leg.

Tex said, "I'd give a month's pay to have seen that."

Cowhands were wiping their eyes and holding their sides, and someone said, "From now on we'll call you grizzly."

When everyone finally settled down, one of the ranch hands said, "We ain't had no Indian trouble for quite a while. I wonder what stirred 'em up?"

"I'm sure they were a bunch of renegade bucks out trying to collect some scalps to impress the young squaws back at camp. For the next few days you boys work in pairs and keep them Winchesters handy," Russ said. "Alright boys, the show is over. Let's get back to work."

At supper, Joe Carville brought up the Indian attack. "They tell me you boys got jumped by a bunch of Apache up on the ridge today."

Mattie Ann walked in carrying a platter of deer steaks. She looked prettier today than she did the first time he saw her, Sam thought as he felt his heart start beating faster.

"What Indian trouble?" A frown creased her pretty face.

Joe Carville said, "Don't worry darling, you're safe. Sam and Jessie had a run-in with a bunch of Apache this afternoon, but they killed half of them. They'll stay off the land for a while."

Mattie Ann turned pale and looked at Sam, her eyes wide open with shock. "You could've been killed."

Tex spoke up and said, "They're still wearing their hair, ain't they?"

"I'm going into town tomorrow," Joe Carville said. "I'll report this to the territorial marshal. In the meantime, you boys do what Russ told you and keep them Winchesters handy for the next few weeks."

Three days later Sam and Jessie were hard at work pulling wire on a new fence in the southeast section when Jessie noticed smoke coming from behind the ridge.

"Hey Sam, look: smoke. What do you make of that?"

"I don't know, maybe we need to check it out. Grab your Winchester and let's go. You go around that big boulder to the right and I'll go around to the left. Let's see what we find."

Sam had to scramble a little to get up around his side. As he stepped past the big boulder, he found a man with a steer down on the ground by a fire. Jessie yelled at the man and, in an instant, the man whipped around and fired. Sam had his Winchester in his hand so he snapped off a shot at the rustler at almost the same instant. Sam saw the man fall, but he couldn't see Jessie.

He yelled, "Jessie, are you okay?"

All he heard was silence. Jessie didn't answer. Sam waited for a few seconds to make sure there were not any more men down there. He crept around the boulders. He was hoping to get a better view of the area where the shot had come from, without showing himself too much.

Leaning out a little further, he spotted Jessie lying on the ground at the base of the boulders. Leaping up, Sam ran to Jessie. He immediately observed the red bloom of blood on his blue shirt. Scooped him up in his arms, Sam ran back to the wagon.

"Hang on, Jessie, old buddy. We're going to get you to the house where somebody can fix you up. Don't die on me."

He gently laid Jessie in the bed of the wagon and leaped up onto the seat. Sam slapped the reins on the startled team's backs and raced all the way to the yard. It was only a mile to the house, yet it seemed to take forever before the wagon bounced and rattled into the yard.

As he raced into the ranch yard, he yelled for help before the team even came to a stop.

Joe and Russ ran out of the house. Joe held up his hand. "Whoa. What the devil?"

The first thing they noticed was the team lathered in sweat and Sam sawing on the reins. He pointed to the back of the bed, trying to tell them to take care of Jessie. No words came out of his mouth, because his throat was too dry—only a croaking sound came out.

Rosa and Mattie Ann raced each other down the steps from the porch. Everybody talked at once. "What happened?"

Sam leaped off the wagon and ran around to the back. He finally got his voice back. "Help me! It's Jessie. He's been shot and needs help. We've got to do something."

Russ hurried to the back of the wagon and climbed up into the bed. He put his hand on Jessie's neck for a few seconds. He turned and stepped down, then reached over and hugged Sam's shoulders. A tear trickled down his weather worn craggy face. He shook his head and said, "There ain't nothin' we can do. He's dead."

"NO! NO! He can't be dead—we were working and he noticed smoke coming from the other side of the ridge. We went to check it out. I saw a man with a steer down by a fire. I heard Jessie yell at him. Then a shot rang out." A torrent of tears cascaded down his face.

Mattie Ann took Sam by the arm and led him to the porch. "Sit down, Sam. Rosa, why don't you get Sam a glass of tea?" Turning to Sam, she said, "Tell us what happened?"

He had to take several deep breaths before he could speak. Taking a big gulp of tea, he said, "We were pulling wire for the new fence. Jessie spotted smoke on the other side of the ridge we were working on. We went to see what it was. He went around one way and I went the other. As I rounded the boulder, I found a man with a steer on the ground, re-branding it. Jessie yelled something to him. The rustler whipped up a gun. I heard the sound of a rifle." He choked back a sob.

"I fired my rifle, hunkered down for a moment to see if there were any more, then I looked over and saw Jessie on the ground. I ran and grabbed him up, loaded him in the wagon, and hightailed it here."

"Had you ever seen the rustler before?"

"Not so's I can tell, but he was about thirty yards away when the shooting happened."

"Is he still up there, or did he get away?"

"I suspect he's still under that sweet gum tree."

Russ and Joe Carville had joined them on the porch. "Russ, send one of the boys to town and tell the sheriff. We'll ride up and see what we find."

A half hour later five riders sat on their horses looking at a dead man lying on the ground. One of the cowhands spoke up. "I recognize that hombre—I played poker with him and some other guys in the Wagon Wheel one time."

"What's his name?" Joe asked.

"I ain't sure about his whole name, but he's one of them Taggerts."

"Okay, leave him lying there beside the steer with the altered brand. It looks like you and Jessie caught one of them red-handed, rustling a steer."

When the sheriff got to the ranch and asked questions, it was obvious he didn't want to tangle with the Taggerts. "I'll take the body into town and send somebody out to the canyon to tell them to come and get him."

Sam had been quiet, telling the sheriff the bare essentials of what had happened. When the sheriff said he would take the body back to town, Sam's head snapped up from staring at the ground. He said, "No—I'll take him home."

Mattie Ann gasped. "No, Sam, you can't. They'll kill you for sure if you take him home."

"They declared war. Now they've killed Jessie. If they want a war, war is what they're gonna get."

"Boy, do you have any idea what you're doing?" The sheriff eyed him like he'd lost his mind.

"Sam, that's not a good idea." Joe and Russ spoke at the same time.

"This can't go on. These cutthroats attacked Miss Mattie Ann. Now they've gone and killed Jessie. They've been terrorizing people in this county." He looked at the sheriff and said, "Why do you put up with these people? You need to clean out that hornet's nest. If you ain't got the stomach for it, then it's up to me."

The sheriff hung his head, then took the toe of his boot and rubbed out a cigarette he had dropped on the ground.

Mattie Ann's face showed she was terrified. "I don't want you to go. You saved me from one of them. I don't want them to get another chance to kill you."

"We can't go on wondering when they're going to come again. They weren't trying to shoot Jessie. He was trying to steal some cows. They killed Jessie because we caught them in the act. Next time it might be someone else. I don't want to have to look behind me every time I leave the bunkhouse."

He walked into the bunkhouse, grabbed his rifle, and walked to the corral to get his horse.

Sam pulled a spare pistol out of his saddlebag, checked the loads in the chamber, and tucked the gun behind his belt. When he climbed into the saddle, Mattie Ann ran over and laid her hand on his knee. Through teary eyes, she stared up into his face, "I'll pray for you. God keep you."

"Vaya con Dios, Senõr Sam." Rosa's black eyes glistened with tears.

CHAPTER ELEVEN
Sam Takes the Body Home

A cold fury burned deep inside Sam as he led a horse that carried a lifeless cargo. The only sound was that of the horse's hooves on the hard ground and the eerie creak of saddle leather. Together they rode a silent pilgrimage of death and coming tragedy. A mile from the ranch, Sam untied the lead rope and turned the rustler's horse loose, with the body strapped onto its back.

He slapped the horse he had been leading on its rump. It would go home with the ghostly load strapped to its back. Sam followed close behind. The horse galloped with the certainty of a homing pigeon, up to a cluster of rundown buildings on a rocky slope at the mouth of a canyon. As Sam looked, he saw no flower, no grass, only bare ground, with ugly, twisted, knurled scrub brush the only greenery visible near the run down shabby cabin.

He thought, *That's a mean looking place—it suits the cutthroats who live here.* The sun sat low on the western horizon when the horse carrying the dead man ran up to the cabin and stopped. Sam had ridden in from the west. He knew that the people in the cabin would face the setting sun when they came out the door. Buck stopped behind the horse that carried the dead body. Sam called, "Hello the house."

The door cracked open and a gun barrel pushed through. "Who are you?"

"My name's Sam McClanton. I work over at the Carville spread and I brought one of your boys home, and a message."

Sam had slipped the thong off the hammer of his six-gun and his hand rested on the saddle horn, inches from the gun behind his belt.

The door flew open and two men stepped out. "Is he dead?"

"I reckon."

"You shoot him?"

"Yep, I sure did. Here's my message. I rode into Cactus Tree town peaceful like. One of your gang drew a gun on me in Cactus Tree. His shot was a mite off and missed. Mine didn't." He pointed at the body draped over the horse. "Now this no good cattle rustler killed my partner. You wanted war. Now you've got it. From now on, I'll kill every Taggert gang member I see."

Out of the corner of his eye, he noticed a curtain move in a window. A flash of gunfire followed. Something slammed into his body. He drew and fired. He aimed a little to the left and above the gun-hand in the window. Then the two men in front of him opened fire. Both faced the sun. Sam's horse shied and stepped sideways, causing them to miss. Sam's bullet hit the one on the right.

Sam's body jerked as another bullet slammed into him. He got off two shots. He hit the one on the right and missed the third man. The buckskin was a trained cutting horse and spun around as Sam clamped his knees into its sides. They raced out of the yard.

His left side was already soaked in blood. He needed to get help. There would be a passel of Taggerts after him, even though their numbers were getting fewer. He was thinning them out pretty fast. For a guy who rode into town only looking for work, he sure rode into a peck of trouble. Slumped low over the saddle horn, he hung on. He had been content to avoid them before they killed his friend Jessie. Now he was filled with rage. He wanted to destroy them. First he had to find a place where he could hole up and tend to his wounds.

The buckskin was mountain raised and as sure footed as an antelope. The horse ran hard and fast for a couple of miles. Sam had a powerful thirst hit him and his head started to feel woozy from the loss of blood. He needed to get to water. He topped a rise and saw a clear, cold mountain stream right below a waterfall. He rode up to the edge of the stream, toppled from his horse, and crawled to the stream for a cold drink.

Sam lay on his belly and drank, letting the water sluice across his face. He listened as Buck slurped water downstream. He lay on the stream bank a long time, semiconscious, fading in and out. He didn't know how long he lay there before a deer appeared through the waterfall and disappeared into the trees. At first he thought he was hallucinating because of the shock and pain, but another deer appeared from behind the waterfall.

He grabbed a stirrup and pulled himself up. He picked up a large stick to use as a crutch, and led the horse to the edge of the waterfall where he had seen the deer emerge. The buckskin shied away from the curtain of falling water. After a little coaxing, they walked into a cave as big as a saloon, right behind the falls.

Sam, weak and exhausted, didn't even take the time to remove Buck's saddle. All he wanted to do was lie down and sleep. One thought kept going through his mind: Those wounds had to be treated.

Pack rats had made nests in the cave, so plenty of fuel was available for a fire. Soon he had a blaze going. Through his foggy thinking, he noticed the smoke going back into the cave. *At least the Taggerts won't see the smoke and find me.*

Sam placed his canteen in the fire and soon had hot water. He stripped off his shirt and found that one bullet had gone through the muscle above the hipbone on his left side. Another bullet had gone through his thigh, but didn't appear to have hit the bone. The pain was so severe that he wanted to scream as he cleaned both the entry and exit wounds. He took his razor-sharp bowie knife and cut the tail off his shirt. He used the material to plug each hole and stop the bleeding.

Sam crawled to the backside of the waterfall and drank his fill of water, then replaced what had been in his canteen. He crawled, exhausted, back to his blanket, and fell asleep next to the fire. Later, he awoke. He was extremely cold. Even wrapped up in a blanket, in the damp cave he trembled violently. Sam wondered if the tremors were caused by the cold or the fever that raged in his body. When he woke, the fire had burned down. He threw on more sticks and crawled back into his blankets.

A COLLISION OF DREAMS

Before falling asleep, he thought he would die if the fire burned out. He had to somehow keep that fire burning. He was in bad shape, and the damp cold in this cave would kill him without the fire.

He must have been delirious with fever. In the middle of the night, a man in a long white robe came and sat by him and kept adding fuel to the fire all night. In the early morning twilight, he could find no evidence that anyone else had been there. Yet the fire was still burning.

Finally, he was fully awake. He fumbled in his saddlebag and found some coffee and his coffee pot. A few moments later, huddled in his blanket, he sipped a strong cup of black coffee. A coyote appeared out of the back of the cave and stopped, staring at Sam. After seeing Sam and his fire, the coyote turned and ran back into the cave.

Sam drank some more coffee, then crawled to the waterfall and refilled his canteen. Even a little exertion left him exhausted. Sam thought, *If I die in here, no one will ever find my body.* Throwing down a challenge to the Taggerts had been a foolhardy thing to do, but an angry fire still burned in him.

He'd made up his mind a long time before he met the Taggerts— evil was not ever going to get the best of him. Yes, there were consequences to pay for doing the right thing, but he had to live with himself. That would be impossible if he let a bunch of cutthroat no-accounts win. He would not die here—he would win. Exhausted and weak, sleep overtook him, and he dreamed about what the world would be like if no one stood up for the right stuff.

The sound of voices woke him. They were right outside the entrance.

"Jake, I'm telling you, he just disappeared. I can't figure it out. We tailed him to the stream. He up and disappeared."

"Well, he ain't got no damn wings. He's got to be around here someplace."

Prickles of fear danced along his spine. Sam thought, *You ain't in no shape to play hide and seek with a bunch of cutthroats.* He gripped his six-gun in his right hand. *If they come in together, you can get a few of them before they get you, but there ain't no way you can get away.*

Sam listened to their grousing, which seamed to go on for a long time. They were mad because they couldn't find any tracks. His hands started to cramp. He shifted the gun to his left hand so he could flex his fingers on his right hand and get the cramps out. His muscles finally started to relax when he heard them mount up and ride away.

Sam turned his gaze to the back of the cave, curious about where the coyote had gone. He shuddered when a thought hit him. *What if there is another way in here? I thought there was only one way in here. I guess I'd better check it out and find out what is back there.*

Part of him wanted to curl back up in his blanket and sleep. He called Buck over to him, then grabbed a stirrup and pulled himself up onto his feet. He gripped the saddle horn with his left hand, then reached down and took the thong off the hammer on his six-shooter…just in case. He held onto the saddle horn, and urged Buck to move toward the back of the cave. Sam was totally un-prepared for what he was about to find.

Deeper in the cave, he took slow, halting steps into the dark tunnel. He shivered with cold and was sweating at the same time. The cave made a hard left turn. Slowly, he rounded the corner. There was daylight in front of him. He was jarred by the realization that this cave did have two ways in and out. "Oh, good lord, Buck, if those guys find this other opening, I'm in real trouble. I felt safe as long as I was behind the waterfall."

Sam and Buck inched closer to the opening. His skin prickled with the realization that he had no idea what he would face when he stepped into that opening. He eased up to the opening and his eyes popped wide open. His jaw dropped as he gawked at what lay before him.

CHAPTER TWELVE
Searching for Sam

Mattie Ann stood twisting a dishtowel in her hands. "Rosa, where can he be? Do you think they killed him?"

Rosa dipped a spoon in the frijoles bubbling on the stove and looked back over her shoulder. "Honey, I don't know. I do know that boy will take a whole lot of killing. Why don't you pray for him?"

"I think I will...Dear Lord, please don't let Sam get killed out there. If he is hurt, put your arms around him and bring him back so we can get him to the doctor. If he is hiding out, please don't let them find him. We want to see him ride back, please. Amen."

"Honey, you just done the only thing you can do. You need to keep doing it till we get him back."

"Rosa, I like him a lot. I wish he was a believer."

"Have you asked him?"

* * *

Five saddle weary men rode single file along the side of a mountain. "I don't get it. Where could that guy disappear to? Do you think he is dead?"

"He could be. We found a bunch of blood on the ground back there by the creek."

"I say we keep lookin'. Anybody with enough guts to ride right in bringing Del-Roy's body is not gonna die easy."

"Last we saw of him he was over east of here. Let's circle around this hill and see what's on the other side of it."

"Timbers pretty thick right in here. He could have climbed up the hill and gone up in them trees."

"If he did, we'd see his horse tracks somewhere. Keep your eyes open for tracks."

"That guys is an old he-coon. If I see that dude, I'm gonna put a bead on him and shoot him as soon as I see 'em."

"Yeah, don't nobody take any chances—as soon as you lay eyes on him, start shootin'."

CHAPTER THIRTEEN
Sam Found Something Special

"Buck, can you see what I am looking at? It's breathtaking. We're looking into a beautiful bowl. Must be fifty acres surrounded on all sides by steep straight walls a hundred feet high. The only way to get into this bowl is through the cave behind the waterfall. In the middle, there's a large pond or a small lake. I've never seen a place like this, so peaceful and beautiful."

With all the strength he had left, Sam pulled himself into the saddle. Buck stood as still as a statue until he was seated in the saddle. Sam felt weak and tired. With his six-gun in his right hand, he encouraged Buck to ease into the bowl. By the time he reached the small lake, he'd run out of energy, and weakness overtook him.

He slowly slid off the horse. Pain shot through him when he fell to the ground. Several minutes passed before he could regain enough energy to start a small fire. After the fire was going, he reached into his saddlebag and dug out his coffee pot.

Sam pulled out bacon and, using his razor-sharp knife, shaved off slices into the frying pan. Soon he had the coffee pot bubbling and the bacon sizzling. The smell of coffee and bacon was delicious and made him realize he was famished. He chewed and savored the flavor until he had satisfied his hunger and thirst. Then he bunched leaves together to make a pillow for his head and stretched out in paradise.

He looked at the position of the sun when he awoke. It was noon. His thirst raged. He placed the back of his hand on his forehead. At least he didn't feel feverish. He searched around for Buck, and found the horse cropping grass nearby. "Well Buck, we're still alive, so far." He crawled on his stomach over to the lake. After a drink of the cold, clear water, he said, "Buck, this water must come from a spring in the rocks over there—it's crystal clear." Lying on his stomach, he drank his fill. His movement was slow to avoid opening one of the wounds again. Finally, he sat up and took in more of his surroundings. He thought, *This place is beautiful and well hidden. I don't think anybody has ever been here.* It's like the first Garden of Eden, with towering oaks, maples whose leaves would be crimson come fall, and now there were wildflowers scattered throughout, like jewels gleaming in the sun. This was the kind of place a man dreamed about owning one day. By the looks of the tracks, there was plenty of game in this place. He looked around and found blackberry vines loaded with succulent fruit. He took a handful and filled his mouth. He discovered the berries tasted good, a little tart and sweet at the same time. He picked another handful and slowly chewed them and gazed at the wonders around him. He had to find out more about this place.

He slept again, and woke up hungry and thirsty. His spirit lifted because these were good signs of a body mending. Even though the bowl did appear to be very well hidden, he didn't dare risk a gunshot because, if his enemies did hear the shot, they would search even harder. He thought, *I don't need for the Taggerts to intensify their search.*

He knew he was too weak to run or fight. The Taggerts would know this neck of the woods. Certainly, they were still trying to find him. He dug around in his saddlebag until he found the little tobacco can with his fishing line and a fishing hook. Worms turned out to be plentiful in the soft ground near the water's edge. Staring down into the water, he said, "I can see fish swimming around near the shore—I just need to catch one."

He sat watching the hook with the worm attached slowly drift deeper in the water. All at once, a big bass knifed through the water and snapped up that worm. The movement was so swift and the attack on the hook so violent that he almost dropped the end of the string he held. Sam recovered and jerked hard on the fishing line, and a big bass came out of the water. He experienced a small surge of excitement. "Now I eat." He gathered some leaves and small sticks together, and spread them on the coals. He blew gently on the coals, and soon had a fire going again.

Taking out his bowie knife, he scaled and skinned the fish and put it on a stick above the fire to roast. The smell of roasting fish made him think of Rosa. He thought, *I guess the Carville's assume I'm dead.* The thought bothered him some—Mattie Ann would be sad. He hoped she wouldn't blame herself for the trouble he'd found himself in because he defended her. The moment his wounds healed enough for him to ride, he was going back to relieve their worries.

Sam had to shift his position to relieve the pain in his leg. He said, "Buck, I'm still too weak to ride back. I can't stand very long even when I use this big stick I made into a crutch."

He found he did best if he scooted around on the ground. Any movement made the wound in his thigh throb like the dickens. After a little exertion, the bullet holes leaked blood. He loved this place, but the thought of dying here and nobody finding his body did not set well.

After he had eaten the fish, he fell asleep. He dreamed of Mattie Ann. His dream was beautiful. In it, he rode up to his own ranch house. She waited on the front porch in a beautiful white dress at evening time. The setting sun reflected off the dress and made her appear to glow.

He woke up, looked at the stars, and realized it was about two o'clock in the morning. He lay there and thought, *Three more hours before sunlight.* He listened and heard no sounds. The night was still. Even the frogs and whippoorwills had gone to sleep. His fire had died down. He felt uneasy. What had woken him?

He felt rather than saw something move. He asked himself, "What was that movement?" He reached for his gun. The bright moon made the night almost as bright as day. His eyes squinted as he tried to see into the shadows. As his eyes adjusted to the light, he realized he was surrounded—by a bunch of curious cows. They bolted when he moved to drag himself to the water's edge for a drink.

A terrifying thought came to him. Where'd those cows come from? There must be another entrance into this bowl! He sat up and added more sticks to the fire. He still had a hard time finding a comfortable position to lie in. Again, his thoughts turned to Mattie

A COLLISION OF DREAMS

Ann. There was no doubt—he was in love with her. *What would it be like to have a wife like her and live in a place like this? She's beautiful and bright. She's proved she has staying power, the way she jumped in to help take care of Jessie. But I've got nothing to offer a girl like her. I'm a drifter with a $30.00-a-month job, and no prospects. I own a horse, a saddle, and a couple of guns.*

He drifted back to sleep and dreamed about what if . . .

CHAPTER FOURTEEN
Waiting to Hear Something

"Daddy, do you think they killed him?"

"Honey, Sam is the kind of guy who takes a whole lot of killing. I don't know. If anybody can ride into that hornet's nest and ride out, Sam might be the man who can. You're worried, but fretting won't help a bit."

"Daddy, at first all I could think about was that man grabbing me. My thoughts were all mixed up. I was shocked and horrified when guns started blasting. The noise was unbelievable, and that man fell right in front of me. I didn't know the young cowboy who took up for me. I assumed I would never see him again. I was so surprised when he showed up here. Now I realize things could have been a lot worse if Sam hadn't stopped him."

"Honey, try not to worry too much. We don't have any idea what happened when he took the body back home. We just don't know."

"But Daddy, it's been four days. Where can he be?"

"Maybe they did get into a fight. I feel certain he is hiding out in the hills until things settle down. Mattie Ann, he might have done the smart thing and kept right on ridin'. There are a whole lot of them and only one of him."

* * *

The next time he awoke the sun peeped into the bowl with the first rays of morning. The stiffness had worked out of his leg some and he'd found the crutch he'd made from a fallen tree branch made it possible for him to stand and hobble around. He needed something to eat besides fish—he needed meat to build up his strength. He spotted deer tracks all around the water's edge, but he still didn't want to risk a rifle shot; partly because of the Taggerts, and partly because he didn't want to disturb the stillness in the valley—the bowl. He remembered the slingshot. The weapon was in the saddlebags. He dragged himself to them and dug out the slingshot. After scouring the ground for suitable rocks of the right size, he dropped a big old fat prairie chicken that was taking off after getting a drink in the lake. He ate well that night.

On the fifth day, Sam managed to throw a saddle on the buckskin and ride around the area. The more he observed, the more he liked his hiding place. "Buck, this grass is deep and lush, and there is plenty of water, and those purple flowers growing along the east wall, they're like large clusters of purple grapes. They're so pretty they almost take your breath away. Well Buck, if you can't fly straight up, I guess there is one way in or out of here: the way we came in, through the waterfall. I still wonder how those cows got here."

The more he looked around and thought about it, he decided, *This must have been an old volcano at one time.* He tilted his head back so he could look at the ridge surrounding the bowl. He found heavy timber, with trees growing up to the edge.

On the way back to camp, a small doe sprang out of the bush right in front of him. He had that ole slingshot all loaded up thinking he would get a rabbit or a squirrel for supper. He let fly with a stone and the rock hit the deer right behind the left ear. She made one more jump and fell. Still too weak to get down and back up onto the buckskin, he tossed a rope around a back leg and dragged the deer back to camp. "Yes sir, a venison steak sure is gonna taste good tonight."

After supper, he spread his bedroll and slept.

Noise and movement woke him. "What was that?" He peeped through slits in his eyelids to assess the situation before he made a move. What he found made his blood curdle. Wolves were eating the remainder of his deer meat.

He reached for his six-shooter. The wolves were busy devouring the deer and hadn't noticed him. He threw bigger pieces of wood onto the fire, sat up, and leaned his gun hand on his knee to steady the barrel. He knew there was no way to shoot them all before the pack ripped him to pieces.

* * *

Mattie Ann refused to go back to town. She stayed at the ranch and sat alone in her room. Sleep eluded her. She prayed, "Lord, please don't let anything happen to Sam. I don't know if he has even noticed me. Even if he did, he may think of me like a little sister. The rest of the cowhands do. I think I'm falling in love with him. I hear the pastor say the prayers of a righteous person avail much. Lord, please don't let the Taggerts kill him."

She thought, *I just told the Lord I'm falling in love with Sam.* Then she thought, *Is that true? Or am I worried because he stood up for me? He is a hired hand. What would Papa say if I wanted to marry a man like Sam?*

* * *

Randolph Taggert called a meeting of the Taggert clan. "That dude has got more guts than a Missouri mule. He kilt Del-Roy and brought him right back here to the house. Now he's kilt Raymond and Ollie. By damn, that's four. We can't kill 'im four times, but we gotta kill him good and dead, before he wipes us all out."

"Pa, I guarantee he's already dead up in them hills somewhere. We followed a pretty good blood trail to the creek. In fact, we found where he laid down to get a drink. Blood is all over the ground. So we got some lead in 'im."

Randolph slammed his hand down on the table and yelled, "I don't want you to quit lookin' until I put my hands on his dead carcass myself. When you find him, don't nary one of you try to take 'im by yourself. This jaybird is mighty handy with them six-shooters. You find him and hightail it back here. This all started over the Carville gal. One of you boys keep an eye on the Carville place. That's where I think he'll show up pretty soon. I'm bettin' he's makin' calf eyes over the gal. Sooner or later, he'll show up, and we'll be out to stop him. I want him dead."

* * *

A COLLISION OF DREAMS

The buckskin jerked on the picket rope and his hooves danced in the grass. Buck gave a nervous whiney and blew through his nostrils, ready to cut and run as soon as he got loose from his tether.

What is the matter with Buck? There is something or somebody else out there in the dark. Something besides these wolves. What does Buck see or hear?

Sam almost jumped out of his socks when a scream split the still night air. Hair stood up on the back of his neck. His grip tightened on the six-shooter. The wolves jumped back like they'd been hit with a hot branding iron. They took off running, dragging the deer carcass with them.

On the other side of the campfire, a pair of big green eyes stared at Sam. Eyes that glowed like they were made of glass. Sam worked hard to keep his voice calm when he spoke to the visitor. "Mr. Cougar, I don't want no truck with you. It's okay with me if you want to go hassle them wolves for the rest of the deer. Help yourself. But if you try to get either of those hindquarters I hung up in this tree, I'm going to shoot you plumb full of holes with this forty-four."

The cougar melted back into the darkness. Sam sighed with relief. Buck stopped his restless stirring. Sam built up the fire, and the blaze rose three feet into the air. He got up and moved the buckskin's tether rope closer to the fire. He placed his bedroll so close to the fire that he felt like, if he got any closer, he would roast.

He knew one thing: He would rather roast than become dinner for a pack of hungry wolves or a cougar. "Buck, I don't like those wolves or that big cat around here anymore than you do. You and me are gonna stay close to this fire until daylight. As soon as morning comes, we're gonna saddle up and get out of here. I hope when we ride out of here we don't ride right back into a shooting war. I really don't want any more of this war. I want to find a place with several hundred acres, like this bowl, where I can build a ranch and talk Mattie Ann into marrying me. Am I asking too much?"

He was quiet for a few minutes, then told the buckskin, "It just ain't right. When I rode into town all I wanted was a job. One of them sorry Taggerts tried to shoot me. Later, one of them no-account Taggerts dry gulched Jessie. I killed three or four of them. It didn't bring Jessie back. Maybe now is the time to let it go. Get back to trying to build a ranch of my own. Buck, you know something? All the time I've been here, I haven't thought about the Taggerts. All I've thought about is Mattie Ann." He laughed. "You know what? I'd rather face a whole passel of Taggerts than that old cougar again."

He didn't get much sleep the rest of the night. When he did doze off, he dreamed of Mattie Ann. In his dream, they settled down in this beautiful place. As he woke, he remembered Jessie. The muscles in his jaw tightened. This wasn't the time to think about marrying. He had no way to know how the fight with the Taggerts was going to end. Even if he wanted to stop the war, they might not let him. After he had fixed some breakfast, he stood up and used the makeshift crutch to hobble around. He walked three paces, then turned to his horse and said, "Buck, we're safe as long as we stay here. We can't win anything' by hiding out. I'm going to get the saddle on you and we are going out of here."

He struggled, but he managed to get his gear on the horse.

CHAPTER FIFTEEN
Taggert Family

Jake Taggert rode in after dropping off a load of moonshine whisky to the Indian village. Sarah Beth met him at the door of their two-room shanty. Her eyes were red from crying. "Jake, I want us to load up and move out of here. We can find plenty of land farther west."

"What are you talkin' about? This is our home. Family's here."

"Yeah, and two of your brothers and two of your nephews are dead. I understand what happened. Billy Wayne tried to get ugly with the Carville girl, then he tried to shoot this young cowboy and got hisself killed. Now another one of your brothers and two of your nephews are dead. I don't want you or either one of our boys getting killed over somethin' Billy Wayne did."

"It ain't that easy, Sarrey, you know that. He's killed four Taggerts. Now we got to get him."

"How? You can't even find him, and every time one of ya'll do find him another Taggert gets killed. I think the man ain't natural. I think he's got the voodoo on him. You better leave him alone. Let's get out of this canyon and find us a new place."

"Quit talkin' crazy, woman. Nobody messes with Taggerts." Jake started for the door.

"Four, Jake. There's four new graves up on the hill and this stranger put 'em there. Leave him alone. Let's just get out of here. If'n your pa and brother want to get themselves killed, that's their business. Do you realize our two sons are the only two left to carry on the Taggert name? There ain't no Taggerts left—just you, your brother, and your pa. I don't like them odds."

He spun around and slapped her with the back of his hand. The blow split her lip and knocked her down. "Don't you ever stick your nose in my business. You keep your mouth shut and do what I tell you." He stormed out the door and slammed it behind him. "We're gonna find him and we're gonna kill 'im."

* * *

Sam rode into the yard at the Tumbling C. From a distance, nobody recognized him. He had a full beard.

Russ glanced at him and then looked at the buckskin. "Man, where've you been? We had about decided you were dead."

"They got some lead in me, but I ain't dead."

Rosa peeked out the back door and spotted him. "Oh my Lord. Mattie Ann, come and see what I'm looking at." The screen door flew open and they both ran out to meet him. Rosa said, "That boy is pale, and look how much weight he has lost. Get him in the kitchen so Rosa can feed him some food."

He eased off the horse and reached back to get his walking stick. Mattie Ann put her arms around him, saying, "You're hurt. Someone help me get him in the house."

The next morning Russ said, "Sam, you ain't in no shape to ride. I want you to spend as much time as you feel like working. Repairin' all the busted bridle and tack stored out in the tack room. Don't push yourself until you get stronger."

Sam started to object, but Russ said, "Just till you're stronger."

The third day he worked in the barn, Mattie Ann showed up with a cold glass of tea. "Take a break and drink some cool tea. Rosa's been making large jugs of tea and storing them in the spring to keep them cool."

"Sounds like a gift from heaven, especially since it's delivered by an angel." Sam smiled at her as he took the glass from her hand.

Mattie Ann inspected the tack he had been working on. She crinkled up her nose and said, "Real blacksmiths do better work."

Sam said, "I'll have you know I'm a full-fledged cowhand who happened to get stuck here fixin' tack. I'm not a blacksmith."

"Well, cowhand, come sit on the porch swing to drink your tea and you can tell me the whole story about what happened while you were missing so long."

"Why, ma'am, you make it downright appealin'. I can drink Rosa's tea and tell you about my wild exploits, or I can just make something up."

"Hmmm... This ought to be good."

Sam walked up on the porch and sat on the swing. *I shouldn't do this. I'm still a $30.00-a-month saddle bum who rode in looking for work. I can't think about starting a ranch of my own until I get this Taggert mess settled—if I don't get killed first.*

Mattie Ann opened the screen door and walked into the kitchen. In a moment, she came through the door with a plate full of donuts. "Okay, cowboy, tell me how you managed to hide out for over a week. The Taggerts are combing the hills looking for you."

"Ma'am, you give me one of them donuts and I'll tell you all the tales you want to hear." She handed the donuts to him. He stuffed one in his mouth and said, "I guess you learned some Greek mythology in school, about Pegasus, the flying horse? Well, Buck's sired by that breed, and when he needs to, he just unfolds his wings and we fly. It confuses the bad guys every time."

Mattie Ann laughed. "If you ever expect to get another glass of Rosa's tea or another donut, you'd better come up with something better than that."

"Okay, you win. You know how much I like Rosa's tea, and I love these bear signs. Never did understand why people call 'em bear signs, anyway. The truth is I found a cave near a stream of clear spring water. I was able to fit both of us into the cave. I made a small fire, bathed my wounds, and cut up my clean shirt for bandages." He was quiet for a moment then said, "Let me ask you a question. Do you believe in angels?"

"I can't say. I've never seen one. Why?"

"The first night I lay on my blanket in the cave burning up with fever. I thought I saw a man wearing a clean white robe sitting by my fire. He kept feeding sticks into the fire to keep the fire going so I never got chilled."

"Sam, I don't understand all about how God works. My Bible does say he will send angels to watch over us. Why don't you come to church with us and talk to the pastor about it? He might have some ideas about how angels work."

"Mattie Ann, I can't go to church. Don't you realize I've killed five or six men?"

"Were any of those men shooing at you?"

"All of 'em were."

"You didn't commit murder, you shot in self-defense."

"Doesn't the Bible say, 'Thou shalt not kill?'"

"The Bible actually says, 'Thou shall not commit murder.' What if you were in the army and your troop was attacked by a bunch of Indians?"

"Jessie and me was attacked by a bunch of Apache."

"What's the difference whether they're Apache or outlaws? Someone shoots at you, you have the right to shoot back."

"Mattie Ann, sometimes I just don't know what's right and what's not anymore."

"Why don't you come to church with Daddy and me next Sunday? You'll like the preacher. He's not a pulpit pounder."

Sam sat his tea glass down on the porch railing and stood. "Right now I've got to go finish the tack room before Russ comes back and skins me. Thanks for the tea and the bear signs."

Mattie Ann watched him walk away and thought, *He is one handsome cowboy. Lord, help me to not be too pushy about getting him into church. It sure would be nice to sit beside him and share a hymnal.*

CHAPTER SIXTEEN
Somebody New Making Whiskey

Morton Taggert, Jr. said, "Uncle Jake, are you sure you know about cookin' whisky? That stuff can be dangerous. Unless it's cooked just right, it can blow up. Pa says a bad batch can poison a fella. He's always done the cookin', but he's gonna be laid up awhile after that lowlander whacked him on the head with his gun barrel. Ma says he had a brain conclusion or something like that."

"Aw hell, boy, don't you worry none. We're just sellin' it to a bunch of savages. Throw some more wood on the fire."

"Pa always says if it ain't cooked right, a bad batch can make you go blind or kill ya. That's pretty dangerous stuff."

"Then don't drink it. Just sell to the Indians. If they all go blind, they can't go on no warpath, now can they? It'd be like doin' a patriotic duty to the country. Pour in some more of that sour mash."

* * *

Sunday morning, Sam leaned against the corral as Mattie Ann and Joe climbed into the buggy. He thought, They are on their way to church. Mattie Ann sure looks beautiful in that pale green dress and white shoes, with her blond hair piled up on top of her head. He felt like she took his breath away. He thought, If I had my own spread, I'd ask that girl to marry me.

Mattie Ann's daddy snapped the reins on the back of the roan hooked to the buggy. The horse stepped out at a spanking trot. Before they left the ranch yard, she glanced over and saw Sam standing by the corral, and thought, If I got that cowboy to start coming to church with us, I'd marry him. He is a good-looking guy. Of course, right now he doesn't seem to have any interest in God. I wonder if God did hear my prayer and send an angel to watch over him that night? If I can't get him to become a believer, the Bible is pretty plain, when it says, "Do not become yoked to an unbeliever." That has never been a problem before.

Sam rested his right elbow on the top rail. As the buggy rolled down the lane leading to the road, he felt sadness settle over him. He thought, *I shouldn't be dreaming about walking down the aisle with somebody like her.* Then he told himself, *You don't have-ta stay a cowhand—there's a lot of land out there that ain't been fenced yet. If a fellow wanted to work hard and wrestle it away from nature, he could build something for himself just like Joe Carville did. I think its time Buck and me took a ride.* He called Buck over to the fence, grabbed a handful of hay, and brushed the horse's back to make sure there were no burs in the hair. Then he lifted the saddle off the top rail and tightened the cinch. He opened the gate and headed north to check out the land. Most of the big ranches, in fact, had only a few hundred acres fenced. They normally fenced around their hay and grain fields. Cattle grazed on the open range.

"Buck, what I need is to find a good spot to homestead, and then buy a few head of cow to get started. If I do well, the first thing I am going to do is come back and ask Mattie Ann to marry me."

His thinking shifted to the Taggerts. "Buck, I'm willing to drop this war with the Taggerts. But what if they come shootin'? How can I ask Mattie Ann to marry me? I don't know if I even have a future. I've got to keep an eye out for the Taggerts."

He rode for a while and enjoyed the quiet of being out on the range. With beauty all around him, the hill to his right appeared to be completely covered in purple sage. He rode to the top of a rocky outcropping and turned to look back toward the Tumbling C. From this high up, the tops of the buildings appeared to shimmer in the haze. "Buck, look down there. That's what we're looking for—a place of our own. Mr. Carville built his own ranch and so can I. Let's keep going. It's out here somewhere."

An hour later, he rode over a hill and fixed his eyes on a beautiful valley that stretched for miles. "Wow, Buck. I've rode a lot of trails, but I've never seen so many shades of green—and look at the colors. Wildflowers are painting the valley with all the colors in a rainbow. This is as pretty as the bowl and a lot more accessible.

"I see plenty of timber on the slopes for building. A man wouldn't be short on water with that river running right through the middle like a blue ribbon. I could stay here forever. I've never seen such deep, lush grass. I would need to put a wire fence around a hundred acres or so to plant hay and grain After I feed the stock I might have some left for a cash crop. Folks back east always need wheat for flour."

When he rode down into the valley, he came to a stream of clear, fresh water fed by a spring that came out of the hill. "I'll build a house on the side of the hill overlooking the valley and have fresh, cold mountain water from the spring."

He noticed several deer that came out of the trees across the valley and started grazing. Movement off to his right caught his attention. A herd of wild horses moved into the valley. He watched them for a while, and it became obvious that the herd came to drink out of the river. His first thought was that a man could trap those horses and start a horse ranch. That herd has some beautiful horses in the group. Then he thought, No, with the railroad coming the need for horses will be less and less. Cattle are where the future is—people have got to eat.

A plan started to form in his mind. "Buck, I've got three months wages coming, and with what I've got in my pocket I'll have a little over two hundred dollars. I'll ask Mr. Carville to loan me a wagon and team. We'll haul wire in here to build a pen for the horses. I'll trap that herd of wild mustangs. I'm glad I learned Fred's method of training horses—that's what I'll use. I'll sell 'em to the army, then take the money and go buy a whiteface bull. After I get a good bull, I'll go back to the bowl behind the waterfall, brand the cows, and have the start of a herd. What if I leave most of the cows in the bowl and bring a few to the homestead at a time? That'll build up the herd on my ranch while the herd continues to grow in the bowl."

A COLLISION OF DREAMS

Sam rode down to the spring and jumped off the back of his horse. He stepped off the space where he would build the barns and corrals, and especially the house. The more he stepped off the dimensions, the faster he walked. He wanted to make it something Mattie Ann would consider living in. He'd have to make this a grand place, with a wide front porch. He wanted flowers around a porch designed so a body could sit late in the evening and look at their cows down in the valley.

"Buck, the first thing we've got to do is go into town and file a claim on the valley before somebody else does, and then I've got to talk to Mr. Carville about drawing my wages and borrowing a wagon."

In his excitement about finding the valley, he hadn't been looking at the sky. Suddenly a loud clap of thunder shattered the stillness of the valley and echoed down through the hills. He glanced up and said, "Oh boy Buck, we may be fixing to be caught out in a storm."

He had also not given any thought to the Taggerts.

CHAPTER SEVENTEEN
Mattie Ann's letter

Mattie Ann sat at her writing desk and penned a letter to her cousin in Denver.

    Dear Sally Jo,

    Daddy and I just got home from church. There is a terrible storm outside, so I decided now would be a good time to write.

    A few weeks ago, I was visiting Aunt Millie in Cactus Tree when a terrible thing happened. As I was walking back to her millinery store from the mercantile, a drunken man ran out the bat wing doors of the salon and almost knocked me off the boardwalk. Then he did the most despicable thing. This dirty, smelly, drunken thing grabbed me and tried to kiss me right there on the boardwalk in the middle of the day. I almost fainted. I don't know what would have happened if this very handsome cowboy hadn't stepped in and demanded that the smelly man turn me loose and leave me alone. Then something equally sickening happened. Right in front of my eyes, the smelly drunk pulled out a gun and shot at the cowboy.

    He missed, then the cowboy pulled out his gun and shot the drunken molester. Sally Jo, he fell almost on my shoes. I had never seen a man killed before. It was horrible.

    Then my Daddy gave the cowboy a job. Now I have a terrible dilemma. I think I am falling in love with him, but I can't get the image of a dead man lying at my feet out of my mind. Oh, he is handsome and I love teasing him. Another thing: He is not a believer. I have invited him to church with Daddy and me several times and he isn't interested.

    He acts like he is interested in me. I am so mixed up. I love being around him, spending time with him, but I just can't see any future with him since he is not a believer.

I don't know what to do?
Your Dearest Cousin
Mattie Ann

* * *

About ten minutes after Sam left the valley, rain started pouring down. It was coming down so hard he couldn't see the trail. He just hoped Buck could see it. Lightning flashed and thunder boomed through the hills. Sam thought, *I've got to get Buck off this hill. I don't want to be sitting up on a horse with a pistol strapped on my hip and a rifle in the saddle boot. I can't see a thing. I don't know which way to turn. If I ride down into a gulley, I've seen what a flash flood will do up in these hills.* He could tell Buck was getting as nervous as he was. All at once, Buck stopped. Sam peered ahead and realized they were on the edge of a cliff. With the rain, he couldn't tell if it was a hundred feet or ten feet to the bottom.

Lightning struck a scrub tree about fifty feet from where he sat. When it lit up the darkness, his heart almost stopped beating. He was at the very edge of a deep canyon.

On his own, Buck turned right and started down a steep trail, one that Sam had never seen. Now Sam was scared. He had to trust Buck to save them both because he couldn't see anything. The trail turned to the right and Sam felt more than saw a dark cave on his right.

* * *

The sheriff walked into the territorial marshal's office, shook rainwater off his slicker, and said, "It ain't for man or beast out there. Have you heard anything about some bad whisky being sold to the Indians?"

"Any whiskey sold to the Indians is bad."

"Yeah, I agree. One of my deputies was talkin' to a fellow from over by the reservation and he says there are a lot of sick Indians. They think it's because somebody sold them bad whiskey."

The marshal twirled his handlebar mustache. "I'd better take a ride over there and check it out."

"If you find out who's sellin' bad whiskey, tell him to keep it out of my county."

"Jake, if I was a bettin' man, my bet would be that the moonshine whiskey is comin' out of your county. Those Taggerts sell more whiskey than anybody."

"Yeah, but we've never been able to catch them sellin' it. And we've never heard of anyone complainin' of bad stuff."

"Maybe there's somebody else sellin' to the Indians? Or somebody new is doin' the cookin' at the Taggerts? You better find out before it causes a big dust up."

"Have you had any trouble with renegade Indians attackin' white folks?"

"Naw, just that one incident when Joe Carville reported a couple of his boys had a shootin' scrape with a bunch of young bucks. I figured they were just flexing their muscles."

"Has there been anymore trouble with the young fellow that got tangled up with the Taggerts?"

"Well, you know one of the Taggerts dry gulched a cowhand of Joe's. That same boy shot the dry gulcher. Then he took the body back home to the Taggerts. I heard he got in a shootin' scrape with them and killed two more. At this rate, pretty soon there won't be any left to plague the rest of us. There wasn't but nine or ten of them and he's already shot four."

"Did they kill 'im?"

"Not accordin' to Joe. They put some lead in 'im. He hid out up in the hills until he was well enough to ride. Now he's back working on the ranch."

"Is this kid trigger happy?"

"I don't think so—at least he doesn't act like it. It all started when Billy Wayne Taggert tried to molest Joe Carville's daughter, right out in broad daylight on Main Street. The kid was just gettin' off his horse and told Billy Wayne to get his hands off the girl. Billy Wayne took a shot at the kid and missed. The kid put two forty-four bullets in a spot this big." He held up his thumb and index finger to form a circle the size of a four-bit piece.

"Do you mean to tell me he put two bullets in a space no bigger than that?"

"I laid a silver dollar on Billie Wayne's chest and it covered both holes."

"If the kid can shoot like that, you better keep an eye on 'im. He may go bad on you. It sounds like he's already killed most of the Taggerts. Not that anybody'll miss 'em."

"Yeah, he could go bad. But every time he's shot anybody, they were shootin' at him. All he did was shoot back. He doesn't sound much like a hardened killer to me."

"Yes, but that sort of thing can mess with a man's head."

"I'll keep an eye out. And I'll let you know what I find out about the bad whiskey. We don't need a passel of do-gooders down here from Washington, crying over a bunch of Indians."

* * *

Monday morning, Sam walked in and told Joe Carville about his intentions. Joe looked at him for a long moment, then said, "Sam, did you get caught out in that storm?"

"Yes sir. I was on my way back when it hit me. Buck found a cave. Well, actually it was more of an overhang, but we were out of the rain and lightnin' and I got a fire goin', so it was alright."

Carville said, "What do you need from me?"

Sam told him about the valley and his plan.

"Sam, I admire a man who wants to get ahead. But if it doesn't work out, you'll always have a job here."

CHAPTER EIGHTEEN
Building the Fence

As Sam rode into town, he remembered the first time he had ridden into Cactus Tree. A lot had happened since then. When he rode in the first time, he was looking for a place to put down stakes and build a life with a good woman. He had now found the place. All he needed now was for Mattie Ann to agree to marry him. He had bet everything on the hope that she would. Of course, he couldn't ask her until he got his ranch established.

The first place he went was the land office, where he filed for six hundred and forty acres in the valley. The way he filed the homestead claim, he controlled the entrance to the valley. That would in effect make him the sole owner of the whole valley.

After finishing at the claims office he went to see the marshal, who had befriended him on that first day in town.

The marshal glanced up from his desk when Sam walked in. "Well, lordy-lordy, look who just showed up in my door. What can I do for ya, son?"

"Marshall, I just filed a homestead for a section of land up in a valley a few miles north of here. I wanted you to know I'll be puttin' down roots, so I'll be around."

"So you're goin' to try your hand at ranchin', are you?"

"Yes sir."

"Where are you going to get cows? 'Cause if I catch you runnin' loose with a brandin' iron, I'll have your hide."

"No sir, while I am in town I'm goin' to buy some wire. I am going to build a trap for wild horses. There is a whole herd of good-looking horse stock in that valley. I am going to trap 'em and train 'em and sell them to the army. When I get enough money, I'm goin' to buy one of them whiteface bulls I've been hearing about from back east."

"As long as you do everything on the up and up, you'll be welcome. I want to see more good men settle around here. Wish you had a family. Families are even better settlers."

"Yes sir. I'm working on that now." Sam grinned and waved goodbye.

***

Sam drove the wagon along the line where he wanted the fence. Every 100 feet he unloaded coils of barbwire and staples. At one point, he disturbed an old cottontail rabbit sleeping in the shade of a cactus plant. The rabbit ran off about fifty feet and sat looking at him. Sam thought, *That old boy is trying to figure out what the heck I'm doing.* Sweat rolled off his body by the time he had all of the heavy rolls of wire and supplies stacked near the spot where he would build the fence. He stood in the wagon and looked all around and thought, *I love the peace and quiet out here in the valley. There ain't a more beautiful place in the world. The whole hillside on the west is still covered in purple sage.*

Sam stood and gazed up the valley and thought, *My plan is simple, but a good one. First, I'll build a strong four-strand barbwire fence about a mile long. The long side will run north and south along the east side of the river. Horses coming for water will find the fence. At first, they'll be unable to get to the water. After a few minutes, they'll figure out that they can follow the fence until they find a way to get past the south end of the fence to the water. When the corral is finished, they'll end up in a corral. I'll divert water from the river, creating a small pond inside the corral.*

He took a whetstone and sharpened an axe. When he was through, he could have used it to shave. He climbed up on the wagon seat and headed for the hills, and thought, *I want trees about six inches in diameter to use for fence posts. I'm not building a fence—I'm building a future, a home, and roots. It ain't much yet, but it is a start.*

For the first time in his young life, he had something he could call his own. As the sun was going down, Sam unhitched the team of horses and untied Buck from the back of the wagon, and led them to water. He picketed the team and turned Buck loose. There was no need to picket him. Buck wasn't going far from Sam or the other horses.

The first thing he did after he saw to the horses was to build a fire and get some coffee brewing. He dug cold biscuits out of his knapsack and sliced bacon into a pan. Before he got into his bedroll, he cleaned his guns.

Sitting with his back against his saddle, he looked across his valley, just soaking in the peace and quiet. While he watched the sun paint the sky in brilliant shades of red and orange, night shadows lowered like a curtain across the valley. Sam sat there and listened to the whippoorwills sing their night song, and the coyotes complaining to the moon. War with the Taggerts seemed thousands of miles away. Before he turned in, he walked to the spring, stripped off his shirt, and bathed his arms, neck, and shoulders. The icy water was like medicine for his aching body and swollen hands.

Sam lay on his blanket and stared at the Milky Way. The stars filled the night sky, like thousands of flickering candles. He dreamed of Mattie Ann. "I wonder if she's thinking about me?" He drifted off to sleep and dreamed of a ranch house that faced down the valley. It had a great view of tall stalks of corn waving in the wind, and whiteface cattle grazing in the valley.

* * *

Sarah walked into Ma Taggert's kitchen. "Ma, we need to talk. The men are all out chasin' this man. They ain't gettin' no work done around here. They're spendin' all of their time roamin' all over the hills lookin' for him. Every time they corner him another one of ours gets killed. I tell you, this man has the voodoo on him, he ain't natural. I'm scared for them to find 'im."

"I know honey, but he has killed four of our clan. They've got to find 'im and kill 'im."

"That's just it, Ma. I hope they don't find 'im, because if they do find him, he'll kill some more of our men. I tell you, that man ain't natural. I want us to move out of this valley. Let's go on to California or somewhere else."

Grandma Taggert wrinkled her brow, like she had troubling thoughts. "Sarah, you're right. I've got two sons and two grandsons buried up there on the side of that hill. I don't want to bury anymore. It ain't supposed to happen like this—your kids are supposed to outlive you." She was quiet for a while, then she said, "But you know Pa. He'll figure out what has gone wrong and he'll learn from their mistakes, and the next time they meet this dude they'll kill 'im dead. Pa ain't gonna quit until they kill that man."

Sarah started to cry. "Or until he kills all of them."

* * *

Blue-silver streaks were just filling the morning sky as the sun smiled over the ridges to the east. Rosa was gathering fresh eggs from the chickens and Mattie Ann was picking fresh tomatoes from the garden. They were getting ready to make breakfast for the hands.

As they both walked back to the house, each with a basket in her hands, Mattie Ann said, "I wonder what Sam is doing today?"

"I'd say he is busy building a home for his new bride."

"Rosa, he doesn't have a new bride."

Rosa swished her hips and did a little dance. "No, not yet. He will soon. If a certain young lady doesn't want him, there are several more young ladies that are all eyeing a good looking man like him."

"Rosa, you are impossible. He hasn't asked me anything yet. Besides, we still have the problem of him not being a believer. That is a big problem."

* * *

Sam's eyes opened to a crisp clear morning. He rolled out of his blanket, crumbled up some dried bark on the coals, and started to blow on it. Flames licked up around the crumbled bark. He added small twigs. Then he had a fire going. He began slicing strips of beacon into a pan. As soon as the bacon finished frying, he dropped sourdough biscuits into the hot grease.

He ate a hurried breakfast and gulped down two cups of scalding hot, railroad spike coffee—cowboys called it that because it was strong enough to float a railroad spike in. Soon he was wide-awake.

The blisters on his hands were still sore from cutting post the day before. He moved slowly because his muscles were stiff this morning. It was an effort to load his tools into the wagon and hitch up the team.

Sam said to the two mares hitched to the wagon, "Okay girls, we've got a lot of work ahead of us, so we best get started." Sam stood in the wagon bed and dropped a post every ten feet along the line where the fence would go. When he reached the end of the line, he climbed down and started to dig holes for the posts to sit in.

His arms and shoulders were strong from years of hard work, but by noon he groaned with the agony of the blisters in the palms of his hands. His body was slick with perspiration. Going back to the spring, he soaked his swollen hands in the cold water to help make the swelling go down.

He reached into the syrup bucket that acted as a lunch pail, and pulled out two cold biscuits and a piece of venison jerky, then washed it down with cold water from the spring. A robber jay hopped near to steal some food. Sam tossed a piece of biscuit to him. "Okay little buddy, at least you are some company. To bad I can't teach you how to set fence post."

He looked at the sun and decided he had about five more hours of daylight. He had placed the poles ten feet apart, which meant that every ten poles equaled 100 feet of fence. He was too busy to think about the Taggerts—although he did work wearing his six-shooter on his hip.

At the end of the day, he looked at what he'd accomplished with satisfaction. He thought, *All together I need about fifty sections. If I can do ten sections a day, I'll have this fence done in five days. I'll need five more days to build a strong corral.*

A COLLISION OF DREAMS

Sam sat in his camp soon after the sun came up the next morning and watched the horse herd come into the valley. The horses stopped when they came to the fence. He pulled his telescope out of its bag and studied them. As he watched, he saw that they were curious about the fence. He talked to himself. "Come on big fellas, the fence won't hurt you. Don't be frightened by it. That's good. Just walk along the fence until you reached the end of the wire, and then you can go around the end to the river and get a drink." *There are some magnificent animals in that herd*, he thought. *I can hardly wait to start training them, using the same method I learned from Fred.*

He was moving the telescope over the herd when he suddenly stopped. "Whoa, look at that big roan stallion. That's one magnificent looking horse." Sam thought, WOW, *what a magnificent stud he'll make.*

All at once, a bird flew straight up from a bush about fifty yards in front of where he sat. The sudden movement caught his eye. What caused that bird to take off like that? With his right thumb, he eased the thong off the hammer of his six-shooter, and then waited several minutes. When he saw no movement after several minutes, he decided he must be seeing things where none existed. He reached for his rifle and climbed to his feet. With careful steps, he approached the bush. Nothing moved. Under the bush, he could see that something had disturbed the leaves under and behind the bush. Whatever it was, or whomever it was, it had moved on. The ground was so hard in that area there were no tracks.

He stood and looked all around. The hair on the back of his neck stood up. He had a feeling that somebody was watching him. After a slow, careful look at every tree and bush where anyone could hide, he told himself, "Well, I don't see anything, and I've got work to do. Might as well get started." He kept his six-shooter loose in his holster and his rifle close by as he got back to work. If he wanted to catch those horses, he had a fence to build.

CHAPTER NINETEEN
Mattie Ann Talks to Rosa

Mattie Ann sat shelling peas into a bowl. "Rosa, I don't know what to do about Sam. He is really good-looking. He is polite, fun to be around, but he will not go to church with us."

"So?"

"Rosa, you know I have always said I will not date a man who is not a Christian. I will not take a chance on falling in love with a man who is not a believer. I have seen too many girls fall in love with a pair of wide shoulders and tight blue jeans. Non-believers don't make good husbands and daddies."

"Child, how many have you actually known? You have been reading those *Gazettes* too much. I think you are already falling in love with that cowboy and you are just too stubborn to admit it. Remember, love conquers everything else."

"No, I do like him a lot. He is very handsome. I'll admit that. He is also the most stubborn man I have ever met. I have asked him and asked him to go to church and he won't do it."

"It seems to me that maybe Sam is not the only one who is being stubborn. Sounds to me like you want him to do things your way and, if he don't, you're trying to get up enough nerve to stop thinking about him, but you can't."

Empty pea hulls rattled as Mattie Ann threw a handful into the hull pan. "Oh, you are as exasperating as he is. I will not be married to any man won't take me to church on Sundays."

Rosa wiped her hands on a cloth and smiled. "Has he asked you to marry him?"

Mattie Ann's cheeks flamed. "No, he hasn't even tried to kiss me. He is the most exasperating man I have ever seen. What am I supposed to do?"

A COLLISION OF DREAMS

"Look girl, the man is a proud man. He is up there all alone, working day and night to build a ranch. He is doing it all by himself, with no help. When he gets the ranch going, he'll come back. In the meantime, we can always pray for him. Why don't we do that?"

"That is a good idea. Rosa, will you pray for Sam?"

Rosa lifted up her apron, kneeled on her thick stubby knees, and said, "Lord, we lift up to you these young lovers. We ask you to watch over Sam as he is working all alone up on his ranch. Protect him, please. Lord, we lift up Mattie Ann. Give her patience and allow her love for this fine young man to grow. We ask these things in Jesus name. Amen."

Mattie Ann used the helm of her apron to wipe tears from her eyes and said, "Thank you, Rosa."

CHAPTER TWENTY
Sam Talks to Mr. Carville

For the next three days, Sam's fence continued to march toward the area where the corral would wait. Each morning, Sam watched the herd, and kept an eye on the bush where he had seen the bird fly straight up. The mustangs were predictable and always came right after the sun came up. Each day the fence grew longer, but they were less curious about the fence and tomorrow he would close the corral. Then he would own the herd.

The next morning after getting a drink of water, the horses took the same trail back up into the hills. By mid-afternoon, Sam had finished the corral. He had nothing more to do today. The fence and corral were complete. Sam hitched the team to the wagon and drove it back to the Tumbling C. He wanted to see Mr. Carville and Mattie Ann, and he sorely missed Rosa's hot cornbread.

With each section completed, his excitement had grown. Today he would see Mattie Ann. That's all he had thought about while he dug postholes, stretched wire, and pounded staples. Mattie Ann acted friendly and comfortable with him. The thing was, Did she think the same way about him as he did about her?

Then he was scared. "What if I ask her to marry me and she says no?" He looked back over his shoulder and told Buck, "As soon as we get that first load of horses sold to the army I'm going to ask Mr. Carville if I can have his blessing to court his daughter. Even if she doesn't love me yet, maybe she'll learn to. I can't ask her to marry me now. The ranch isn't finished. Buck, we've got some hard work ahead of us if we want to get things ready for a lady to come live at the ranch. We've got to go back to the bowl behind the waterfall and catch some of those wild cows so we can build us a herd, and then we've got to build a house. Not just any old house, but one that will make Mattie Ann proud."

Russ saw Sam drive in as he walked out onto the front porch of the bunkhouse. "Park the wagon out back of the barn and I'll help you unhitch. Where've you been? We'd about decided them Taggerts got you again."

"Naw, just working. I built a mile of fence and two corrals."

"Whoopee, I'll say you've been workin'. Well, come on up to the house and put your boots under Rosa's table. After bein' out there on your own, you're sure to want some of her cookin'."

"I'd be lying if I said I hadn't thought about it every time I made biscuits in my skillet or fried up some bacon. I did find some berries to munch on."

"Mattie Ann's been frettin' ever since you left. I think she'll be glad to see you're in one piece."

"I missed Mattie Ann about as much as I missed Rosa's cooking."

As they stepped through the back door, Russ laughed and said, "You better not let Mattie Ann hear you say it like that."

"Say what?" Mattie Ann asked.

Russ said, "Sam has been up in them hills so long he was saying old Buck had started to look as pretty as you."

Mattie Ann blushed, and then said, "So you're saying I look like a horse?"

Sam was getting flustered and turned red. He stammered, "I never said no such a thing. Russ here is just trying to get a rise out of you."

Rosa was setting a platter of tortillas on the table. She said, "All right, you two quit pickin' on the boy, and let him eat some of my huevos rancheros. He looks like he lost some pounds. He needs some of Rosa's cookin' to fill him out again." Leaning closer to Sam, she whispered conspiratorially, "She's been mopin' around here for two weeks lookin' for you every day."

Later, Sam and Mattie Ann sat on the porch swing. Mattie Ann said, "You know today is Saturday—why don't you spend the night and go to church with Daddy and me tomorrow?"

"Mattie Ann, I can't. I've got to go to town and see if I can hire me a helper to break horses. I don't think I can do it by myself. Besides, it's too dangerous by myself. If I got thrown and broke a leg or something, no one would know about it until I was found dead."

Right after noon Sam rode into Cactus Tree. He slipped the thong off the six-gun before he got into town, then he paid a visit to the marshal first. "Howdy marshal."

"Well, hello, Sam. Have you had any more trouble out of them Taggerts?"

"No sir, I'm hoping I don't."

"I heard awhile back you'd had some more shootin' trouble with them."

"Yes sir, one of their clan dry gulched my saddle partner, Jessie. He was a good boy. I shot the dry gulcher, then I tied his body onto his horse. I turned the horse loose and followed it back to their cabin. Some dude tried to shoot me through a window while I was talking to two of them standing on their front steps. I saw the gun out of the corner of my eye and shot just a little to the left and above the gun hand. Them two on the steps cut loose. They got some lead in me before I got one of them."

"Wow, that makes four Taggerts you've shot. At that rate, you're gonna clean out that nest of snakes for me. You better watch your back trail real close. 'Cause you know, they're still lookin' for you. I hear tell old Randolph is just a rantin' and ravin' to find you. The only reason you haven't been found is because you've been workin' up on your own place, not out movin' around. But sooner or later one of them is goin' to run across you."

"I appreciate the warning. I'll be on the lookout. What I'm here for is, I need to hire a man to help me break some wild horses I've got penned up. I'm gonna sell 'em to the army so I can buy a whiteface bull. Can you recommend anybody"?

CHAPTER TWENTY-ONE
Outlaws Can't Find Sam

One by one, the outlaws gathered around the supper table. Ma Taggert said, "You boys get them hats off so I can say grace."

The men removed their hats. Ma bowed her head and said, "Lord, we ask your blessing on this family. We are just trying to scratch out a living in a hard land. We ask your blessin' on Pa and the boys as they try to provide for us. Amen."

After supper, the men gathered on the porch to smoke and drink a little of Pa's moonshine. Randolph said, "Well, where's he at?"

"Pa, we don't know. He must ah left the country. He ain't been to town and he ain't been seen at none of the other ranches around here."

"You boys ain't looking hard enough. He's still around. I feel it in my bones. We'll find him. In the meantime, we need some supplies. Junior, you and Pete ride over to the main road, stop one of them stages, and ask them rich folks riding on it to contribute some of their wealth to the poor folks in this area. Don't shoot nobody unless you have to, and keep them bandanas over your faces. That lazy sheriff won't bother us as long as you don't shoot nobody."

* * *

"Here comes the stage. Pete, get that bandana over your face." Leveling a double-barreled shotgun at the stage drive and guard, Junior said, "You boys keep them hands up in the air and nobody won't get hurt. All we want is for the rich Christian folks to contribute a little to the poor in this area."

Pete opened the door of the stage and pointed a gun at the three men and one woman inside. "Good mornin', folks. If you would step outside real peaceful like, you can be back on your way in a moment and you'll feel good about making a small donation to help the poor box in this region. Don't none of you gents try to be a hero, 'cause this old forty-four has a hair-trigger and at this range there ain't no way I'm gonna miss."

The lady stepped down, turned to her fellow passengers, and said, "This is ridiculous. Why don't one of you men shoot these filthy no-good robbers? If my John was here, they'd both be dead by now."

"Now ma'am, that ain't no way for a lady to talk. You don't want to see one of these good men get killed. 'Cause that is what will happen if one of them tries to follow your suggestion. Who knows — when bullets start flying, you might get caught right in the middle of it."

Her eyes went wide when she thought of where she was standing. All three men were now standing on the ground, and one by one Pete took their guns and tossed them to the side of the road. Junior held the driver and guard under the barrels of his shotgun. Pete took of his hat and held it in front of each man. "Please put you wallet and that fancy watch in the hat."

When he came to the lady, he said, "Maybe I should search you, to see what you've got hidden in all them ruffles"?

"Don't you dare touch me."

"Well ma'am, touching you would probably be like scratching an old boar hog. You take that little purse you've got there and dump it in the hat and y'all can be on your way. Driver, you pull that stage forward about fifty yards — these folks need to stretch their legs a little after all that riding. Fellows, after we are gone you can walk back and get your guns. Y'all have a pleasant trip."

He backed away as the stage pulled forward.

CHAPTER TWENTY-TWO
Sam Hires Juan

"As a matter of fact, I do know somebody. I've got a Mexican boy here in jail, a good boy—hard worker. He's got one problem: He's only five foot seven and weighs about one hundred and forty pounds. When he gets to drinkin' too much tequila, he thinks he can whip every redneck in the territory. He'll work, and if you keep him out of town. I won't have to keep him in here. His name is Juan. You want to meet him?"

"Yes sir, but how much is it going to cost to bail him out?"

"I'll let him go for nothing if you promise to take him out of town when you leave. Come on back and you can talk to 'im." On the way back to the cell the marshal called out, "Wake up you no-good Mexican. I've got somebody here to see ya."

The prisoner was short and rather handsome, with a devil-may-care persona about him. One look at the boy and Sam could tell he was accustomed to hard work. What little flesh he had was all muscle.

"Juan, this here's Sam. He owns a ranch up north of here. He's lookin' to hire someone. He asked me if I knew a good man he could hire to help him break wild horses. I told him no, but that I had a no-good Mexican back here I was tired of feedin', so he could have you."

Juan sent a half smile, half smirk at the marshal, and then turned to Sam. "Senõr, if you want to break wild horses, I'm your man. I can ride anything with hair on it."

"Have you had breakfast yet?"

"No, Senõr Sam, the service is lousy in this jail. They don't serve no tequila, no tortillas, no frijoles, no nothing. The service is lousy." His big grin showed even, white teeth in a Latin tan face.

"That's the problem now: Too many places sell this wetback tequila. That's why I've got to keep feedin' him. Sam, you'll be doin' the town a favor if you'll take him so far out into the sticks he can't find his way back."

"But, marshal, think of the senoritas. They'll be so sad and broken hearted if Juan is not here to sing love songs for them."

The marshal shook his head and glared at the boy, but Sam could see the smile he tried to hide.

Sam and Juan walked over to the Cactus Flower Café. Sam ordered two eggs and a slice of ham. Juan wolfed down three eggs and a half dozen slices of bacon. Over breakfast, Sam said, "I've built a trap for wild horses. I haven't caught any yet. I've got about six coming to water every morning at the water hole in my trap. There's a larger herd in the valley. I want to trap those first six and train 'em, then sell 'em to the army. After we get these sold, we'll try to catch the larger herd. I want to buy a whiteface bull and start a cow herd with the money I get from sellin' the horses."

"Senõr, Juan is a good horse breaker. I can ride anything. I have broke a lot of horses."

CHAPTER TWENTY-THREE
The Horses

After breakfast, Sam loaded a few supplies onto the packhorse and the two of them headed for the ranch. Sam kept scanning the area as they rode along. He remembered the bird that had flown off the bush a few days before. He couldn't shake the feeling that he was being watched.

Riding into his camp that evening, Sam showed Juan his trap, with the pool of water inside. "Juan, see the second section of fence on this side? The two of them act as a funnel into the trap. The fences narrow down to an opening into the corral."

"Si, senõr."

"We'll mount a swinging gate on the other side of the opening into the corral, then attach a rope to the gate. We'll bury the rope in the sand. The wild horse will walk over the rope and not see it. As soon as the horses are in the corral, all we have to do is grab this end of the rope and jerk, and the gate will slam shout. We'll have cut off any chance of escape for the mustangs. They won't get hurt, they'll just get trapped."

Nodding his head, Juan said, "You veeery smart Senõr Sam."

Daylight was crowding out the night the next morning when the sunrays began to paint streaks of silver and blue in the eastern sky. Sam pointed to the north end of the fence and said, "Look! Here they come. Be real quiet. The end of the rope is right here at our feet. I tied knots in the end so our hands can't slip. When they get in the corral, we'll both grab it and snatch the gate closed. Don't move around until they are all in the corral. The moment they're all in, we'll jerk the rope and slam the gate closed. Then we'll have us some horses to train."

Sam glanced around. He still couldn't shake the feeling that someone watched them. He shook it off. He was getting as jumpy as a newborn colt. This was the start of building his ranch. Soon he would be able to ask Mattie Ann to be his wife. A smile spread across his face.

CHAPTER TWENTY-FOUR
Mattie Ann Gets Sick

Mattie Ann woke weak and feverish. Her body ached all over. "What is wrong with me?" It took some effort to get dressed. When she walked into the kitchen, the room started to spin.

Rosa looked around as Mattie Ann fell. She ran to her and yelled, "Mr. C, help!" Rosa stretched Mattie Ann out on the floor and put her fingers on the girl's wrist, feeling for a pulse. She found a pulse, but it was fast and unsteady.

As Rosa knelt by Mattie Ann's side, she felt the floor shake. Joe Carville thundered across the floor in his western boots and raced through the kitchen door. He saw Mattie Ann stretched out on the floor with Rosa by her side. "What is it? Rosa, what happened?"

"I don't know, Mr. C, but we've got to get this girl to the doctor. She is burning up with the fever."

Russ came in the back door. Joe looked up and yelled, "Russ, get a team hooked up to the buckboard. I've got to get Mattie Ann to the doctor."

Joe Carville knelt by his daughter. He prayed, "Lord, please don't take Mattie Ann. I can't take any more. You took her mother—at least let me keep Mattie Ann."

Rosa jumped up, ran to the water bucket, and returned with a cool, damp rag. She sponged Mattie Ann's face. She said, "Mattie Ann, honey, you're going to be all right. We'll get you in to see the doctor. He'll make you better. You just hang in there, baby."

They both heard Russ's boots on the back porch. The door flew open and Russ was framed in the opening. "Boss, the buggy is right here."

Joe Carville scooped his daughter up in his arms. "Rosa, grab a blanket and come with me." Rosa climbed up into the buggy seat and Joe placed Mattie Ann in her lap. He then covered Mattie Ann with a blanket. He ran around and jumped up into the buggy, then looked back at Russ. "Russ, you'll have to see that the guys get some breakfast." With that, he snapped the reins on the back of the team.

Russ stood there and watched as the buggy made a cloud of dust as it raced down the lane and out onto the road. *Joe is going to kill that team before he gets to town.*

A lathered-up team of horses wheeled into Main Street and stopped, heaving for breath, in front of the doctor's house. The wheels had barely stopped turning when Joe Carville was out of the buggy and scooping his only daughter up in his arms. Without stopping to knock, he banged the front door open and scurried into the doctor's office.

The doctor was working on some notes when the door flew open. He glanced up and saw Joe Carville with his daughter in his arms. "Put her on the examining table." He grabbed his stethoscope and asked, "What's the matter?"

"We don't know. For a few days, she's been complaining of feeling poorly and having a sore throat. Then this mornin' she just passed out."

The doctor called his nurse in, then turned to Joe and said, "Okay Joe, you get out of here and let me examine her. I call you back in a minute."

Rosa sat in one of the cane-bottom chairs that lined the wall in the front room. Joe Carville couldn't sit. The sound of Joe's boot heels on the hardwood floor kept pace with the ticking of the grandfather clock in the corner. He thought, *I've never heard a clock tick so loud in my life.* He walked to the clock and turned to retrace his steps, when suddenly an earth-shattering sound erupted behind him. Instinctively, he ducked and spun around. The sound struck nine more times, and only then did he realize it was the clock striking the hour.

Finally, the doctor opened the door and walked out. "Joe, we'll need to keep her here for a few days. She is really sick. I believe she has rheumatic fever. The most common treatment for the fever is bleeding, whereby you take a surgical instrument, open a vein in the patient's wrist, and allow blood to drain out."

"How do you know when you have let out enough?"

"The theory is you watch their lips. When the patient's lips turn blue, you have drawn off enough. I've read about some newer treatments that I want to try. I've never liked the bleeding method. Joe, I want you to help move her into my treatment room. The nurse will stay with her until the fever breaks. The thing about rheumatic fever is, it usually settles in the patient's joints—but sometimes it affects the heart or some other organs. We'll just have to wait and see."

* * *

The morning was beautiful, but he couldn't shake the felling that he was being watched. Not a cloud was in the sky. Only a very slight breeze from the south put them downwind of the mustangs. Time stood still as Sam and Juan hunkered down behind low brush and waited.

The horses were suspicious, even though they had already watered here several mornings in a row. Sam thought, *Today they can tell something is different.* Soon three horses entered the corral. Sam held his breath. He whispered to the horses, "That's right. Get a drink and eat some of that fresh hay." Sam watched the first three push their noses into the water for a drink.

All at once, one of them snorted and jumped back. As soon as that horse spooked, all three raced out of the corral. There was a lot of milling and shoving in the area between the fences.

"Juan, what spooked them?"

"I don't know senōr, but I theenk I saw somethin' move in the brush on the other side of the corral."

They sat horrified and watched as the herd race out of the valley. "Juan, grab your rifle. Let's go see what startled the mustangs. You go around the corral to the left. I can get under the fence in that little gulley over there on the right. Keep your finger on the trigger. We don't know what we're going to find over there."

Sam lay on his back and slid under the fence in the little depression caused by the small gulley. As he started to rise up he spotted an Indian aiming a rifle at Juan. Without taking time to aim, he fired from the hip. He missed, but the Indian whipped his head around. When he saw another gun pointed at him from that side, he decided this was bad medicine. The Indian gave out a war whoop as he whirled and dashed back into the brush. A few moments later, they heard a pony race away.

"Juan, are you all right?"

"Si, senõr. Juan theenks you save his frijoles today."

"We'll have to keep a sharp eye out. He'll be back. Next time he'll bring some friends with him."

The next morning the horses were back. This time they seemed a little more skittish, taking a few careful steps toward the water. One of the mustangs, on dancing hooves, bravely inched toward the water in the corral. It was as if all the other horses crowded into the opening and watched to make sure that first horse was going to be okay. After a few more minutes, all of the horses slipped into the corral.

"Look at that, Juan: They are like a bunch of kids, bumping, pushing, and nipping each other out of the way to get to the water."

NOW! SWISH, THUMP, the gate slammed shut. Some of the horse went wild, snorting, squealing, and running around the corral. Sam had built it strong. They were not going to get out.

"Senõr Sam, that is a mucho good-loookin' herd. I think right now they don't like you so much."

"They'll settle down. All I want us to do at first is bring a bunch of hay and throw it to them. We'll do that every day for a few days. Soon they'll get to liking the fact that we're feeding them. Then we'll take one horse at a time and move it over to the small round corral. I'll show you how I want to train 'em."

He thought, These magnificent animals are going to allow me to ask Mattie Ann's daddy for her hand in marriage. Life was going to be so sweet. He could imagine his little boys growing up here.

CHAPTER TWENTY-FIVE
Training the Horses

Sam was anxious to get back to the Tumbling C. Wow, he really missed seeing Mattie Ann. He wanted to tell her about the horses. Doggone it, he wished he could ride over there right now. But he couldn't go—this was a critical time in training the horses.

Juan was impressed with the gentle way Sam trained the horses. Each day they would select one horse from the corral. They would rope that one and pull it into a smaller round corral. Sam would stand relaxed in the center of the round corral. In his left hand, he held the end of the rope. He turned with the horse as it raced around the corral until the horse was lathered with sweat. After a while, the horse would get the idea that it was going in circles. It would stop and stand looking at Sam. All the while, Sam was talking in a soft, soothing voice to the horse. He wanted the horse to get used to the sound of his voice.

When the horse stopped running around the corral, Sam would walk with slow, deliberate steps up to the horse. As he approached the frightened animal, he spoke softly. At first, with slow, gentle movements, he placed his hands on the horse. The horse would jerk away and run around the ring. Sam would walk back to the center of the round pen, holding the end of the rope. When the horse stopped, again Sam would repeat the slow, even steps back to the horse, saying, "Take it easy, big fella, I'm not goin' to hurt you."

This time, when he walked up to the horse, he would put a halter on the animal. Soon Sam had the mustang quieted down and led him around the ring. This would go on until noon. Then Sam would say, "Okay big fella, we're gonna to take a break." He'd pour water for the horse into a trough in the round corral. Under a tree in sight of the corral, he sat and ate his lunch. While Sam was doing this, Juan was cutting hay and throwing it to the horses still in the corral. By the end of the second day, Sam had a saddle on the horse. After he led the

A COLLISION OF DREAMS

horse around the corral a few times with the saddle on, he would put his foot into the stirrup and step into the saddle. He sat in the saddle as the horse proudly carried him around the ring.

The first time Juan saw him do that, he was amazed. "Senōr, he does not buck? I've never seeeen a horse that did not buck the first time someone sat on heeem."

"When you try to ride him in the morning, he'll buck. Right now, he's tired and a little confused."

Sam had built a small pasture beyond the round corral. After his day of lessons, rather than turn the horse back into the big corral with the other mustangs, they turned him into the small pasture with their two horses.

The work was hard, but they were building a home, a future. Sam was so glad that he had chosen this valley. There seemed to be nothing to disrupt the peace and quiet of the valley. *I can't wait to bring Mattie Ann out to see how much we have got done.*

* * *

Mattie Ann opened her eyes and found that she was in a strange room. She looked to her left and found her aunt in a chair by the bed she was in. "Aunt Millie, where am I? What is going on?"

"Honey, you are at the doctor's home. You fainted and your daddy brought you in."

"Why do I feel so weak and clammy?"

"Your fever just broke real early this morning. Here, let me get some water into you." She lifted Mattie Ann's head with her right hand as she lifted a cool glass of water to her parched lips.

"Aunt Millie, what happened?"

"You've had a bad bout with <u>rheumatic</u> fever. The doctor said that once your fever broke, we needed to get you to drink plenty of water. Do you think you could eat some breakfast?"

"Right now, I just want to go back to sleep."

When she awoke again, the doctor sat by her bed. He reached over and took her hand in his. With a sad, concerned look on his face, he said, "Mattie Ann, there's something I need to talk to you about."

One week later, Mattie Ann sat in Rosa's kitchen. Rosa dried the plates she had just washed. "You miss him, don't you?"

"Rosa, I'm so confused. Sometimes I think he's falling in love with me and sometimes I think Sam doesn't even notice me."

"You seeely girl. Why you think he work so hard to build a ranch—for heem-self and Juan?"

"He has never asked me to marry him. Rosa, there is no way he'll want to marry me after I tell him what the doctor told us. Then there is still the other problem. I guess after what the doctor said, it doesn't matter if he is a believer or not."

"Mattie Ann, don't get all riled up—that boy loves you, and you are in love with him. I can see it as plain as day when I look at each one of you. He hasn't asked you because he doesn't think he can talk to you until he has something better to offer you. Mattie Ann, that boy loves you. He won't care what any doctor said. You just keep praying and let God work out the details."

* * *

Each morning Sam rolled out of his blanket and looked carefully around. He knew Indian's liked to attack at dawn. After breakfast, he and Juan would bring in the horse Sam had trained the day before.

The mustang would buck a few times, just to keep Juan honest. Then Juan would take it out to the pasture and ride it around in the pasture while Sam started training a new horse. After a few days, they had ten horses ready to deliver to the army.

Juan said, "Senōr Sam, for two months we've been workin' so hard, the senoritas they are gettin' lonely. Juan needs to go to town and sing some love songs for the senoritas."

Sam laughed. "Okay, you lovesick Latino, why don't we deliver these mustangs to the fort? I'll pay you and you can go sing your love songs. You've got two months pay coming. I'm only going to give you one. I'm will hold the other one back to bail you out of the marshal's jail."

"You very wise senõr, that is why you the boss. Juan is just the singer of love songs."

On the way back from the fort after they delivered the horses, Sam said, "Come on in, I'll buy you one drink." Sam sat his empty glass on the bar and said, "I'm going to stop by the "Tumbling C before I head back to the ranch."

"Ah, could it be that senõr Sam is going to sing some love songs his-self?"

Sam left the bar and walked over to see the marshal before he left town. As he stepped through the door into the marshal's office, he said, "Morning marshal."

"Hello Sam, what brings you to town?"

"To tell you that I just sold my first load of horses to the army—and to warn you that Juan is in town singing his love songs."

"That dad-gum Mexican. I was hopin' you could keep him out there a little longer. He's goin' to get himself killed one of these days. He'll jump on a wild cat when he gets a little tequila in him, he don't care."

"Well, I hope not, because he's a good hand—he can rope anything. I saw that yahoo rope a jackrabbit the other day. Marshal, have you heard anything more out of the Taggerts?"

"Well, not directly. But the county sheriff was in here the other day, tellin' me that someone's been sellin' some bad whiskey to the Indians. Me and a couple of deputies are ridin' over there this afternoon to check it out. Of course, those darn redskins won't tell us a dang thing."

"Well, I'm heading to the Tumbling C. I can't wait to see Mattie Ann and eat some of Rosa's cooking. Who knows—by this time next year I might be getting married."

CHAPTER TWENTY-SIX
What Will the Future Hold?

The doctor closed his bag and chewed on the stem of his glasses before he spoke. "She is still weak, but I think she is past the worst of it. It will take some time for her to get her strength back. With Rosa's cooking, plenty of rest, and this Texas sunshine, she should get a lot better. We won't know for a while what long-term effects it is going to have. This disease is vicious and unforeseen things can crop up. We will deal with them when they come."

Mattie Ann thought, *He said "when" they come, not "if" they come.*

Joe shook the doctor's hand as he climbed into his buggy. "Doc, thanks for coming out to check on her. I was so scared we were going to lose her there for a few days when we first brought her to you."

"Now that she is better, I'll tell you—I was scared too. See you." He snapped the leather reins on the horses and wheeled out of the ranch yard.

* * *

As Sam rode into the ranch yard, he thought, I like the way the Tumbling C lays out. I need to remember this when I lay out my yard. In fact, I need to come up with a name like the Tumbling C—that's a good name.

Tex stepped out of the bunkhouse as Sam rode in. Sam looked down at Tex and said, "Howdy, Tex. How's things at the Tumbling C?"

"Pretty good, now that Mattie Ann got all right."

"Wait a minute. What do you mean, 'since Mattie Ann got all right?'"

A COLLISION OF DREAMS

"Well, she almost died." He hooked his right thumb toward the house and said, "But she's better now. The doctor just left a minute ago."

Sam never heard the last part. He fell off the horse and sprinted for the back door. Joe Carville stepped out onto the back porch as Sam hit the bottom step running full tilt. "Whoa, cowboy. Is somebody chasing you?"

Sam stopped to catch his breath and blurted out, "Is Mattie Ann okay?"

"She is for now."

"What happened?"

"She came down with the fever. Rosa and I took her in to doc's house. He kept her there for a week. She's home now. Go on in to see her."

"When did this happen?"

"Two weeks ago."

"Why didn't somebody come and tell me?"

"Well, we were kinda busy. Besides, why should we?"

That stopped Sam cold. I guess they had no reason to. I have never asked to court her.

"Mr. Carville, Mattie Ann is mighty special to me. I was just worried about her."

Joe Carville smiled, clapped Sam on the shoulder, and said, "She's mighty special to me too, son. How's your ranch coming?"

"It's doing good, sir. I just sold my first load of horses to the army. We've got a bunch more up there to train. Then I'm going back east to get me a registered whiteface bull."

"That's great, Sam. Go on in and say hello to Mattie Ann. She'll be glad to see ya."

When he walked through the door, he stopped. Mattie Ann sat in a chair with an afghan spread over her lap. She looked peaked, pale, her color gone.

GEORGE DALTON

When she looked up and saw him, she threw the afghan off and jumped up, wrapping her arms around his neck. "Oh, Sam it's so good to see you."

"Mattie Ann, I'm so sorry. I didn't know you were sick. I would've been here sooner. You look a little pale. Are you all right now? Do you feel better?"

"I'm much better. How is the ranch?"

Sam looked at her and decided it was just the light. After she got up and moved around, she looked okay. In fact, she looked beautiful.

Rosa stepped in and said, "Sam, why don't you two come in to the kitchen and let me set some lunch on the table for you?"

After lunch, Mattie Ann said, "Why don't we ride down the creek and back?"

That suggestion brought a tinge of excitement to Sam. After all, he never got to see her without a dozen cowhands hanging around. Who knows—maybe he could steal a kiss or two between here and the creek.

They talked all the way to the creek. He told her all about the ranch house he planned to build. "I've got a spring right outside the kitchen and I think I can get some pipe and have running water in the kitchen." As they rode along, he reached down and took the thong off his six-shooter. His sixth sense again told him they were being watched.

"I've never heard of running water inside a house."

"When I was at the boys' ranch we got a magazine delivered to the school that had a picture of a house with water piped into it."

"Well, mister big shot, you'll have the only piped-in water in the territory."

"Just think how jealous your friends will be if you are the only one with running water in the kitchen."

"Well, first of all, I haven't agreed to marry you yet."

"No, because I haven't asked your dad for your hand yet."

A COLLISION OF DREAMS

She spurred her horse, and as she raced away she yelled back over her shoulder, "Well then you can marry my daddy."

Buck wasn't about to be left behind—her horse didn't get two strides before Buck was at full speed. As they caught up with her, Sam scooped her off her horse in his right arm and kissed her soundly, all while slowing Buck to a stop.

When the kiss ended, he was still holding her to his side. She looked flushed when she looked up at him and said, "Maybe you shouldn't marry my daddy after all."

He lowered her gently to the ground, then he stepped down. Taking her hand, he started walking back toward the ranch house. All at once, he thought he saw light flash off something metal, like a gun barrel.

He said, "We better get back. As much as I would love to stay right here, I'd better get back up there and check on those horses I left penned up."

As Sam rode out of the yard at the Tumbling C, he was the happiest man alive. He could still taste the kiss on his lips. It was so wonderful that he forgot about being watched—until a bullet whizzed past his head. First, he heard this funny buzzing sound, then the rifle report. Sam looked back over his right shoulder. He saw six riders come out of the trees, firing at him. Instinctively he clamped his spurs to Buck's side. As Buck raced and weaved among the trees, he angled up toward the crest of the hills. He rode hard for a group of trees. Buck raced straight into the grove of trees until he was out of sight, and then doubled back.

Sam cut across the face of the hill. Soon he waited behind some brush beside the draw. He stopped at the crest of the hill. He could see them spread out. They were being cautious. They'd missed him in the surprise attack. Now they knew he could shoot back. There was a draw off to his left. He looked and saw one of the Taggert riders angle into it. He was a youngster, no more than seventeen, but he carried a rifle that was full-grown. Sam waited until the youngster was just

GEORGE DALTON

past him, and then threw a loop over the boy's head and shoulders. The rope pinned his arms to his side. With a jerk on the rope, the rider flew backwards off the horse. Of course, the horse, being a western-trained horse, stopped immediately.

Sam walked up to him and saw that he wasn't hurt. He could see the terror in the boy's eyes. "Are you going to kill me?"

"Stand up boy and turn around." Sam pulled the boy's hands behind him, then tied them together with a pigging string. He reached down and unbuckled the boy's gun belt, then picked up his rifle and smashed it against a tree. Sam lifted the boy back onto his horse with his hands still tied behind him. He took the reins and tied them to the saddle horn. He looked the frightened boy in the eye and said, "You tell your ma that I never intended to kill anybody. All I want is to be left alone. If they keep coming after me, you are gonna need a lot more space in that graveyard. Do you understand?"

The boy just nodded his head.

Sam slapped the horse on the rump and it ran back toward the east. *Well, that took care of one.* Now he had five more to worry about.

That night, Sam camped in a dry camp high up on a ridge about five miles from his ranch. He didn't dare light a fire and give away the location of his camp. They could chase him all over these hills, but he wouldn't go near the ranch. He only hoped that Juan was not in jail. Sam needed him to take care of the horses.

The sun was peeking over the ridge in the east when Sam looked down the hill and saw five riders strung out below him. As he watched for a few minutes, he had another idea. One of the Taggerts was riding up a trail that would intersect the one he was on. There is a very steep drop-off on the other side of the trail. If he got to the intersection of the two trails first, he could rope one of those young sapling trees and bend it back as far as it would bend without breaking.

He got his trap set, then sat behind some rocks and waited. Soon the rider came into view. When the rider was in the right spot, he stepped out. Their eyes met and, as the rider started to bring his rifle up, Sam pulled the slipknot that held the tree back. That young tree snapped back, slapping the horse—rider and all—off the hill. They went head over teakettle, tumbling down the hill.

At that moment, Sam saw another rider draw up and look across the valley at all the commotion. Just as he was trying to figure what all the commotion was about, his horse reached down to get a drink of water from the stream. Sam's bullet splashed water in the horse's face. The horse reared up like it had been shot and the rider flew off the horse's rump and landed on his own rump. Sam watched the horse run off, holding its head to one side to avoid stepping on the reins. Then he saw the rider limp along behind the horse, holding his behind.

Sam looked at the rider who had been swept off the side of the hill. He and the horse limped badly.

Sam sat up on a rock ledge and wondered where the other three riders were. Out of the corner of his eye, he saw them ride toward the two on foot. He told himself, "I'm sitting with a cedar behind me so I'm not worried about them spotting me. From this vantage point, I can see everything they do. I do have a dilemma though. I can ride off the backside of this hill and be at the ranch in an hour. If I do that, they may find my tracks... then my ranch. If I don't go and those horses run out of hay—that would be bad."

"Maybe Juan is back and the horses are being taken care of." He turned his head and looked back at his horse, then said, "Buck, what if he's lying up there in jail and the horses are dying for lack of food or water?"

CHAPTER TWENTY-SEVEN
The Dead Cougar

It was dark when Sam rode into his valley. He could see a campfire burning. He stopped a short distance from the fire and called out, "Hello the camp."

Out of the dark on the side away from him the heard, "Ah, Senōr Sam, I hear a horse coming. I don't know if it is you or a boyfriend of one of the senoritas. So I geeet my Winchester and went in the rocks until I am sure. Where have you beeen? I have beeen working the horses all the day. That must have been some song you sang at the Tumbling C, no?"

Sam told him about the men who shot at him, then said, "Now that I know you're here and the horses are safe, I'm going back."

"But Senōr Sam, these men they are trying to keel you. You can sing no more love songs if you are dead. Here you are safe. Don't go back."

"You are right amigo, but I'm going to see if I can't discourage these hombres from shooting at me anymore. You take care of the horses until I get back."

"Oh, Senōr Sam, there is one thing. Look at what I keel this morning." He held up the carcass of a dead cougar. "He was scaring the horses something awful, so I keel him."

Sam looked at the carcass and an idea came to him. "Give me that thing."

"What you going to do with a dead cat, senōr?"

"I'm going to make some men very uncomfortable."

He had a hard time getting Buck to let him get in the saddle while he held that dead cougar. Eventually, they worked it out and he left the ranch with the dead cougar wrapped in an old blanket tied behind his saddle. It was close to midnight when he spotted their campfire. He had to stay downwind until he was right near their camp. Sam

A COLLISION OF DREAMS

unwrapped the dead cougar and tied it to the end of his rope. He then spurred Buck and they charged up out of a draw. Sam screamed at the top of his voice and raced into the camp dragging that dead cougar. Those horses smelled that cougar and bolted out of there like the devil had just charged through camp with a fiery pitchfork. Sam gave chase, dragging the cougar, and those horses didn't stop running until they were back at their barn, which was a good twelve miles away.

Patting his horse on the neck, Sam said, "Okay Buck, I think we've dealt enough mischief for one night. Let's go home." Sam took a round-about way back to his ranch. He wanted to confuse a tracker as much as possible. He judged by the stars that it must have been about two in the morning when he hailed his camp again.

Sam poured a cup of black coffee from the pot sitting in the coals, then rolled up in his blanket. Sam slept soundly until rain started pouring down. Sam grabbed the blanket and pulled it over his head, then sat and watched the rain coming down in buckets when he heard, "Senõr Sam, next can we build a barn?"

"Well Juan, the good news is that those men who shot at me won't find any tracks now. Besides, they have a long, wet walk home."

"You keel their horses?"

Sam then told Juan what he had done with the dead cougar.

The next morning it was too muddy to work the horses. They took their axes and cut runners for a sled. Sam took Juan's horse and Buck and hooked them to the sled. The two men made several trips back and forth as they hauled flat stones from the river for a foundation on which to build a house. Mixing river sand with crushed limestone, they made a mortar to use between the stones. Soon they had a solid floor made of stone, and the spaces between the stones were filled with mortar.

"Tomorrow we'll start the walls up."

The walls went up fast. Sam said, "Juan, I laid out the house to capture the best view of the valley and to utilize the most breezes.

GEORGE DALTON

We'll build the kitchen at one end of the stone floor then leave a breezeway eight feet wide. Next, we'll build one large room with a large fireplace, and two sleeping rooms off that. Each bedroom will have a small fireplace in it. I want lots of windows all around to let in the breezes and light. On each window, I want to install strong shutters that can be closed in case of an Indian attack."

Sam said, "Juan, you are a good stonemason."

"Senõr Sam, I think your lady, she will like very much."

"I hope so, Juan. I hope so."

The next morning, Sam rode over to the Tumbling C. He ate lunch with Mattie Ann and Joe Carville. Joe wanted to know how the ranch was coming. Mattie Ann got all excited when he described the house. Rosa got excited when he told them he had running water piped into the kitchen.

Mattie Ann insisted that she and her daddy ride back with Sam and see the place.

It was late when they finished eating supper so they decided to spend the night in Sam's new unfinished house. After Sam cooked breakfast, Mattie Ann and her dad left to go back to the Tumbling C. Sam and Juan took the sled and axes to start cutting timbers for the roof. They also cut enough wood to build window shutters and doors.

Sam stopped every few minutes to look all around. He watched the birds and other critters to see if anything disturbed them. Mostly he watched the horses—wild mustangs are better than watchdogs. They would warn you if a stranger came around.

Between cutting hay for the horses and wood for building, it took them ten more days to get the roof on. "Juan, if it rains now, we at least have a dry place to sleep."

Two afternoons later, Sam was fitting a doorframe in place when he looked out and found himself looking into the black eyes of twelve young Apache braves. They sat on their horses and stared at the house. One of the Indians said something and pointed at the building.

Without turning his head, Sam said, "Juan, slide my Winchester over here."

"Why you need a Winchester to set a doorframe?" Then he looked out. "Holy Mother of God, that is the whole Apache nation I think. Maybe they just come to trade."

Sam said, "I don't have anything to trade—guess I could trade you."

"You are not so funny, senōr. Then again, maybe the Indian maidens would like Juan's love songs."

"How good do you think you would look to the young maidens, Juan, without any hair?"

"No senōr, the senoritas would not like that. They love to run their fingers through Juan's hair."

"They could run their fingers as much as they wanted to if they had it hanging in the wigwam."

"Senōr Sam, that's not so funny. What are they doing, just sitting there?"

"I don't know, but they can't hurt us as long as they stay there. They sure don't have anything that will shoot through this stone wall."

Sam and Juan kept working. Each man was sweating more as the minutes dragged on, even though the temperature remained the same.

After a long time, the Indians turned their horses and rode away. For many a moon, the Apaches told stories around the cooking fires about the wigwam made of stone.

No more Indians or Taggerts attacked Sam and Juan, so they got a lot of work done. Sam started to relax. His excitement grew with each task they accomplished.

They would have gotten a lot more work done if Sam hadn't had to run over to the Tumbling C every week. His excuse was that he needed some home cooking. They finished out the house and actually got the water to flow from the spring through a copper tube into the kitchen.

After the house was finished, they got serious about training horses. Most of the horses were less frightened than before. They started to trust the two crazy men who brought them feed every day. In the group of mustangs was one big roan stallion that stood fifteen hands at the shoulder.

"Juan, we're not going to sell that roan—I want to keep him for breeding stock."

"Si senõr, he is magnificent animal."

By late fall, they had thirty-three more horses ready to deliver to the army. "Juan, after we deliver these, I want you to come back here and see after the place. I'm going to go back east and buy a prize bull."

"Si, Senõr Sam, but Juan, he will need to stop in town and sing a few love songs."

CHAPTER TWENTY-EIGHT
Sam Meets a Girl on the Train

Sam caught the stage in Cactus Tree and rode to Mule Shoe, where he could catch the train back east. He had heard about these new whiteface cattle being imported from Scotland. They carried a lot more beef per cow than the rangy longhorn. He left his horse and Winchester with the livery stable man there in Mule Shoe. Then he went to Caprock Café for breakfast before he boarded the train.

He left his Winchester, but kept his six-shooter. Sitting there drinking his coffee, he had to admit he was a little nervous about riding that train. After all, the ticket agent had told him the train could go up to thirty miles in a single hour. That was more than a normal day's ride. In just one hour. That was hard to believe.

***

The council of chiefs gathered in Chief Running Deer's lodge. Chief Running Deer, who spoke the white man's tongue, said, "Our people are sick and many of our braves cannot see out of their eyes. They cannot hunt; they cannot shoot. They are like old squaw that must be led around by the hand. It is caused by the bad firewater sold to them by this white man they call Taggert. He sells braves bad firewater. The braves shared with the young squaws and now they are sick."

One of the younger chiefs started shouting in Apache: ZASTEE LIGIA NUBDEE NETDAHE (which means "Kill all white people, death to all intruders").

Chief Running Deer cautioned, "No, we must report this to the army and let them handle these bad people. If we go on the warpath, the army will attack us. No matter how just our reason, the army will not allow the Apache to go on the warpath anymore."

The young chief spat in the dust and spoke in Apache, "The white man's army does not tell the Apache what he cannot do."

A COLLISION OF DREAMS

The debate raged on, far into the night. However, since they didn't have any whiskey to fuel the fires of passion, fatigue finally adjourned the meeting. A new meeting was scheduled one moon from then.

* * *

Sam bought a whiteface bull and a six-month-old bull calf. They were loaded into the stock car and he was headed back to the ranch. He had settled down in one of the cushion seats and planned to take a nap, when a beautiful young girl of about sixteen or seventeen hurried onto the car. She appeared to be running. Sam thought, *The train is not due to depart for several more minutes. Why would she need to run?*

A nasty old man with unclean clothes and tobacco stains in his beard stormed onto the train. As he rushed through the door, he knocked an older couple out of his way. Then he spotted the young girl. Grabbing her by the arm, he snarled, "Sally Jo, you get off this train and get back home where you belong."

The girl screamed, "Turn me lose, you're not my pa, turn me lose." She was crying. He jerked her up out of the seat.

Sam stepped out into the aisle. "Get your hands off that girl."

The man whirled around and glared at Sam. "You shut up and tend to your own affairs and keep your nose out of my business."

Sam reached down and with his right thumb pushed the thong off the hammer of his six-shooter.

The man threw the girl back into the seat and lunged at Sam. He met the man with a short right, straight to the end of his big red whiskey nose. Sam felt the big nose shatter when the blow landed. Blood splattered from the man's face.

The man then became a raging bull. He battered Sam back down the aisle of the train. They stood toe to toe, slugging it out for several seconds. Sam whipped an uppercut to his midsection. You could hear the wind go out of the man.

At that moment, the conductor and a deputy sheriff ran onto the car. The conductor pointed at the man. "That's him, get him off my train." After they had hustled him off the train, the girl came to Sam and said, "Sir, thank you for taking up for me."

Sam wiped the blood off his skinned knuckles with a bandana and asked, "Who was that guy?"

"He's my step-father. My ma died a couple of months ago. Since then he's been trying to make me his new wife." Shivering, she said, "I hate him. He treated my ma something awful. I don't ever want to see him again. Not as long as I live."

Shoving the bandana back into his pocket, Sam asked, "Where are you going?"

"My mother's sister lives in Denver City, and I wrote her. My aunt said I could come live with her."

"This train doesn't go all the way to Denver City."

"Yes sir, I know, but I had enough money to buy a ticket to the end of the line. I thought I could get a job working in a café or something and earn enough to get a stage ticket on to Denver City."

Sam thought, You poor kid. You have no idea what those end-of-the-line towns are like. You will be like a lamb in a pen full of wolves. Reaching in his pocket, he pulled out one hundred dollars.

"Here, this will buy you a ticket on to Denver City."

"Oh sir, no. I can't take your money."

"Consider it a loan. My name is McClanton. When you get settled down you can pay me back by doing the same for someone else that needs it, okay?"

"Sir, my name is Sally Jo Ackerman. My father was Doctor Ackerman, but he died three years ago of influenza. Last year my ma married that awful man. I was back east at school when she wrote to tell me she had met a real nice man and had gotten remarried. I graduated and came home, which was the first time I met him. That was also when I found out that all he did was drink liquor and gamble away my mother's money.

A COLLISION OF DREAMS

Mother told me she was going to go see a lawyer and file for a divorce, but she caught the influenza and died before she could do it. Sir, my father was a wonderful man. I have no idea why she married that no-count sniveling idiot. I am so sorry. I know a lady is not supposed to talk that way."

"No offence taken, ma'am. Now if you'll excuse me." He went back to his seat and tipped his hat down over his eyes.

When the train came to his stop, Sam hated to get off because he hated to see the young lady go on by herself. "Sally Jo, when you get to the end of the line, go get you a ticket on the next stage to Denver City. If there's a sheriff or town marshal, go introduced yourself to him. He'll look after you until you can get on the stage. Good luck."

Sam went to the livery stable and retrieved Buck and his Winchester. He put a lead rope on the bull and the calf and headed for the ranch, with a stop at the Tumbling C on the way.

When he rode into the Tumbling C ranch yard, it was almost suppertime and the whole gang was quickly out to see the new bulls. After supper, Sam asked Joe Carville, "Sir, can I have a word with you in private?"

"Sure, come on in to my office." When they walked into Mr. Carville's office, it smelled of wood stain. A fire glowed in the fireplace. "Do you want a drink of cognac?"

Sam took the glass Mr. Carville handed him and swirled the amber liquid. For some reason, he was nervous about this talk with Mr. Carville.

Joe asked, "Sam, how is your ranch coming?"

"Sir, we are doing well. I have a dozen head of horses that we have trained and I've already sold forty-three head to the army. We've got the roof on the house, as well as the window shutters and doors on. I don't have any window glass in yet, but as soon as I get some more money in I'll order it. We still have a lot of work to do. We've got to build a barn and put up a lot more hay before winter sets in."

"That Mexican boy's turning out to be a good hand, isn't he?"

"Yes sir."

"Okay Sam, what was it you wanted to talk to me about? Do you want to buy some cows to go with those two good-looking bulls out there in the pen?"

"No sir, I would like to ask your permission to court your daughter. And I've already got some cows."

"Whoa, let's talk about one thing at a time. Where'd you get any cows?"

"Mr. Carville, you remember when I took that Taggert fellow's body back and they shot me full of holes?"

"Yeah."

"They hunted all over for me and couldn't find me. The reason they couldn't find me was I found a cave hidden behind a waterfall. I hid in there and then I discovered that the cave had a back entrance. It opened into a big bowl that had about fifty to one hundred acres of the best grass and water you'll ever see. I also discovered about fifty head of cattle living back there. Same of them are old."

"Are you serious?

"Yes I am."

"How do you plan to get them out of there?"

"What I'd like to do is borrow a couple of your hands for a day or two and brand the cows with the brand I registered while I was in town. Then just drive them out through the waterfall."

"Why do you need my hands?"

"Because the rest of the cattlemen in this area respect you, and if you tell them where I got those cows, they'll believe you."

"Sam, I'll give you credit—you're thinking. What was the other thing you mentioned?"

"I want to start courting your daughter, sir."

Joe laughed then said, "If I said no to that, I would have to leave the county. I'd have Mattie Ann and Rosa both after me." He stood up, reached across, and shook Sam's hand. "Son, you have my blessing. You better treat her right or I'll take a horsewhip to ya."

"You don't haveta worry about that, sir."

"Sam, I do have one question. What about the Taggerts?"

"Sir, I don't know. I've decided that I'm not going to go hunting any of them. If they come after me, I'll just have to cross that creek when I get there."

"Sam, I'm not too worried about them coming after you. So far, you've handled them pretty well. What if they come shooting at you and Mattie Ann is with you? That worries me. Come to think of it, I heard that the army and the sheriff was looking into them selling some bad whiskey to the Indians. Maybe the army will take care of the Taggerts for you."

CHAPTER TWENTY-NINE
The Kiss

"Rosa, what are they talking about? He's been in there for a long time."

"Honey child, you are just gonna have to be patient. They may be talking about cattle and range conditions. I don't know."

"Rosa, that man drives me crazy. Sometimes I can't keep my eyes off him and sometimes I don't ever want to see him again."

"Who are you trying to fool, girl? You are in love if ever I saw anyone in love."

"You would think he would want to talk to me. Instead, he spends all day talking to my daddy. I have half a mind to go back to town and let that banker's son start courting me. He knows how to be a gentleman. The longer he stays in there the madder I am getting. I may just go back to my room and not even talk to him."

When Sam walked out of Joe Carville's office, Mattie Ann and Rosa were both standing in the parlor looking at him.

"Miss Mattie Ann Carville, your father has just given me permission to start courting you, so you better start getting your wedding dress made."

"Oh, you think so, do you? I haven't said yes to anything yet. In fact, I don't remember a loose-jointed cowhand even asking me anything yet."

Rosa spoke up and said, "Will you two quit that. Now get out there and take a walk in the moonlight. Maybe it will bring some sense to both of you."

Sam offered his arm to Mattie Ann. As they walked out the door, he said, "I'll have you know, Miss Mattie Ann Carville, that I am not a loose-jointed cowhand. I'm a ranch owner with running water in the house, and a fireplace in every room."

"Why do you think I'm walking in the moonlight with you? It's just because of the running water."

They both laughed as they leaned against the corral fence. "Seriously Mattie Ann, you look absolutely beautiful in the moonlight."

"As pretty as those new whiteface bulls?"

Sam took her in his arms and their lips melted together. When they broke, he said, "I have never wanted to kiss a bull—not even a whiteface."

"Oh Sam, I love you, but there is something I need to tell you."

"Mattie Ann, I was thinking we would be married in the spring. I'm going to be so busy getting ready for winter and getting the ranch through this first winter. Come spring, we'll have the house finished and I'll have another bunch of horses to sell to the army. You can then pick out the furnishings you want for the house."

"Yes, but Sam, spring seems a long way off. I don't want anything to happen. What if I lose you? Don't you go chasing off after any more of those Taggerts."

"Come morning I'm going to get these two bulls and go straight to the ranch. I don't know how much work I'll get done—I'll be wanting to run back over here to see you every day."

"I won't let you come every day. I'll want you up there getting ready for a wedding next spring. Oh Sam, it is going to be so grand. We'll have the biggest wedding this county has ever seen."

"We'll definitely have the prettiest bride this country has ever seen."

CHAPTER THIRTY
The Letter

Mattie Ann stood at the end of the lane watching Sam ride away. As she started to turn back toward the house, she saw Mr. Thornton coming with the mail.

"Good morning, Mattie Ann. I don't often see anybody waiting for their mail. You must be expecting something important."

"Good morning, Mr. Thornton. No, I'm not expecting anything. I walked down the lane with Sam and when I turned around to go back, I saw you coming. Therefore, I waited. What have you got for us?"

Mr. Thornton reached into the leather bag sitting on the buggy seat beside him. "Looks like I've got a couple of bills for your daddy, and I've got a letter addressed to Miss Mattie Ann Carville."

"Let me see that. Who would be sending a letter to me?" She took her long fingernail and flipped it open.

> Dear Cousin Mattie Ann,
>
> I don't know where to begin. I am sure Aunt Millie told you my mother died. After she died, I couldn't live with my stepfather anymore so I ran away and came here to Denver City to live with our aunt. I got on the train, but before it pulled out of the station, Luther rushed onto the train and grabbed my arm. He tried to jerk me off the train. It was most humiliating.
>
> I don't have any idea who he was, but this very good-looking cowboy stood up for me and told Luther to take his hands off me. Luther threw me back into the seat and charged the cowboy. Mattie Ann, I was terrified, but it was thrilling to watch. That cowboy hit old Luther right on his nose and then punched him in the belly and knocked the wind out of him. Then the conductor and a deputy sheriff ran onto the train car and arrested Luther.

A COLLISION OF DREAMS

Then that good-looking cowboy asked me where I was going. When I told him I had a ticket to the end of the tracks and planned on getting a job to earn enough money to purchase a ticket on the stage to Denver City, he insisted on loaning me enough money to purchase the stage ticket. When I tried to object, he said to consider it a loan, and that I could pay him back by doing something for some other person sometime after I got settled. I am sure I will never see him again, but I will never forget him either.

It sounds like your cowboy is also both handsome and gallant—you better not let him get away.

Your dearest cousin,
Sally Jo

CHAPTER THIRTY-ONE
The Prettiest Girl in Town

Sally Jo sat brushing her hair. She enjoyed the reflection of the snow-covered mountains out the window.

Her aunt walked into the room and sat down on the edge of her bed. "Sally Jo, when are you going to get out and meet some of the young men around town? I know that young man at the bank has been asking you out. He seems nice and he is good-looking. Why don't you go?"

"I don't know, every time I go in there he asks me to go on a picnic or to see a play or something. I just can't stop thinking about that man I met on the train. I never believed in love at first sight, but I have never had a man affect me like he did."

"I know, dear. You were scared and alone and he protected you. Any young lady loves a knight who comes to her rescue. You need to move on with your life. You are a beautiful young lady and there are plenty of young men standing by waiting to fall in love with you. There is no way you'll ever see him again. For all you know he may have a wife and children. He was apparently handsome and he certainly was a gentleman for loaning the money to you for the stage ticket. However, you need to move on with your life."

"I know. I know."

CHAPTER THIRTY-TWO
Getting the New Bull into the Bowl

Sam led the bull and the calf as he rode into his ranch. He saw that Juan was training a white horse with brown splashes on his flank and shoulders. It was a proud, magnificent animal. Sam watched them work together and thought, *That is why I like to train. The mustangs still keep their pride.*

When Juan saw Sam, he stopped and walked over, propping his elbows on the top corral bar and his right boot on the bottom bar of the corral fence. "Senõr Sam, that's one good-looooking papa bull and baby bull. When you want to go get the cows?"

"Juan, I've been thinking. What if we went in there, drove out the old range bull, and put this new bull in there with the cows? Just left them in the bowl all winter. They'll probably be safer in there than out here on the open range. After all, they've been wintering in there for a while already."

"But what if the old bull, he not want to go? After all, he has been singing heez love songs in there for a long time."

"Then you'll just have to talk some of that smooth Mexican talk to him like you do the senoritas."

"Ah, the senoritas. Juan has not been to town for so long, Senõr Sam. Juan is sick in his heart. He longs to see the senoritas and hear the melody of their voices."

"Okay, you Mexican Don Juan, let's get these two in the pasture with the horses for now, and ride over to the waterfall. I want to see what condition the cows are in now."

As they approached the waterfall, Sam could see that some brush had grown up, making it even harder to see the cave behind the falls. Sam got down and, taking his bowie knife, trimmed some of the new growth. Just as he started to get back on Buck, they heard the distinct

A COLLISION OF DREAMS

crack of a rifle shot over in the hills. This was followed by a whole burst of firing, and then it was quiet.

"Senõr Sam, what was that?"

"I don't know. It sounded like somebody's in a fight, and not far away. It's none of our business. Let's get into the bowl before it becomes our business."

They had a difficult time trying to get the horses to go into the area behind the waterfall, but soon they rode out into the valley-bowl. It was just as beautiful as the last time Sam had seen it. "Juan, look at this—isn't this amazing?"

Pointing back at the cave, Juan said, "Senõr Sam, is that the only way in or out?"

"No Juan. If you've got wings, you can fly out."

"Senõr Sam, you not so funny."

Riding around the area, they counted sixty-six head of cattle. They found one old mossy horn bull and three younger bulls. "Senõr Sam, look at the horns on that old bull. You may have to shoot that one. He looks like one mean hombre."

"Here's what we're gonna to do. I'm going to get a rope on one of his horns and then I'll make a loop around the tree over there." He pointed to a tree on his left. "That bull will try to charge me. I want you to get a rope on his other horn and get it wrapped around that tree over there. He pointed to a different tree. Don't you dare miss, Juan, or he'll kill me or Buck—possibly both. He will be killing mad when that rope gets on his horn."

"Okay, Senõr Sam, I don't know. Juan hardly ever misses, but this is too dangerous. That big beast probably weighs 1800 pounds. Those horns are as sharp as grandma's needles. Look at him—he is just standing there looking at us with the devil in his eye."

All at once they heard some more shooting, but it sounded farther way. "Look at it this way, Juan: All we have to face is one old bull instead of a bunch of guns, like somebody is doing right now."

"I think Juan would rather face the guns, senõr."

"Let's get this over with." Sam made a loop in his lariat while he rode toward the bull. The old bull stood his ground, and glared at Sam and Buck. As soon as that rope snapped on his left horn, that old bull bellowed so loud it seemed like it shook the walls of the bowl. He lowered his head and charged. Buck, a cutting horse, could turn on a dime. That is all that saved them. The old bull was fast—much faster than Sam or Juan had expected.

Juan was so startled at the speed of the bull's charge that he hurried his throw and missed—it went over the bull's head. Sam and Buck rounded the tree expecting the bull to be caught between the two ropes. Sam looked back just as the monster bull rounded the tree and 1800 pounds of rage bore down on them.

* * *

The general looked up when they walked into his office. "Marshal, what brings you out here today?"

"General, I'm still hearin' some rumors about the Indians being mad because somebody sold 'em some bad whiskey. They are threatening to go on the warpath. Have you heard anything about it?"

"No, but I have been hearing some rumors about the Indians getting hold of some bad whiskey."

"I know for sure they did. Me and two of my deputies went out to talk to the Indians, but they wouldn't talk to us. They did admit they had some bad whiskey. Several people were sick, but they wouldn't say where they got it. You and I both know it was probably the Taggerts."

"Yeah, except old Randolph Taggert has never sold any bad whiskey before. I wonder if we have somebody new in the territory, trying to start up in the whiskey business. Have you got anybody new that has moved in recently?"

"The only new person I've heard about is Sam McClanton. He's the one who has shot five or six of the Taggerts."

"Maybe Sam is killin' off the competition?"

"I don't think so. Sam is building him a ranch up in the hills. He's the one you boys have been buying horses from."

"Oh him. You are right, I doubt if he has been trying to take over the moonshine business from the Taggerts."

"The rumor I'm hearin' is the younger braves want to take a bunch up in them canyons and wipe out all the Taggerts. Of course, if they get started, there's no way of knowin' where it'll stop."

"If we could get the Indians to tell us for sure where they got the whiskey, we could take a bunch of marshals backed up by a squad of troops and arrest them all."

"Maybe I could just deputize this Sam fellow and send him in there by himself. Did you hear what happened when a whole passel of them Taggerts chased him into the hills over by Pine Creek the other day?"

"Naw, what happened?"

"The way I hear it, late the next afternoon, six of 'em came limpin' home. It seems he scared off all their horses and sent them walkin' home."

"They walked all the way from Pine creek? Pine creek must be ten or twelve miles."

CHAPTER THIRTY-THREE
The Bull

Sam yelled, "Juan, shoot that thang, shoot that thang!" Every time Juan tried to shoot, he couldn't. He was afraid that he was going to hit Sam or Buck. They were running around in a circle so fast that Sam and Buck ended up between him and the bull. The bull was bellowing. Buck was squealing. Sam was yelling.

There was so much noise that Juan couldn't hear himself think. Dust was filling the air. It got so thick you couldn't tell which one was the horse and which was the bull. All at once, the bull made one more loop around the tree. The rope wrapped around the trunk so tight the bull found his head snubbed tight to the tree. He bellowed and butted the tree and pawed the earth. All he managed to do was shake a couple of very frightened squirrels out the tree and onto the ground. All of the other cows ran to the far side of the bowl. They didn't know what was going on, but it sounded terrible. Buck stood to one side, his sides heaving. He was gasping for air.

Sam yelled, "Juan, I told you not to miss when you threw that rope."

"Senõr, you can tell your grandkids how you caught old mossy horn all by yourself. People will probably be singing songs around campfires about the day you caught that old mossy horn all by yourself."

"Very funny. Why didn't you shoot that thang when I was yelling for you to?"

"I couldn't, you and Buck were running around so much. I was afraid I would shoot you."

Sam lifted his hat and mopped sweat from the hatband, saying, "There was a time when I was hoping you would shoot one of us. I didn't much care which one. I don't ever want any thang that big and that mad after me again."

The bull was still bellowing and shaking the tree for all it was worth. Sam rode in a wide circle around the animal and wrapped the rope around his other horn. The second rope snubbed his head even tighter to the tree. "Now old boy, you and that oak tree can fight all you want to, but you are going to lose. When you've calmed down, we'll come back and turn you out into the big wide world beyond the waterfall."

As they rode out through the cave, they could still hear the old bull bellowing and scraping the tree. "Senõr Sam, do you think he'll keel himself?"

"I doubt it. It's like training horses—once they realize that running in circles is a waste of time, they calm down. Once he realizes that tree is not scared of him, he'll calm down."

On the way back to the ranch, Sam shot a young buck deer. "Now we can have some fresh meat."

"Senõr Sam, it's getting cool at night—I think I'll chop up some of that deer meat and make some chili. I saw some wild peppers and sage growing along the riverbank, and there are some wild onions near the spring."

As they arrived back at the ranch, they found fresh tracks of unshod horses that had been there. Sam looked at the tracks. "Juan, what do you think? Are those tracks of another group of wild horses that wandered in here and saw the horses we have in the pasture, or have we had a visit from a bunch of Indians?"

"I don't know, Senõr Sam. The tracks go around the house and then go to the pasture fence."

"Juan, we've had it too good here for to long. I think those are Indian tracks. Do you remember the bunch that showed up here once before?"

"Si, I remember. But they didn't attack us, they just looked and rode away."

"Yeah, but think about all that shooting we heard yesterday. What if that's a bunch of young bucks wearing war paint? I think we had better keep our Winchesters with us. We better sleep in the stone house for a while."

That night they slept in the house with the shutters closed. It was cool outside, so inside at night was not uncomfortable. The next morning after breakfast, Juan said, "You know what we need, senõr? We need some chickens, so we can have fresh eggs for breakfast."

"Well Juan, why don't I get some pigs and then you can have bacon and eggs?"

"Better yet, senõr, why don't we get a Rosa to cook the bacon and eggs, so I don't have to eat your cookin' every day?"

"Why you ungrateful Mexican bandit, from now on I'll make you do all the cooking."

Juan rolled his eyes and looked up at the sky. "Please, mother of God, look out for us." Laughing, they saddled up and headed for the waterfall. "Do you think we'll find the old bull dead?"

"I don't know, he could've killed himself, but I hope not. I hope we can just get him out of there and turn him loose."

As they rode through the cave, all was quiet. "Well Juan, either he has calmed down or he's dead, because I don't hear him."

They were caught totally by surprise by what they found when they rode into the bowl.

**

The sheriff walked into the marshal's office. "Duncan, the Taggerts came in and reported that they had a running gunfight with a bunch of Apache back in the hills yesterday."

"Did anybody lose his hair?"

"They said they killed a couple of braves, but you know how that goes—unless you can count the bodies, you never know if you have killed an Indian or if they just went to the ground."

A COLLISION OF DREAMS

"I talked to the army the other day—they're going to look in on the Indians. If we could find out for sure that the Taggerts were the ones who sold them the bad whiskey, maybe we could round up the Taggerts and avoid a war breakin' out. You know what happens when a bunch of hot-headed braves start putting on war paint. They start raiding everything in sight. They won't stop with just the Taggerts."

"Every outlying ranch like the Tumbling C will be in danger."

"I am not too worried about the Tumbling C. They have a lot of guns around there, and some men who know how to use 'em. I worry about some of the smaller ranches and those sodbusters."

"Maybe you and I should ride over to the army together and see what they've found out."

"I can't go today. Why don't we go first thing in the mornin'?"

"Okay, let's meet at the café and after breakfast ride over to talk with the general. I'm sure he don't want another Indian war to break out any more than we do."

Unbeknownst to Sam or the marshal, at that same moment Mattie Ann walked into her daddy's office. "Daddy, let's ride up to Sam's ranch and see how they are doing."

"Honey, I just can't right now. I have these taxes that have to be posted by the end of the week. How are you feeling?"

"I'm feeling a little stronger. What if I get Rosa to ride with me? She and I could ride up there tomorrow morning right after the guys finish breakfast, and we could be back before suppertime."

"I don't know honey, I hate to see you and Rosa go off without any of the men with you. You remember when those Indians attacked Sam and Jessie up on the ridge a while back? Besides, are you sure you are up to it?"

"Oh Daddy, you worry too much. I'm fine. Rosa and I'll be alright in broad daylight. I want to see how much Sam has got done on my house."

"Let me think about it—we'll talk about it later."

Mattie Ann left the office and went to the kitchen. "Rosa, can we pack a lunch for Sam and Juan tomorrow morning? Right after the guys get through with breakfast, you and I could take the buckboard and ride up to see how much Sam has got done on the house."

With a twinkle in her eye, Rosa said, "Mattie Ann, child, are you sure it's the house you want to go see?"

"Well yes, if I am going to live there, I want to see how they are building it—and yes, I miss Sam too."

"What does your Daddy think of your idea? Have you talked to him about you traipsing off around the country without any of the men with you?"

"I talked to him, and as long as you are with me he shouldn't be worried."

"Mattie Ann Carville, I know you all your life and I heard what you just said. Your daddy didn't approve of this, did he? Anyway, are you sure you are up to a ride that far?"

She said, "Yes, I'm getting stronger. Well, he hasn't said yes yet, but he will. We can always take a rifle with us if you are scared of buggers?"

"Mattie Ann, it is not buggers that I am worried about. You still haven't got your color back."

"I'm fine. Maybe the fresh air will be good for me."

CHAPTER THIRTY-FOUR
Surprise Behind the Waterfall

What they found when they rode out into the sunlight in the bowl was a shock.

The bull was down and six Indian squaws had it almost butchered. Sam and Juan sat absolutely still. Both men were astonished. Until now, they didn't think anybody knew about this bowl but them. They both took time to survey the scene. Three stalwart braves stood guard over the squaws while they worked. Not that the squaws by themselves were any picnic when it came to fighting. Just as Sam reached back to slip the thong off his six-shooter, a brave jumped him from behind.

A strong arm wrapped around his neck. Sam knew the other hand would hold a knife. Sam kicked his feet out of the stirrups and went off the horse backwards. When he hit the ground, the Indian lost his hold. Sam was on his feet quick. So was the brave.

The Indian still held the knife in his hand. He held it down low with the razor-sharp cutting edge turned up. All at once, he leaped at Sam.

Sam had wrestled enough while at the boys' ranch. He reacted quick as a wink, and with the palm of his left hand he slapped the point of the knife away from his body. Sam grabbed the wrist of the knife hand in his right hand. He threw the Indian over his shoulder. With a thud, the Indian hit the ground. When the Indian came up this time, Sam kicked the hand holding the knife and the knife flew into the air.

The Indian reached down to retrieve the knife and Sam whipped his six-shooter out of its holster and slammed the barrel over the Indian's head. The Indian hit the ground, out cold.

"Is he dead?"

A COLLISION OF DREAMS

"No Juan, but he'll have a headache for a while. Can you speak any Apache?"

"Si, I speak some."

"Tell them they can have all the meat from the bull. We're friends with the Apache. We live in the tee-pee made of stone."

The Indians had all stopped work and stared at the downed warrior. "Juan, tell them he's not dead. He'll help eat the meat from the bull in their lodge tonight. Tell them he's a brave warrior. He fought well and he will live to fight again."

The Indians had rigged travois to haul the meat. They made room on one of them for the downed brave. Sam and Juan sat on their horses and watched as the Indians filed out of the bowl and took the meat with them.

"Senõr Sam, why did you not shoot him? You had the gun in your hand."

"Because he was a warrior protecting the women from his tribe. He didn't deserve to die."

"Senõr Sam, Indians don't think like you. Now they think you weak. His medicine was too strong. They will think that is why you didn't keel him. Now he will come back to keel you for sure."

As they rode back, Juan said, "Senõr Sam, we need to build a brush lean-to for the horses. Except for your horse and my horse, all of the others were running wild in these hills last winter."

"First we'll need to cut and stack a lot of hay. Then we'll build a smokehouse, fill it with meat, and start the fires going. And then we'll build the lean-to."

An antelope sprang from the trees right in front of the riders. Both men fired and the antelope went down. It took only a few minutes for them to skin it out and cut the choice cuts of meat. They wrapped the meat in the hide and bound it to the back of Sam's saddle. "When we get home, Juan, let's dig a pit where we want the smokehouse to be. We can start this meat to roasting tonight. Tomorrow we can haul down some logs and build a smokehouse around the pit."

"Si, we can build the smokehouse in one day, maybe two—you are better hunter than Juan. I cut hay, you keel meat for the smokehouse."

The next morning, at first light, they took axes up into the hills and started to cut logs the size needed for the smokehouse. It was almost dark when two very tired lumberjacks limped back into camp.

"Senōr Sam, Juan is a cowboy, he is no lumber Joe."

"You mean lumberjack, and I agree with you—I'm not a lumberjack either."

"I would rather go fight the bear," Juan said, "than chop any more wood. That is not work for a vaquero."

* * *

Mattie Ann sat in the kitchen and ideally stirred a spoon round and round in a cup of coffee that had already gone cold.

Rosa put bread in the oven, turned, and said, "Mattie Ann, did you tell Sam what the doctor said?"

Mattie Ann bit her bottom lip as tears rolled down her cheeks. She said, "I couldn't, he was so happy."

"Mattie Ann, honey, you've got to tell him what the doctors said."

"I know, it's only fair, but I love him so. I want to marry him. I'm afraid he'll change his mind."

"Honey, I know life is not fair sometimes. If he really loves you, it won't matter."

* * *

Sam and Juan were dead tired after cutting trees all day and then building a rack to roast the meat. After supper, Juan was soon fast asleep. Nights were cold, so they both slept in the house at night. As each man rolled up in his bedroll, they didn't think about the antelope meat hanging above the fire pit.

Sam lay wrapped up in his blankets and thought about Mattie Ann. He imagined what it would be like to be married and have

A COLLISION OF DREAMS

several kids. He didn't want to build a ranch. He wanted to build a home for a family.

An hour before daylight, a noise outside the door woke him. He grabbed his Winchester and flung the door open. As he whipped up his rifle, he squeezed the trigger. A loud bang shattered the still night and echoed off the walls in the house. His bullet struck a big grizzly bear behind his left shoulder and killed it.

Juan was sound asleep when that rifle bullet exploded inside the room. He tried to leap up and his feet tangled in the blankets. He sprawled on the floor still tangled in the blankets. When he tried to jump back up his arms were tangled and he flopped around like a fish thrown on the riverbank. "What? Where's shooting? Who's shooting?" When his eyes cleared enough to focus, he saw Sam leaning against the doorframe, laughing at him. "Oh senõr. I think Juan is shot."

Sam was laughing hard, so he held on to the doorframe to keep from falling. "No, you're not shot. Get up and help me dress out this bear. He'll make a lot of fat meat." They skinned out the bear and hung the chunks of meat in the tree until they could get the smokehouse finished. Then they took the liver and fried it for breakfast. No one noticed the pair of eyes that watched them from the side of the hill.

Early the next morning Juan climbed up on the top of the new smokehouse. Sam handed short logs up to Juan. These formed the pitched roof. Suddenly, an arrow struck the side of the smokehouse with a thud and a twang. Juan dropped straight down through the unfinished roof. He almost fell into the fire pit. Sam jumped through the doorframe and spun around it so that he was now inside too.

Indians on horses raced around the yard. They yelled, screamed, and shot arrows at the smokehouse. The logs were thick enough that no arrow was going to go through. Their biggest problem was that Sam and Juan were both trying to get in position to shoot out the door at the same time. The opening was too narrow for both of them to look out.

Sam said, "Juan, you cover the door. I'm going to climb up there and shoot out through the hole in the top."

Sam opened fire from the top of the smokehouse. The shooting was fast and furious for a few seconds. Indians rode in a tight circle around the smokehouse and at this range Sam and Juan couldn't miss. After a few minutes, the attack broke off. Four bodies lay on the ground. Sam said, "Looks like we drove 'em off."

Juan didn't answer. Sam turned and glanced down into the smokehouse. He saw Juan lying on the floor with an arrow stuck in the front of his shirt. Sam leaped down, and with trembling hands ripped open Juan's shirt. The arrow had gone into his chest high on the left side. His breath was labored, but he was still breathing. Sam rubbed his fingers over Juan's back and found the arrowhead just below the skin.

Sam picked up Juan and ran to the ranch house, where he laid him on a bench they had built. Sam was very careful as he rolled Juan over on his right side. Then took his razor-sharp knife and slit the skin on Juan's back. He took hold of the arrow shaft and broke it in half. With clenched teeth, he sucked in a deep breath, grabbed hold of the piece of shaft stuck in Juan's chest, and pushed it on through.

"Don't die on me, you lazy Mexican. I need you to help get this place ready for winter." He walked over to the shelf in the kitchen and took down the bottle of whiskey. He thought, *This is sure a waste of good whiskey*. Sam took a piece of cloth and wrapped it around the arrow shaft, then soaked it in the whiskey. He pushed the whiskey-soaked rag through the hole, all the way out the back.

Juan moaned when he did this. "I know it hurts old buddy, but we've got to keep the infection down if we can. You hang in there. I'll doctor you the best I can."

When he had finished dressing the wound, Sam covered Juan with blankets and started a fire in the fireplace. After he had done all he could for Juan, he went back out to the smokehouse and added some mesquite wood to the fire pit.

He noticed that the Indian bodies were gone. While he doctored Juan, the Indians had slipped back and removed the bodies. "Just as well—this way I won't have to bury 'em."

Sam tended to the stock and came back in to check on Juan. When he touched Juan's forehead, he could tell his fever was up. He went to the spring and drew a pail of cold water, then dipped a piece of cloth in the cold water and placed it on Juan's forehead. Then he shaved some meat into a pan, covered it with water, and poured in a lot of salt. He soon had a broth simmering. He gently lifted Juan's head and told him, "Juan, I know this's going to hurt but you need to get some of this broth in you. You've lost a lot of blood and we need to replace the salt you lost and get some fluid in you."

He held the cup to Juan's lips and poured small amounts of the broth into his mouth. Juan managed to get the entire cup down. Sam kept thinking, *What am I going to do if he dies? I'll never get this place finished before spring by myself.*

The next few days dragged by. Sam tended to Juan and the stock. He missed Mattie Ann. Yet he couldn't leave Juan. Each time he went out, he was afraid he would find him dead when he came back.

On the third long lonely day, Juan briefly opened his eyes. Sam said, "Man am I glad to see you open your eyes. I am tired of using up good drinking whiskey on you."

Juan mumbled, "What happened?"

"You don't remember us getting in a fight with a bunch of redskins?"

He looked and Juan was back asleep.

Each day he was awake a little longer as he regained his strength, and by the end of two weeks he was still stiff and sore but he was back in the saddle.

Sam told Juan, "You hang around the house and work on gaining more strength. I'm goin' to the Tumbling C. I've got to see about Mattie Ann."

As Sam cantered across the hills north of the Tumbling C ranch house, he could see the hands out tending the stock. The ranch looked so peaceful. "Buck, that is the way I've always pictured how a home will look. Just think—in a few years we'll have some young'ens running around the yard. Mattie Ann will be in there baking bread or pies or something. I can't wait for spring. I wish the wedding was tomorrow."

When he stepped up on the back porch, Rosa opened the door. "Come in, Sam."

"Where is Mattie Ann? Is she okay?"

"She is resting right now. She still hasn't got all of her strength back yet. I'll go up and tell her you're here."

A few minutes later he looked up as Mattie Ann came down the stairs. Wrapped in a pink robe, it was obvious she had just woken up. Her face lit up in a smile as she saw him standing there. "Hi handsome, I've missed you. Where have you been?"

They sat down on the sofa and he told her how Juan had been shot by an arrow.

"Oh Sam, that's terrible. Is he all right now?"

They talked about the ranch. What he and Juan had done. All the time they talked, he had an uneasy feeling that something was not right—in fact, something was terribly wrong. What was it?

Mattie Ann took both of his hands in her hands and looked him in the eye. "Sam, I have something to tell you. Please listen. Hear me out. First, I love you. I love you with all my heart."

"Mattie Ann, I love you too."

"Sam, don't talk. Let me say what I need to say. You remember when I had rheumatic fever. The fever damaged my heart. Sam, we can't get married. I can never have any children for you. I am so sorry. I wanted so badly to be your wife." Tears ran down her face as she said, "And give birth to your children, but the doctor tells me that I can never have any children."

Sam was stunned. He couldn't believe what he had heard. Not Mattie Ann. She was so full of life. He reached and pulled her to him, held her and stroked her hair. He couldn't even think of words to say. She started to sob softly.

Sam took her shoulders in his hands and held her back at arm's length. "Mattie Ann, I'm not in love with children. I'm in love with you. In the spring, we'll get married and I'll take care of you. We don't need kids. I just need you. When we are old and grey, we'll sit on the front porch in our rocking chairs and watch the wind bend the wheat stems in the field."

"No Sam, I love you too much. If I can't be a complete wife and mother for you, I won't tie you down to a cripple."

"Mattie Ann, I'm going to be back every few days from now until the day we are going to get married. Now you go on back up stairs and rest. Let that beautiful little heart of yours get stronger. I've got to go back and get a home ready for a beautiful bride." He pulled her to him and kissed her gently.

CHAPTER THIRTY-FIVE
The Storm

Ma Taggert sat the steaming bowl on the table. "You boys eat while it's hot."

Randolph sat down at the head of the table and said, "Old woman, get me some buttermilk. You know I like buttermilk with my corn bread."

All talking stopped while they stuffed food into their mouths.

Leaning back in his chair, Randolph lit his pipe. "I still don't know why you boys can't find that feller. He's around here somewhere."

"Pa, we have rode all over every trail in the territory. I heard he was in town the other day, but I never seen him."

"I think he left the territory. He probably got tired of hiding out from us and left."

"He ain't left. Y'all keep lookin'. We'll find him and kill 'im. In fact, I've got a new idea how we can find 'im."

* * *

Sam and Juan decided to go check on the whiteface bull again. As they rode out, Sam said, "Look at all the beauty around us, at the brilliant fall colors of the trees, orange, red, yellow, with a dark green pine tree thrown in every so often just to add color."

"Aw senõr, Juan appreciates beauty. That is why Juan needs to go into town and see the beautiful senoritas."

Laughing, Sam said, "Okay amigo, let's go over to the bowl, check on the bull, and then get the hay moved up. When we are done, we'll head for town."

When they arrived at the waterfall, Juan asked, "What we do if the Indians are back?"

"Hopefully we won't see any Indians. If we find a bunch of Indians butchering a whiteface bull, I'm going to go on the warpath

A COLLISION OF DREAMS

myself. I've staked everything on that bull and the young one back at the ranch. Of course, the young one won't be of any value for another year or two."

Sam reached down and pulled the thong off the hammer of his six-shooter, then pulled the Winchester from the saddle scabbard. "Better get ready in case they are here."

Guiding the horses through the cave into the bowl behind the waterfall, they came out into bright sunlight in the bowl-valley, Sam leading the way. He stopped his horse just outside of the cave. "Look at that, Juan—have you ever seen anything as beautiful as this? Look at all those beautiful white flowers over there next to the east wall. Look at how green the grass is this late in the year. No wonder the cattle look so fat. A man could just ignore what was going on in the rest of the world as long as he stayed here."

After they had looked the bull and cows over, Sam said, "Juan, if we want to get back before dark, we'd better head on back."

"Senõr Sam, let's just move in here and stay."

"It's sure tempting, but I don't think Miss Mattie Ann will go for that idea. She has already been planning on how she can fix up the stone house. At least she was before she got sick."

As they rode out through the waterfall, they were surprised. The wind blew much harder out here than down in the bowl. "Whoa, Juan, looks like we may have a storm coming in."

"Si, Senõr Sam, look at the lightning in that storm. This one is a bad bear."

"Better get your slicker out, it looks like we may need it."

They hadn't gone two miles when the storm hit. Thunder boomed off the canyon walls and rolled down the canyon. Sam yelled, "We better find a place where we can hole up and wait this monster out."

Lightning split the sky again, then the rain started coming down in sheets of water. Sam spotted a group of young cedars that grew close together. Standing in his stirrups, he reached up, grabbed the tops of two cedar trees, and pulled them together, tying a pigging string around them. Then he grabbed two more and tied the four together. With his razor-sharp bowie knife, he chopped off the lower branches that grew all of the way to the ground. He handed the branches he cut off to Juan, who wove them back into the tops of the trees. They soon had a cave cut into the cedar trees that were tied together, forming a tee-pee.

Tying their horses under the larger trees, both men were able to scramble into the cedar tree tent. In there, they were reasonably dry, as the branches on the cedars shed almost all of the water while the storm raged around them. Sam quickly got a fire going, then reached into his saddlebags and pulled out a sack of coffee and a pot. Within a few minutes, he had coffee brewing.

The branches that had been cut off and woven back into the tops of the trees made the structure almost watertight. Very little water leaked in. They were warm and dry, with strong black coffee to drink and pieces of jerky to chew—while a fierce storm raged outside! It was as dark as midnight and rain poured from the night sky. The lightning was so fierce that the hair on Sam's arms stood up, and when he looked at Juan, he saw that the hair on his head stood up too. "In the morning, at first light, we'll ride by the ranch and check on the horses, then ride to town. I'll stop by the Tumbling C on my way back."

CHAPTER THIRTY-SIX
Kidnapping Mattie Ann and Rosa

Mattie Ann walked into the kitchen, where Rosa made biscuits. "Rosa, I told Sam that I couldn't marry him."

Rosa wiped her hands on her apron and turned to look at Mattie Ann. "What did he say?"

"He is stubborn man Rosa. He said he didn't care about kids; we were going to get married in the spring anyway and he would take care of me."

"Mattie Ann, let me ask you something. If he was sick, would you still marry him?"

"Well sure, but I can't have any babies for him. He's always talked about having a ranch and kids. The doctor says I can't ever have any kids."

"Honey, there is so much in life we can't control. You love heem and he loves you. You don't know what the future holds. He could get shot by an Indian, or one of them Taggerts, or gored by a bull. You are worried about your heart. Fate could take him before it takes you. Get married. Enjoy what time fate allows you two to have together. In this day and time, life is short. Grab the moment and love him."

"Oh Rosa, I love you. Since Momma died, I am so glad I have you to talk to."

They spent the next several minutes like two schoolgirls, looking at the beautiful pictures in Mr. Barlow's catalog. "Look at that four-poster bed. Aw, look at that lamp. Look at that settee." Mattie Ann's spirit lifted. Finally, Rosa said, "If I no get these biscuits made, you weel be looking at some mighty unhappy hands. You better put that book down and help me get lunch on the table."

"Okay, but as soon as lunch is done, I want to take the buckboard and run up to see the new house."

* * *

A COLLISION OF DREAMS

Sam and Juan did not know that Mattie Ann and Rosa were coming to the ranch. After they checked the horses, Sam said, "Okay Juan, let's go let you sing some love songs."

As they approached town, out of habit, Sam slipped the thong off the hammer of his six-shooter. He reached into his pocket, pulled out some money, and said, "Juan, here is $30.00. I'm still holding back one month's wages. That money is going to bail you out of jail if you forget that you are a lover and not a fighter again."

"Juan is a lover of beautiful senoritas, not a fighter. However, sometimes the beautiful senorita has a boyfriend who is a fighter. Then Juan ends up in jail. Right now, Juan is going to the mercantile and get him a new shirt to wear when he goes to the cantina."

Sam went in to see his friend the marshal.

"Sam, I'm glad to see you. Have you seen any Indians around your place?"

"Well, when we were building a smokehouse a bunch of young bucks attacked us. Juan took an arrow in the chest, but he is doing alright now. Then we were gone the other day, and when we got back, there were a lot of unshod pony tracks around the place. I wasn't sure if another wild horse herd had come through or if it was Indians.

We ran into a bunch of Indians one other time. We had an old longhorn bull snubbed to a tree and when we got back a bunch of squaws was butchering him. Before we could say anything one way or the other, a brave jumped on my back with a knife and we had a little go 'round."

"He obviously didn't kill you."

"No, and I didn't kill him either. I did whack him on the head with my six-shooter, so he'll have a sore head for a while."

"Sam, if you don't beat all. Why didn't you kill that Indian if you had your gun in your hand?"

"Because they weren't attacking us. They just found an old bull tied up to a tree and were butchering it. All that brave did was try to protect his womenfolk, so I gave them the meat and sent them on their way."

"Like I said, if you don't beat all. Most white men would've killed that Indian just for spite. Anyway, keep your eyes open. There are rumors that somebody sold the Indians some bad whiskey and they are killin' mad about it. You know how Indians are if they go on the warpath—they'll attack the outlyin' ranches first."

"It was probably the Taggerts that sold them the whiskey. Why don't you go lock up the Taggerts and maybe the Indians will hear that, and stay on the reservation?"

"Two reasons. Just like you said, it was probably the Taggerts—but nobody knows for sure. I can't lock a man up until I am sure, and old Randolph Taggert has never sold any bad whiskey before. Therefore, I'm thinkin' we may have somebody new in the territory. In fact, the army suggests it might be you."

"Why me?"

"Just because you're new."

"Well, it ain't me. I've been too busy training horses for the army."

"That's what I told them. When they found out it was you they had been gettin' horses from, they decided it wasn't you too."

"Well marshal, I've got to get some supplies and get back out there. I just stopped by to warn you Juan is in town and he has a month's wages on him." Sam reached into his pocket, pulled out $30.00, and handed it to the marshal.

"What is this for?"

"That's Juan's other month's wages. I held it back to cover his bail. I need him out at the ranch, so if you've got to lock him up, turn him loose as soon as he sobers up."

The marshal laughed. "You'll do, Sam, you'll do."

Sam stepped through the front door just in time to see Juan with his back up against the wall in front of the mercantile. Two Taggert men faced him.

One of the men said, "Are you the greasy Mexican that works for that no-good killer named Sam?"

A COLLISION OF DREAMS

"Si, I work for Senõr Sam, but no killer."

"Then I'm just goin' to kill you and send him a message."

They hadn't noticed Sam on the boardwalk in front of the marshal's office.

"I'm right here. Tell me yourself."

Caught off guard, there's such thing as reaction time. It took Taggert a moment to register what had happened. Then he reached for his gun.

Sam slapped his gun and flame and smoke shot out of its barrel before Taggert's gun even cleared leather. The other man found himself looking down the barrel of two guns when Juan drew his pistol also.

Sam said, "You Taggerts are pretty dumb. I could've killed a half dozen of you when you chased me up in the hills. Instead, I let you walk home. I thought the walk would clear your brains for you."

The door to the marshal's office crashed open. He raced out with a scattergun in his hands. "What's going on out here?"

Juan pointed his gun at the man lying on the ground. "That man told me he was going to keel me because I work for Senõr Sam. Then Senõr Sam stepped out the door and that hombre tried to shoot Senõr Sam and got heemself kilt dead."

The marshal pointed to the other Taggert standing there, turning white all around the gills, and asked Sam, "What're you going to do with that one?"

"He didn't do anything, he was just standing there, so I'm going to let him go home and bury his kinfolk."

He turned back to the Taggert man and said, "Now I suggest you go home and make that cemetery plot a lot bigger, because if any more Taggerts come after me, you are going to have some need for some more gravesites."

The marshal said, "Dang it, Sam, come on back in here. You're killin' me with all this paperwork."

Turning to Juan, he said, "Mexican, go on down to the cantina. Sam here has already posted your bail, so get drunk and then get back up to the ranch."

Sam gathered up the supplies he needed, and two hours later rode into the yard at the Tumbling C. Joe Carville met him as he stepped down from the saddle. He asked, "Where are the girls?"

"What girls?"

"Mattie Ann and Rosa, they went up to your place early this mornin' to see how you were comin' with the house."

"Juan and I left at first light. We went into town for supplies. I'm sure they're all right. They're probably just busy lookin' at the house. I better get on up there to make sure."

"Let me grab my hat and a gun. I'll go with you."

Side by side, they galloped across the hills. By the time they arrived at Sam's ranch it was late in the afternoon. There was no sign of the girls.

"Sam, I don't see any tracks that look like they've been here."

"Mr. Carville, I don't either. The ground is still wet—that buckboard's tracks should be plenty visible."

Joe Carville had an anguished look on his face. "I should've never allowed them to come alone."

"Let's head back and see if we can pick up their trail before it gets too dark to see."

"Sam, I'm sorry. Mattie Ann wanted to see you and the house. I first told her no, but she wanted to come so bad, I gave in. I'm sorry."

"Mr. Carville, we're going to find those tracks and then we're gonna find Mattie Ann and Rosa."

They arrived back at the Tumbling C just at dusk. Each man hoped to see a buckboard parked in the yard. It wasn't there.

"Sam, we might as well go on into the house—it's too dark to see anything now. In the morning, we'll get all of the boys together and spread out until we find those tracks."

The toe of Joe's boot caught on the top step as he started in, and he almost fell into the house. His shoulders slumped. He appeared to have aged thirty years since morning. The memory of losing his wife two years before was just too fresh, and now this. His hands trembled as he poured a stiff shot of whiskey into a glass.

Sam took the two horses to the corral and put them up. Russ rode up. He took one look at Sam and asked, "Sam, what's the matter?"

"Mattie Ann and Rosa have disappeared."

Alarmed, Russ asked, "Sam—what do you mean, 'disappeared?'"

"They're gone, Russ. This morning Mattie Ann talked her daddy into letting Rosa and her ride up to my place to see the house. Juan and I had gone to town. We didn't know they were coming. They never got there."

"How do you know they never got there?"

"They were in the buckboard. There are no buckboard tracks anywhere around my place."

"Have you looked for their tracks between here and there?"

"That's what Mr. Carville and I've been doing for the past two hours. We found nothing. At first light, we can track it outbound from here."

Together they walked into Joe's office. Russ said, "Boss, I better send one of the boys in to tell the sheriff and the marshal."

"You boys sit down and have a drink. Russ, we might as well wait until first light. No use taking a chance on getting one of the boys hurt riding in the dark. There ain't nothing anybody can do between now and daylight."

Tears ran down his rugged face. Here was a man's man. A man who had built an empire with his bare hands. He had fought cattle rustlers, Indians, weather, storms, and snow up to the rooftop, but he hadn't been able to keep the influenza from taking his wife. Now someone had taken his only daughter. He turned and looked at the other two men in the room. "Boys, if you've got any connections with the man upstairs, now is the time to trot'em out, 'cause all we can do between now and daylight is pray."

CHAPTER THIRTY-SEVEN
The Meeting in the Chief's Lodge

While Mr. Carville, Sam, and the boys were gathered in Mr. Carville's office, Chief Running Deer had all of the council gathered in his lodge. As soon as the council was seated around the lodge, Chief Running Deer said, "What have you done bringing two white women here?"

One of the warriors spoke in Apache. If anybody had been translating, it would have meant, "The white eyes must know the pain he has caused the Apache. My wife Little Dove is dead. I say we kill these two, so the white man can know pain, like my pain."

One of the older men of the council spoke. "We have known peace for many harvest moons. Already you may have brought the army down on us. As soon as they find out we have these women, they will destroy all of us. I say we take them back immediately, with a peace offering."

Another of the young warriors spat in the fire and shouted in Apache words that meant, "Never! We have bowed to the white man enough. I say we put on the paint and drive them all from our land."

One of the older chiefs said, "Listen to me, my brothers. I have been to the white man's cities back in the east. They have many men, many guns, and many horses. They will destroy the Apache nation forever if you persist in this foolishness. We must take the women back unharmed."

Another chief said, "The white eyes with the silver star on his chest—he say if we will tell him who sold the whiskey to the Apache, he will arrest the seller of bad whiskey and put him into the white man's prison."

One young warrior jumped to his feet, yelling at the chiefs in Apache words that meant, "Do you hear what you are saying, old men? They will arrest him. He will live many more summers in the white man's prison. Running Bear is dead—he will never see another

A COLLISION OF DREAMS

summer. Beaver Claw is dead. Little Dove is dead. No—they must die. The white man must also die. IT IS THE APACHE WAY!"

Another young warrior spoke up. "If the old fathers are afraid to fight, then let them step out of the way of the warriors. I say we kill these two and hang their hair on the lodge poll. Then put their bodies back into the sled with wheels. Let their horses take them home, but leave their long hair hanging in the camp."

CHAPTER THIRTY-EIGHT
Searching for Mattie Ann

Before daylight, Joe Carville and the men made some coffee. No one wanted to eat. As soon as it was light, they swung into the saddle and started to follow the trail left by the buckboard. They were a grim-faced, heavily armed group of determined men. The only sound was the clomp of horse's hooves and the creak of saddle leather.

One hour after sunup, a rider galloped a tired, hot, lathered horse into Cactus Tree City. The first place he went was to the café. "I need to find the marshal or the sheriff."

The waitress said, "They're around somewhere. They were just in here eating breakfast about an hour ago."

He wheeled around and ran out the door, then glanced both ways. He didn't see either man on the street. His boot heels made a thundering sound that echoed down the street as he raced down the boardwalk. He ran all the way to the marshal's office. It was closed and locked. Whirling around, he dashed down to the courthouse and burst into the sheriff's office. "I need the sheriff."

A white haired deputy said, "You're too late. Maybe I can help you. He and the territorial marshal left for the fort early this morning, before daylight. What do you need, son?"

"Somebody has stole Joe Carville's cook and his daughter." Years later, he would be teased about the order of importance he placed on the hostages.

"Slow down, son—what do you mean by somebody stole 'em?"

The cowhand gasped for breath as he blurted out, "The two women took a buckboard to go up to Sam's ranch—they wanted to look at the new house he's building." He had to stop to take a breath and said, "Sam and Mattie Ann is planning on getting married come spring. He's building her a new house. Somebody got 'em before they got there."

"I'll let the sheriff know as soon as he gets back—probably won't be till late this evening."

* * *

Joe Carville and Sam found where the buckboard had turned off the trail. "I wonder why they turned this way? I don't see any other tracks, like somebody made 'em turn," Joe mused.

One of the men shouted, then pointed to the buckboard parked near a patch of mountain laurel. It was just sitting there. The horses were munching grass. They had obviously been there all night because all of the grass was eaten down where they could reach. Russ looked in the buckboard. "Well, I don't see any blood."

"I see some blood on the ground over here. I'd say one of the gals shot somebody."

Unshod pony tracks told the story. Apparently, the women had turned off the trail to pick some flowers for Mattie Ann to take up to the new house. While they were picking flowers, a band of Indians had attacked them. Mattie Ann or Rosa had managed to get off one shot before the Indians got them.

Slim said, "What do you think they'll do with them?"

"You don't even want to think about it," Russ said. "We've got to get 'em back."

About that time, a horse raced over the crest of the hill. All eyes turned to see. It was Juan. He slid his horse to a stop and said, "I was sleeping in the jail, and a deputy came in and told me what happened. I came as fast as a horse could go. What can Juan do?"

Staring at Juan, Sam said, "The first thing you need to do, Juan, is calm down—we can't understand you when you get all excited." Turning to Joe Carville and Russ, Sam said, "The trail left by the Indian ponies shouldn't be hard to follow. They have a whole day's start on us, so I say we get moving and hope they hold Mattie Ann and Rosa for a day or two while they figure out what to do with them. My guess is they were taken by a bunch of hotheaded young bucks and maybe the older heads will cool them down some when they get to camp. That is, if they took them back to the main camp."

Someone said, "There are only twelve of us, and there are maybe two hundred of them. Maybe we should go get the army."

"No, we don't have time. Indians are notional," Sam said. "They can decide to kill the women at any moment. We've got to follow those tracks and see where they lead us."

As they followed the tracks, they were soon in a tree line on the side of a valley. When they looked down into the valley, all of them could see what appeared to be about a hundred tee-pees. The tee-pees were arranged in concentric circles around a main lodge. Sam watched the village though a spyglass. He could see that two warriors guarded one lodge.

There appeared to be a meeting going on in another. That one was likely the chief's lodge, with an open courtyard in front of it.

* * *

While Sam watched the Indian village, Randolph Taggert's wife Myrtle stood with her hands on her hips. "I say enough is enough. Take down your still, load it all on the wagon, or leave the dang thing here. It has brought us nothin' but trouble. We have buried six boys on the side of that hill. Randolph Taggert, you have buried two of my sons and four of my grandsons. I want you to put a stop to it. I say let's pack up and get. Now we even have the Indians down on us. How are you going to sell anymore of your brew to them?"

"It ain't my fault that Jake didn't cook it off right. If that no-count fellow hadn't whacked me on the head, I'd have been doin' my own cookin'. I ain't ever cooked a bad batch."

"Randolph, sometimes you've just got to know when to fold your cards and ride away. We were goin' west when we found this place. I say let's get in them wagons and get. I hear tell they have found gold out in Californy and those miners will want some whiskey. Why don't you go sell it to them? If that's what you want to do?"

"Woman, that's crazy talk. I ain't gonna let one man run me out of my home."

"Then I'm gonna go ahead and make you a gravestone because that man is gonna bury you up there on the side of the hill. Don't you understand? If you leave him alone, he'll leave you alone."

He slammed his fist down on the table. "I'm gonna kill 'im. Do you hear me, woman? I'm gonna kill him. Me and the boys have got a plan. You just stay out of the way."

CHAPTER THIRTY-NINE
Sam Tries to Trade for the Women

It was mid-afternoon and Sam had studied the Indian village. He'd searched for a way to slip in there and get the girls out. From here, the village looked so peaceful. Squaws washed clothes in the stream. He saw kids play on the open grounds in the center of the village. While he watched, a hunting party rode out to the south. He assumed they were a hunting party since they weren't wearing war paint.

Off to the south of the village he could see where they had all of the horses in a large rope corral. If he hadn't followed the tracks of the party that had kidnapped Mattie Ann and Rosa, he wouldn't have guessed that this was the group that took them. Everything looked so peaceful.

The wind picked up. It was strong out of the north, and the temperature dropped. Sam glanced back over his shoulder and said, "I think we're about to get a norther."

"Yeah, look at that lightning way off to the north," Joe said.

"That's all we need is for a blue norther to blow in."

"The Indians know it too. Look at all the firewood the squaws are dragging up."

Sam concentrated on the spyglass. He said, "Mr. Carville, I've got an idea. Why don't we round up a couple of steers? I'll drive them in there and see if I can trade for the girls back? I want to see if I can trade 'em for Mattie Ann and Rosa."

"It might work, Sam. You know how notional Indians are, and they know winter is coming on. Maybe you and I should both drive the beeves in."

"No, we don't want them to capture both of us. If they get me, you can still try to figure out a way to rescue all of us."

A COLLISION OF DREAMS

Joe Carville sent a couple of cowhands to round up two fat steers and drive them back. Time seemed to stand still until they showed back up with the steers. Sam watched the village through the spyglass. He saw squaws enter the tee-pee where Sam thought the women were held. They all assumed that the squaws brought food to Mattie Ann and Rosa.

Joe Carville said, "Sam, it drives me crazy because we didn't know how the women are being treated. As frail as Mattie Ann is, how is she holding up? Sam, let me go. Let me be the one to drive the steers in and try to make the trade."

"No sir. With all due respect, I recognize one of those braves down there—he's the one I fought with at the waterfall. Maybe he'll remember that I saved his life once, and that he owes me."

"Sam, you can't count on that. Indians don't think like we do."

"Sir, I know it is your daughter and your cook down there, but it is my future wife. It has to be me."

Joe Carville looked long and hard at Sam, then said, "I understand, Sam. Watch you step. It's going to be a tricky situation."

Sam rode out of the trees and drove the two fat steers in front of him. Several Indians started at him as he came out of the trees. Five young braves leaped onto their horses and raced to meet him. Their loud yells echoed through the canyon.

He kept his eyes straight ahead and continued to drive the steers toward the camp. Sam rode into the camp surrounded by the braves, who whooped and hollered. As they arrived at the center ground, a group of older chiefs stepped out to meet them.

Sam held up his hand in the sign of peace and said, "I come as a friend of the great Apache. I bring gifts to the great chief and the great Apache nation."

One of the young braves sneered, "Apache have no friend."

Sam ignored him. He chose to keep his eyes on an old white haired chief who appeared to be the man in charge. "I bring these two wo-haws as a gift to the great Chief Running Deer. I would talk with him."

A young brave said, "Maybe we'll just kill you and keep the wo-haws."

"It's not the Apache way. I know the Apache way. If a guest comes into the village on his own, he will not be harmed so long as he is in the village."

For the first time, the older white haired chief spoke. "I am Running Deer. You are brave coming to the Apache nation. Come into my lodge and we will hear what you have to say."

The chief's lodge was a large tee-pee. Sam sat down where the chief indicated that he should sit and the chief sat cross-legged on the ground across from him, surrounded by twelve braves. "Why do you bring wo-haws to the Apache?"

"It's going to be a hard winter. I would like to trade these two wo-haws for the two isdzans your braves captured and brought here."

As he said these words, he held his breath. They might decide to keep the cows and kill all three of them.

CHAPTER FORTY
The Fight

The marshal rode into the fort just before sundown. A young trooper on guard at the gate said, "Good evening marshal, what brings you back again?"

"Son, I need to see the general again on urgent business."

"Come with me, sir."

The general had just sat down to supper when the marshal walked in. "Well marshal, you're just in time for supper. Pull up a chair and sit."

"General, we've got more problems."

"How's that"?

"Somebody kidnapped Joe Carville's daughter and that Mexican cook of his."

"When'd this happen?"

"Sometime yesterday morning, I guess. The two women were in the buckboard. They were driving up to Sam McClanton's place. Joe's daughter wanted to look at the house Sam's building. You remember Sam and Joe's daughter is supposed to be married in the spring? I guess the girl wanted to see how Sam was comin' along with the house. They never got to Sam's place. I guess Sam and Joe have got everybody out lookin' for 'em."

"How did you hear about it?"

"One of Joe's hands came racin' into town on a lathered up horse."

The general thought for a minute. "There ain't much we can do before daylight. Do you suppose the Indians got 'em"?

"Well general, here's what I'm thinkin'."

* * *

A COLLISION OF DREAMS

Sam sat cross-legged and listened to the heated debate as it raged around him in the lodge—some of which he could understand. The younger braves were angry because a white man had sold some bad whiskey to them and killed members of their tribe. Now they wanted to kill white people, and they had three right there. Some of the older warriors argued against putting on the war paint. The young warriors were adamant that they wanted revenge.

Sam thought, *At least they didn't take my guns. I can take a few with me. Probably the best I can hope for.* He spoke up and said, "The great Chief Running Deer is a wise chief. Many fine young braves will die if they put on the war paint. There'll be much wailing in the lodges. Let me have the two isdzans and I'll ride with the chief to see the army. After we tell the general what has happened, the army will make the men prisoners who sold the bad firewater to the Apache. They will put them in the prison. They can never sell any more bad firewater to anybody."

Walks-With-Wolves shifted his weight. He was now balanced on the balls of his feet. He reached down and gripped the handle of his razor-sharp hunting knife. He was thinking, *In one leap I can spring across the lodge and gut the white eyes like gutting a deer.*

Another young brave leaped to his feet and spit into the dust. "They must not be allowed to live until they are old men in a white man's prison. Is Little Dove going to live to be an old squaw? Is Tall Bear going to live to be an old warrior?"

One of the older warriors spoke. "We must do as the white man says. The white eyes are too strong. There are too many white eyes and they have many guns."

"Ha—the white man is weak. This one," he pointed at Sam, "was too weak to kill Walks-With-Wolves when we fought behind the waterfall. Next time, I kill him. He's too weak to kill Walks-With-Wolves, but I kill him."

Sam stared at him and didn't blink. Then he spoke. "A great warrior does not confuse strength and weakness. I spared Walks-

With-Wolves not because I'm weak, but because my medicine is stronger than his."

Walks-With-Wolves leaped at Sam, who sprang to his feet with the speed of a mountain lion and struck Walks-With-Wolves with a right cross to the chin, knocking him into the wall of the tent. Infuriated, the Indian spun around and jerked out his hunting knife with the long sharp blade.

The chief's voice cracked through the air. "STOP! Walks-With-Wolves, you will not attack a guest in the council lodge. Put your knife away and sit down." Two very large Indian warriors leaped to their feet. They were bodyguards for the chief.

Walks-With-Wolves trembled with fury as he glared at the two bodyguards and then at Sam. "I'll kill this white eyes, and all the white eyes I see."

Sam looked to the chief and respectfully sat back down, then said, "Great chief—I'll fight Walks-With-Wolves. If I win, you allow me to ride out and take the wa-sie-un isdzan (white woman) and nakai-ye isdzan (Mexican woman) with me. You keep the two wo-haws. I'll go to the army and get them to go get the men who sold the bad firewater to the Apache. If Walks-With-Wolfs kills me, he can hang my scalp on his lodge pole."

The chief turned to the two stalwart bodyguards who stood between Sam and Walks-With-Wolves. "Take the white man out of the lodge while we discuss his offer."

* * *

While all this was going on, the general and the marshal talked into the night. They tried to think of a way to stop the outbreak without a lot of bloodshed. "General, what if I take a squad of your troops and my three deputies, go in there and arrest the Taggerts, then take them with us to the Indian village? If the Indians see we have them in custody, maybe we can convince the Indians to take off the war paint."

A COLLISION OF DREAMS

"Dang it man, we can't just arrest people without any proof. You said yourself old man Taggert ain't never sold any bad whiskey before."

"General, do your regulations allow you to take them into protective custody because of the impending Indian trouble?"

"Only if we go out and round up everybody in the area. If we tried that, you would hear a squawk all the way to Washington."

* * *

Sam could see the gleam in Walks-With-Wolves' eyes as the big guards escorted him from the lodge. He thought, *Mattie Ann and Rosa are right over there in that lodge. Could I possibly overpower these two, get them, and escape?* He took another look at those two stalwart braves. He knew that was a foolish notion.

Sam could hear much heated discussion inside the chief's lodge, but he couldn't understand the words. Finally, a brave pulled back the door flap and motioned them back into the lodge. The chief looked at Sam and said, "The council has voted and decided to take your challenge. You and Walks-With-Wolves will fight at first light. If you win, then you and the prisoners will be allowed to ride away. If you do not win, Walks-With-Wolves will hang your scalp from his lodge pole—and the scalp of the two isdzans. His wife Little Dove was one of the Apache who died from taking a drink of the poison firewater."

The chief pointed to the two guards standing beside him and said, "They'll take you to their lodge and you'll sleep there. They'll guard to see that you are not harmed before the fight."

Sam thought, That is rich. I may have my guts spilled all over the council ground at first light. They are going to guard me to make sure nothing can happen to me before then.

In the middle of the night, as Sam lay trying to sleep in the lodge with the two warriors, the stillness of the night was destroyed by the most blood-curdling scream Sam had ever heard. It was loud and sounded like a mixture between a cougar, a panther, and a woman's scream. Sam bolted straight up off his mat with his six-shooter in his hand. His first thought was, *What have they done to Mattie Ann?* At the same time, both warriors shot up with spears in their hands. All at once, the quiet was shattered with another terrifying scream from the other side of the camp. Sam breathed—at least it wasn't Mattie Ann. The first one cut loose again. Every horse in the Apache's rope corral bolted and started to run down the canyon. They could hear the horses' hooves as they raced away. Whatever had made the loud scream appeared to be chasing the horses. Now Indians appeared in front of their lodges. No one was sure if he wanted to come out.

The scream had moved way off down canyon. Even the village dogs were gone. One of the older warriors asked, "What was that?"

Sam remembered having seen Juan take a hollow of log and stretch a piece of rawhide across one end, like the head of a drum. Then he took a pigging string, coated it with pine rosin and feed it through a tiny hole in the center of the stretched rawhide. When he pulled the rosined pigging string through the rawhide, it made a sound like the sound they had just heard.

Sam spoke up and said, "It's the spirits—they don't approve of the Apache taking the isdzans prisoners. You've lost your horses tonight. The spirits will come back tomorrow night. If any harm happens to the wa-sie-un isdzan (white woman) and the Nakai-ye isdzan (Mexican woman), the spirits will return and tomorrow you will lose your squaws. You must let the isdzans go, even if I lose the fight with Walks-With-Wolves."

One terrified warrior said, "That thing will scare all of the game away."

"That is true. The Apache will have no game all winter and no squaws to keep the lodge warm. You must let the isdzans go."

Walks-With-Wolves hadn't said anything. All at once he pointed to the eastern sky and said, "It's first light—I'll kill the white eyes and the evil spirit will go away. He brought the evil spirit." He whipped out his knife. As he charged, he held his knife with the cutting edge up.

Sam tried to slap the point away from his body again like he had done the first time they'd fought. Walks-With-Wolves wouldn't fall for that again. This time he ripped up and cut a gash on the inside of Sam's left arm. Blood gushed from the wound.

Sam kicked the big brave on the kneecap with his boot heel. The Indian almost went down. With his right hand, Sam wrapped a bandana quickly around his left arm to slow the blood flow. The Indian came in bent low, with the gleaming razor-sharp knife in his left hand. Sam noticed the change and suspected what the Indian would do. The Indian tried to flip the knife to his right hand. At that same instant, Sam hit him square in the mouth with his left fist. The blow smashed his lips to a bloody pulp against his teeth.

The unexpected blow caused Walks-With-Wolves to miss the knife with his right hand. Walks-With-Wolves snarled in fury and charged, catching Sam in a giant bear hug and bending him over backwards. His intent was to break Sam's spine. Sam slugged the Indian on each side of the head. His knuckles pounded the Indian's ears bloody. The power was going out of his punches, the pain in his back was so severe. Sam knew he had to do something. The powerful arms of this big man were going to break his back.

Sam threw up both feet and fell over backwards. The move caught Walks-With-Wolves leaning foreword off balance. He was so intent on his attempt to snap Sam's spine and had not expected this move. They both hit the ground. Walks-With Wolves lost his grip when his forehead slammed into the hard-packed ground. Sam flipped over and was on his feet first. Quick as a cougar, Walks-With-Wolves flipped over and came up with his knife in his hands again.

Sam knew he didn't want to face that knife. He had wrestled a lot in the boy's home and remembered some of the moves. Surprised he still had power in his legs, Sam jumped into the air and drop-kicked both boots heels into Walks-With-Wolves' chest. The kick knocked the big brave over backwards. Before the big Indian could get back to his feet, Sam grabbed the arm that held the knife and slammed it over his knee. Walks-With-Wolves lost his grip on the knife.

The Indian gasped for breath because Sam's dropkick had knocked the wind out of him. While the big Indian tried to get his breath back, Sam grabbed him and threw him to the ground. He scooped up the knife and pressed it to Walks-With-Wolves' throat.

The knife was razor-sharp and blood started to ooze from the skin where the knife was held. All Sam had to do was flinch and he would kill Walks-With-Wolves. Face-to-face, Sam could see the hatred in the Indian's eyes. He held the knife on the brave's throat for several seconds then jumped back and walked to the chief and presented the knife to him.

"Great chief, please accept this knife as a gift to the Apache chief. Walks-With-Wolves fought bravely and well. He's too good to die today. Our deal was, if I win the fight, you'll allow me and the isdzans to ride away. How the fight ends is my choice. I don't choose to kill Walks-With-Wolves."

Sam turned and started to walk out of the lodge. All he wanted to do was go to the lodge where the women were being held. Get them and go. There was a furious yell behind him. Sam spun around and found Walks-With-Wolves with a spear in his hands. The Indian charged.

Walks-With-Wolves' steps faltered. His legs buckled and he fell with his face to the ground. Then Sam saw that Chief Running Deer had thrown the knife Sam had just given him. It was imbedded all the way to the hilt in the center of Walks-With-Wolves' back.

"White eyes, your medicine is too strong. I could not let Walks-With-Wolves bring shame to the Apache. You won the fight. Take the isdzans with you and take the curse away so the horses and the game can return."

"The Apache nation is my friend. The chief is welcome at the lodge of the stone any time."

Chief Running Deer said, "Ka-dish-day."

"Farewell to you too, my friend." Sam walked over to the lodge where the women were kept.

* * *

Ma Taggert said, "Pa, you and the boys are spending all your time huntin' for this fella and you are not huntin' any meat to put up for winter. How are we goin' to feed all these kids all winter if you don't kill a deer or two and get a couple of hogs butchered?"

"Stop that worrying. I'm gonna take care of ya."

"How? I don't see any supplies laid up for winter. It will be here before you know it."

Slamming his hand down on the table, Randolph said, "Nag, nag—that's all you do anymore." With that, he stomped out the door and slammed it behind him.

CHAPTER FORTY-ONE
Coming Home

The pastor said, "Sally Jo, thank you for joining the choir. You sing beautifully."

"I enjoy it. The other choir members take it so seriously, yet they have welcomed me in."

"Well, we'll see you at choir practice Tuesday evening."

As she stepped out of the church, a tall, handsome young man stepped up. "Miss Sally Jo, can I walk you home?"

"Thank you Dennis, that is nice of you." She slipped her hand into the bend of his elbow.

"Sally Jo, can I tell you something?"

"Sure."

"I think you are the prettiest girl in these parts."

"Thank you Dennis, that is so sweet of you. How is it a handsome man like you don't already have a girl?"

"I don't know who to ask if I can come courting you, Sally Jo. Your pa being dead and all."

She thought about it a moment and said, "I guess you would need to ask my aunt. But Dennis, I am just not ready to start courting right now."

"Oh, do you already have a beau back home?"

"No. I need time to settle in, I guess." *What I need is to find a way to meet that cowboy from the train again. I have no idea how to find him.*

They stopped in front of the gate at her aunt's house. "Dennis, thank you for taking time to walk me home. I guess I'll see you Tuesday evening at choir practice."

"Yes you sure will." Tipping his hat, he turned and walked away.

"Well, Sally Jo, did I see a handsome young man walked you home?"

"Yes."

A COLLISION OF DREAMS

* * *

Sam pulled back the flap on the tee-pee and stepped inside. His eyes swept the room. Both women sat on a bearskin on the floor. Mattie Ann didn't look good. She looked pale and scared. Sam reached down and lifted her off the mat.

Mattie Ann's tears wet his bare shoulder. "Oh Sam, I was terrified. We could hear the fight. I was so afraid you'd get killed."

Cuddling her close to him, Sam chuckled and said, "You were afraid that pretty blond hair of yours would be hanging on the top of a lodge pole." He tilted her head back and kissed her. "And so was I." Sam turned to Rosa. He said, "Are you okay?"

"Si, Mister Sam, Rosa is okay."

Mattie Ann looked down, saw the gash on his arm, and said, "Oh Sam, you're hurt."

"We'll deal with that when we get back to the Tumbling C. Right now, we've got to get out of here. There is a blue norther on the way here and we want to be home before it hits."

Sam carried Mattie Ann out and set her gently on his horse. Taking the reins in his left hand, he turned and said, "Chief Running Deer is a great chief of the Apache nation. He will always be welcome at my fire."

When Mattie Ann saw her father, she slid from the horse and threw herself into his arms.

As soon as they were back in the buckboard, Mattie Ann said, "Sam, I still want to go see the house."

Later, when Mattie Ann and all of the others from the Tumbling C rode away, Sam turned to Juan. "We've got a heap of work to do before spring. Did you see the list that Mattie Ann left for me? Tomorrow morning, we'd better get busy and build those lean-tos for the horses. My joints tell me the weather is really fixing to move in on us."

CHAPTER FORTY-TWO
Taggert's Arrest

The marshal and three of his deputies, followed by twelve soldiers from the fort, were ready to mount up and head for the canyon where the Taggerts lived. The marshal said, "Men, we're going to arrest every Taggert male over eighteen years old. I hope when they see the size of this group they'll give up without a fight. However, ride with your eyes open. I don't want to lose a single man on this raid."

They rode into the yard just as the sun crested the ridge in the east. The troops caught one of the Taggerts milking a cow. Another one was forking hay to the horses. A deputy pointed his six-gun at the one milking the cow and said, "Stand up real slow and keep your hands where I can see 'em."

The man who was forking the hay looked up and saw the bunch ride up. He dropped his hayfork and ran. One of the deputies whipped his lariat off the saddle horn and dropped a loop over his head before he got past the end of the corral.

The marshal mounted the back steps and stepped into the kitchen as the old man sat down to breakfast. "Taggert, keep your hands on top of the table."

"What's this all about? You can't come bustin' in here, this is private property."

The marshal removed his hat with his left hand and said to the older lady who stood by the stove, "My apologies, ma'am, for bargin' in." Turning his attention back to the old man, he said, "Taggert, you're under arrest. I'm gonna take you and your boys in."

"What for?"

"To start with, I'm haulin' you in for sellin' whiskey to the Indians. It may turn into a charge of murder for sellin' bad whiskey and killin' a few Indians. Now stand up real slow and keep your hands where I can see 'em. This old forty-four of mine has a real touchy trigger."

* * *

Sam was riding back from testifying in court against the Taggert gang. When he left the county seat the morning before, the sky was clear. This morning he noticed a red hue in the western sky and thought about the old saying, "Red sky in the morning, sailors take warning." He thought, *Ranchers need to take warning*. He then mounted up and headed on home. He was halfway home when the wind picked up. The temperature dropped about twenty degrees. He reached back into his saddlebag, dug out his coat, and pulled it on. "Well Buck, it looks like we better get along. We don't want to get caught out in this."

A west Texas blizzard roared down on him. Large snowflakes filled the air. Sam turned his collar up and hunkered down in his buffalo-hide coat. He lost the ability to see landmarks. His only option was to trust the horse to find its way home.

* * *

Juan loved working for Senõr Sam McClanton, but today he was worried. He wished the boss would hurry up and get home. He did not like the looks of the weather. Driving the team, he hauled the last 500 pounds of hay up to the corral as a violent north wind assaulted him. He left the hay on the wagon, quickly unhitched the horses, turned them into the corral, and fought his way through the storm toward the house. The strong wind pushed against his back, shoving him forward and causing him to stumble as he stepped up onto the porch.

From a kneeling and almost prone position, he reached out and grabbed the door latch to try to pull himself up as the blistering wind tore the door from his hand, sending the door swinging savagely on its hinges to slam against the wall inside.

Once inside, Juan struggled with all his might to push the door closed, inch by inch, until he heard the latch click. He fell to the floor

GEORGE DALTON

gasping for breath. Juan stayed there motionless for a few moments to rest as his mind once again turned toward Sam, his boss and best friend, out there somewhere in this storm. Juan thought this must be the worst and most frightening of the storms he had seen in his lifetime.

Grabbing two handfuls of wood chips, he threw them onto the coals in the fireplace. Kneeling on one knee, he blew on the hot coals, and soon blazes licked up around the chips and a small bright flame emerged. When the chips caught fire, he began to add larger sticks, and within minutes a warm fire danced in the big kitchen fireplace. The vapor trapped in the wood started to hiss and pop, causing small embers to fly out of the fire and scatter like little diamonds on the stone floor.

Juan held out his hands toward the fire and rubbed them together to spread the warmth. He looked into the blaze and inhaled the familiar and comforting scent of burning wood. He thought, *A warm fire feels good, especially during a cold and bitter storm.* The only sound he could hear was the high-pitched scream the wind made as it blasted around the eves of the house. His thoughts turned to Sam. *Where can Senōr Sam be? What can Juan do to help him?*

"When Senōr Sam gets back he'll want hot coffee and tortillas. I know what I can do. I can knead some dough and roll out a batch of tortillas." As his strong hands shaped the tortillas, he kept thinking, *Senōr Sam, he is best boss Juan's ever had. Senōr Sam had to go to the county seat to testify in the rustler's trial. I hope he is still in town and not out in this storm.*

Something banged against the side of the house. *What was that?* He thought, *I guess the wind blew something against the house. I wish Senōr Sam were here.* Juan turned the tortillas and stirred the beans bubbling in the pot. His thoughts immediately went back to Sam. If Senōr Sam was on his way home when the storm hit, how can he survive in this?

Something banged against the side of the house again. He hurried to the door and tried to peek out. As soon as he released the latch, the wind slammed the door back into his face. He was temporarily blinded as he tried to wipe away the snow and ice that now coated his eyelashes and eyebrows. Seeing nothing and feeling pain from the harshness of the snow and ice and the bitter cold wind, he abandoned his quest to see what had caused the noise outside and again struggled with all his strength to push the door closed.

As the door inched forward, he heard the welcome sound of the latch catching. He let out a sigh of relief and rested his shoulder against the door briefly. As he turned around, he looked at the big clock on the mantel that showed seven o'clock. It ticked its slow monotonous tick-tock, tick-tock.

Juan walked to the fireplace, reached into the wood box, and added more wood. He felt warmth on his hands as he held them out to the fire, and rubbed his face, still cold from the icy wet snow and ice pellets that had been blasted onto his skin by the storm. Juan realized that this storm was not going to end soon.

A thought came to him: *This room will be warm, but the rest of the house is going to be ice cold. I'll move our bedrolls in here where it's warm.*

Juan took his heavy coat from the wall hanger, buttoned it up, turned up his collar around his neck and face, and released the latch as he struggled to hold the door in place as he stepped out and pulled it shut. The wind seemed to have gotten stronger and the temperature much colder as he hunched his shoulders and stumbled across the breezeway into the other side of the house. The cold bit into his arms and legs as he tried to hurry across the open space.

His legs moved like both were in molasses. He thought, *My legs already feel like they are frozen—no one could survive in this for long.* Snatching up both of the bedrolls and wrapping them around him for additional warmth and protection, he waddled back to the door to the breezeway and prepared himself to face the bitter cold again.

With his hand on the door latch, he paused before opening it, fearing the storm blast he knew was going to hit him as soon as he stepped back outside. *At least we can sleep here in the kitchen where it is warm. I am glad we have a large stack of firewood in the breezeway out of the snow.*

He stirred the big, black iron pot, watched the steam rise and the beans bubbling as the aroma of beans and ham hock filled the room. Like a soldier on guard, he paced the length of the room and stared at the big clock. It read 7:30. He went back and stirred the beans. All he heard was the sound of the wind howling around the house and the constant tick-tock of the big clock on the mantel. *What was the thing that bumped into the house? Where can Senōr Sam be? Could it have been him trying to get in?*

He checked the tortillas, moved them into a Dutch oven, and looked at the clock. It read 8:00.

The fire hissed and sputtered when a piece of ice fell down the chimney. Juan thought, *Should I go out and search for Senōr Sam? What if he is hurt out there?*

Juan thought he heard a new sound. He ran over and jerked the door open. A blast of cold ice-laden air almost took his breath away when it hit him in the face. *I can't see anything when I open the door. How can I find him if I go out and search?* It again took all his strength to force the door shut. Tick-tock, tick-tock. The clock now read 8:30.

Juan was not a praying man, but he found a rosary, hung it over the fireplace, and said, "Holy Mother, what can Juan do? Please send an angel to help my boss, Senōr Sam."

Exhaustion finally drove Juan to sit down in one of the kitchen chairs. He dozed off to sleep.

* * *

Sam couldn't feel his feet anymore. It was as if they were gone. His entire body felt beaten by the fierce wind and ice pellets hammering into him. Fear crept up in him. He felt disoriented.

If he could just find shelter and get out of the wind, he could build a fire. Ice pellets were under his eyelids. He was completely blind. There was no way to see anything. At least the horse was still walking—all Sam could do was hang on and hope the mustang could find shelter.

The horse stumbled and went down on his knees. But a wild mustang is a magnificent and resourceful animal, and it scrambled back to its feet. The horse stood trembling. Slowly, Sam felt the horse start to walk again. The sound was dreadful—the wind howled and screamed around his head. The bitter cold, the unbearable sound, and the slashing, blowing snow gave Sam vertigo, so he wasn't sure if the horse was moving or not.

Poor Mattie Ann—who is going to take care of her now? Then he said, "God, if you can hear me, please take care of Mattie Ann. She is so precious."

CHAPTER FORTY-THREE
Mattie's Worry

Mattie Ann sat wrapped in a soft warm throw by the fireplace in her daddy's big house. She listened to the howl of the wind as it beat against the windows and said, "Oh, I hope Sam and Juan are in the house where its warm. They sure don't need to be caught out in this blizzard."

She shivered under the throw. "I feel so cold even though the fire is going. It must be from listening to that wind. It sounds like someone crying." Mattie Ann glanced over at her daddy and said, "Do you think Sam is all right? What if he got caught out in this blizzard?"

"Honey, that stone house should be easy to keep warm. I'm sure they scooted inside and got a good fire going when they saw this thing coming. They'll be safe and warm. I just hope we don't lose any stock. A blizzard like this can kill anything caught out in it."

Tugging the cover closer around her, she said, "Daddy, I am scared. This is a bad storm. It must be ten below out there."

"It probably is, but I am sure Sam and Juan are sitting around the fire eating some of Juan's chili."

"Oh Daddy, I hope you're right, but I am so terrified. I just can't shake it."

"Do you want me to pray for them?"

"Yes, let's do that."

Joe got up and knelt down on one knee beside her chair. "Dear Lord, we come to you tonight because we are afraid. We ask that you watch over Sam and Juan tonight. Make sure they're warm and sheltered from this awful storm. If one of them is out in the blizzard, take his hand and lead him to safety. Please Lord, calm Mattie Ann's fears and bring her peace. Amen."

"Thanks Daddy. I know in my heart God will look out for my Sam. I just wish this storm would hurry up and pass. I want to see him ride over here. Then, I can see for myself that he's okay. I don't think I could survive if something happened to him. I can't lose him now. It is only a few more weeks until we get married."

* * *

The door blew open with a crash. A blast of ice-cold wind filled the room. Coated in a layer of snow and ice, Sam stumbled and fell into the room.

Juan awoke with a jerk. "Senõr Sam—Juan was starting to get a leettle worried. Sit down, I have the coffee hot. It will get some warmth back in you. You need some hot frijoles and tortillas. I bring the bedrolls into the kitchen, much warmer in here. Where have you been? Sit here by the fire. I get the coffee and hot beans. Wrap up in the blanket. Senõr Sam, how did the trial go? Did the judge send the outlaws to prison?"

With teeth chattering, Sam had a difficult time answering Juan's questions. "Yeah, I told—told—the—the judge how I caught—one of them re-branding a steer. The sheriff told—how he found some more steers—with altered—brands at their place. The judge gave them—ten—years."

"That is good, senõr. They are a mean bunch."

Sam's jaw felt raw and cold when he rubbed with his hand over the stubble of a beard. Still wrapped in a blanket near the fireplace, he sipped the scalding hot coffee and glanced up at the clock. It read 10:00. Now his teeth had stopped chattering.

He looked up at Juan and said, "You're going to think I'm crazy. Maybe the cold causes people to see strange things. I was totally lost. The snow was blowing so hard I became disoriented. I couldn't find shelter to get out of the storm. I didn't know what direction to go to get home. My horse was cold and tired, and he started to falter. Snow and ice got into my eyes. I was blind. The sound of wind was so loud, I couldn't see or hear anything except the storm.

"Juan, all at once, a man dressed in white riding a white horse appeared right in front of me. Even though he was dressed in white and the horse was white, I could see them plain as day though the blowing snow. He motioned for me to follow him. I did and he led me straight home. Then he just disappeared into the snow."

Sam watched Juan walk over and kiss a rosary hanging over the fireplace, and say, "Thank you Holy Mother, for sending an angel to guide Senōr Sam home."

Sam sat there sipping the hot coffee for several more minutes and finally said, "I'm not sure I believe in any angels. Nevertheless, I sure can't explain what I saw."

* * *

Sarah said, "Ma, we are out of food for the kids. Little John went out and killed a few rabbits to keep us going but with this blizzard he can't kill anything." Ma Taggert looked at the hungry kids and wanted to sit down and cry. She said, "Sarah, I don't know how we are goin' to survive this terrible winter with all the men folks off in prison. I sure do wish we'd stayed back in Kentucky. It all goes back to Billie Wayne tryin' to get fresh with the Carville gal and then tryin' to shoot that stranger. Billie Wayne was always the wildest one of the bunch. I don't know how we are goin' to make it, but I've been saying my prayers every night. God will provide some way."

"Ma, I sure wish he would come on—my kids are gettin' mighty cranky when they're hungry."

CHAPTER FORTY-FOUR
Rescuing the Women and Kids

When Sam and Juan woke the next morning, the blizzard still raged. Juan built up the fire, fried some ham, and warmed up the beans for breakfast.

The warmth of the tin cup full of hot coffee felt good as Sam wrapped his hands around it. He stared at the fire for several minutes before saying, "Juan, I've been thinking about the outlaw gang. They left a bunch of women and a passel of little kids up in the canyon. With the men all gone to prison, they're gonna starve up there. Soon as it gets good and light, I'm gonna go out and butcher a steer, and take the meat to those women."

"Senõr Sam, theeez idea, she is not good. Theeze people in that gang tried to shoot you many times. They even shot at Juan. No, theeez is not good idea."

"I know, Juan, it's a stupid idea—but I can't let women and kids starve. I'm going."

"Senõr Sam, if we must do it, let's use the sled—it will go better in the snow."

"Juan, you don't haveta go with me. I can't ask you to go out into this storm."

"Senõr Sam, if you go, the only way you can leave Juan here by he's self again is if you shoot heem. No, senõr. Juan, he will go—but he will go quickly."

Sam and Juan found all of the cattle bunched up in a canyon, against the north wall out of the wind. Sam took out his rifle, shot a steer, and field-dressed it in the snow. After they got the meat loaded onto the sled, Sam said, "Juan, I can do this without you—you don't have to go with me. You can go back and keep the fires going at the ranch until I get back."

"Senõr Sam, theez women and kids need theez meat, si?"

"Yes, I'm afraid they do."

"Do you even know how to get there, Senõr Sam?"

"I know where I took the rustler's body after I had a shootout with him and killed him. I'm sure he left a family behind—a wife and maybe some kids. I had no choice—it was either him or me. We'll ride our horses and lead the team pulling the sled."

After they had gone a short distance, Juan said, "Senõr Sam, in places the snow is deep and makes going hard. Juan is hunkered down in his buffalo skin coat with the collar turned up and his hat pulled down low. He is still freezing."

"Juan, you should have stayed back. This storm is vicious. Some of these drifts are as much as six feet deep in places. There must be twenty women and kids out there with no food. We've got to push on. Juan, we need to get off and walk to keep circulation in our feet to avoid frostbite."

A little later, Juan yelled to be heard above the storm. "We have a big problem. We don't know what is underneath the snow."

"I know. While I was walking a while ago, we must have crossed a frozen stream. I slipped on the ice. My feet shot out from under me and twisted my knee. Now it hurts real bad. I guess I'm gonna have ta get back on and ride."

"Senõr, do you know where we are?"

"Not for sure. I'm having a hard time finding landmarks. The snow covers everything and makes them look different. It'll be getting dark pretty soon and the temperature will fall even more. We need to find shelter. I'm also having trouble breathing—the bandana covering my nose and mouth is coated in ice."

"Senõr Sam, if you make it and Juan does not, will you see that I get a good grave marker?"

Sam strained to be heard over the storm. "Juan, I'll give us one more hour, and if we don't find their cabin, we'll find a sheltered place to make camp and build a big fire."

"Senōr, Juan is tired. We have fought through the snowdrifts all the way. In the last hour, we have covered only maybe two miles. Juan is thinking we are not going to make it."

"Hang on, Juan, let's get to over the top of that ridge and we'll see if we can find shelter on the downwind side. We've got to make it. If we die, those women and little kids will die a horrible slow death by starving."

As they topped the ridge, they stared into the storm and could see nothing. Their hands and feet were painfully cold and they were really beginning to feel despair and hopelessness. They had come this far and failed. Sam took another look, this time by slowly turning his head from side to side.

Sam squeezed his eyelids down to slits and tried again to see something through the storm. *Was it my imagination, or did I see a light?* He pointed and said, "Juan, I see a light. I think it's the cabin."

As they neared the light, Juan said, "Be careful, senōr—those women can shoot same as a man. They may not think you are coming to help 'em. It will be bad to get killed thirty feet from their door."

Juan and Sam staggered and slid down the hill. Sam called out, "Hello, you in the house." As quick as a lightning flash, the lamp was blown out. "Miz Taggert, we've brought two sides of beef for the young'ens."

The door opened a crack and light from their fireplace silhouetted the barrel of a shotgun poking out. "Who are you? We don't know you."

"No ma'am, you don't know me. My name is Sam McClanton. I heard that you folks needed some meat, and I ain't gonna let no women and kids starve. I own a ranch up north of here. We slaughtered a steer and brought it to you." He stepped close to the door and held up a large chunk of beef wrapped in feed sackcloth.

The gun barrel lowered. The door opened. An older woman stood there. The wind whipped snow around her. "You came through the storm to bring us this?"

A COLLISION OF DREAMS

Yelling so he could be heard above the wind, Sam said, "Yes ma'am. You take this and feed the kids. We'll hang the rest in your barn. Meat won't spoil in this weather. We'd like to sleep in the barn tonight, and come daylight we'll be gone. If that's all right?"

She squinted her eyes and stared at them. Her lips quivered like she didn't know what to say. Her hand shot out and took the chunk of beef.

Sam turned around and walked back to the buckskin, then caught the reins and led the horse into the barn. He said, "Juan, rub down the horses with dry straw. We'll put them in the stalls and feed them."

The two frozen, exhausted men got a fire started in the center of the dirt floor and soon the aroma of hot coffee filled the air. As they gulped down the thick, strong black coffee, Sam's gaze took in the surroundings and he said, "Juan, this heat will rise, so let's climb up and bed down in the hayloft."

Wrapped in a blanket and snuggled down in the sweet-smelling hay, warmth slowly seeped back into their bodies. Juan said, "Senõr Sam, can you smell that? The women are cooking the beef now."

"That means those kids were hungry."

"Senõr Sam, you are good man."

Before Sam could reply, he heard the rhythmic sound of Juan's snoring. It seemed only a short time later when he thought, *What is that noise? It's a roster crowing.* He lay there listening for a moment as he thought, *The storm must have already passed. It's still and quiet.* The only sounds he could hear was a horse stomp every now and then the sound of a rooster crowing. *Is there any fire left?* He thought, *I'll peek over the edge of the loft and see if the fire we started last night has any coals left. Oh man, all I see is grey ash. I wish Juan would wake up. He appears to be sound asleep. The last thing I want to do is crawl out of this warm blanket.*

After a few minutes, Sam reached out and shoved his feet down into his icy cold boots. Sam grabbed his blanket, wrapped it around his shoulders, and raced down the ladder. With the glove on his right hand, he brushed the ash back, revealing glowing red coals. Sam gathered some straw, spread it on the red coals, and started to blow on the coals until a small flame licked up and started to burn the straw. Sam added small twigs, and when they caught fire, he added some larger logs. He wrapped the blanket tighter around him and sat down by the fire. Sam's gaze eventually traveled upward until he looked right into a pair of black Mexican eyes and heard the sound of Juan laughing hysterically.

"Senõr Sam, I thought you were never going to wake up."

"You sorry Mexican bandit. I ought to leave you right here with all those women and a passel of kids—that would serve you right."

About that time, the hinges creaked as the barn door swung open. A small boy of about eleven or twelve stood in the doorway. "My grandma is makin' hot cakes and wants you to come eat breakfast."

They followed the boy into the house, and as they stepped in through the back door, Sam noticed how warm the room was. It seemed like an eternity since he'd been really warm.

As Juan and Sam glanced around the room, they saw several women of all ages and a bunch of kids. It seemed that all the women were thanking them and telling them what a great thing they had done. Sam did notice one boy, who was about sixteen, glaring at Juan and him in a mighty unfriendly way.

The older woman said, "It's a good thing what you and your friend are done, being out in that storm. You're now here with us where you can enjoy the food you brought us and enjoy being warm. Please sit down and enjoy some hot cakes with us."

"Thank you, ma'am. We hung the rest of the beef up in the barn so varmints can't get at it. It was a large steer so it should last you a while."

When they sat down, the older woman bowed her head and prayed for the food and the safety of their menfolk who were gone from them.

After they had eaten, Sam said, "Thank you, ma'am, for the breakfast. Now ma'am, even though me and your menfolk had some trouble, if you and the young'ens need anything, send someone to my place and we'll help if we can."

CHAPTER FORTY-FIVE
Naming the Ranch

Even though the temperature was still well below freezing, the sun was out and no wind blew, so it was almost pleasant as they rode back to the ranch.

"Juan, we need to come up with a name for the ranch. You know, like the Tumbling C."

"Si senõr, you could call it Juan's Love Song Ranch."

Sam laughed and said, "I don't think so. I might have all the lovesick senoritas for miles around."

"Senõr Sam, that would be good. Then Juan would get more work done; he wouldn't have to ride so far to sing his love songs."

Still laughing, Sam said, "I'm going to get you married off so I can stop hearin' about those blasted love songs."

"No senõr, just think how sad all of the other senoritas would be if Juan married just one. No, that is a bad idea, senõr."

Finally, Sam said, "I'm going to call it The Wild Horse Ranch after all everything has happened because of those Mustangs we trapped. Even to our small herd of cows. I'm going to register the 'W-H' brand."

The blizzard came back that night and Sam worried. *What if something happens to Mattie Ann while we're stuck out here?* As each new day dawned, his uneasiness multiplied. The storm lasted three more days, in which time there was little they could do. Each day they would bundle up and go out to check on the horses. They seemed to be doing fine huddled under the lean-tos.

Sam looked at the weather and debated whether he should strike out for the Tumbling C or not.

He and Juan took axes and chopped holes in the ice so the animals could drink. On the third day he said, "Juan, I'm sure glad you've got that smokehouse full of wild hog meat. I really like that chili you made out of pork and deer meat, mixed with wild onions and peppers. We're okay, but I'm real worried about Mattie Ann. I can't wait to get over there and check on her."

"Si, when it is cold outside Juan's chili makes you warm inside. Maybe soon you can ride over to the Tumbling C."

The days passed monotonously slow. They broke ice so the stock could get water, forked hay to the horses, and gathered more firewood. On the fourth day, the sun came out and the wind stopped blowing. It didn't feel so cold. Sam stood and stared out the door.

He said, "Juan, today I'm goin' to the Tumbling C." As he rode along, the sunlight reflected off the clean, new snow. The world was a beautiful place. Sam was so filled with love and joy he started to sing an old song called "A Great Speckled Bird" he remembered from the chapel service at the boy's home.

He and Mattie Ann sat for the next few hours in the living room. She talked about the plans for their wedding. Sam felt a glow inside. His world was complete. She looked so happy and healthy. It was easy to forget what the doctor had told them.

"Sam, this is March. Next month is April. In one more month we'll be married. Isn't it wonderful?"

All at once, a cold chill swept over Sam, and he shivered. He thought, *There is an old saying that when you feel that, someone just stepped on your grave.*

"Oh Sam, it is going to be so grand. We'll have the biggest wedding this county has ever seen."

"We'll definitely have the prettiest bride this country has ever seen."

CHAPTER FORTY-SIX
Encounter with a Rattlesnake

Sam had checked on the cows, and as he rode back to the ranch, he daydreamed about the upcoming wedding and was not fully alert. All at once, Buck gave a sudden bolt and reared up. The move was unexpected and Sam was thrown from the saddle.

When he hit the ground, the bone in his left thigh snapped. Buck, like all western-trained horses, ran only a short way, stopped, and came back. Sam lay on the ground, the pain in his leg almost unbearable.

First, he looked to his horse. Something was wrong with his front leg. Buck limped badly and his right front leg was already starting to swell. Then Sam saw the rattlesnake. He whipped out his six-shooter and killed the snake.

Buck went down and started to thrash around. The venom was obviously getting into Buck's heart because he went down on the ground and started to thrash around. He was in terrible pain. Sam already held his .44 in his hand, "So long, Buck. I'm sorry old pal. I won't let you suffer like that."

With tears in his eyes, he shot the horse between the eyes.

He then told himself, "Sam old boy, you're in serious trouble—you have a broken leg, and your horse is dead. You are miles form the ranch house and you will probably go into shock." He looked around for anything that might help. "That willow over there might help keep the pain down and prevent me from going into shock." He dragged himself over to the dead horse and stripped off the saddlebags. Then he dragged himself to the tree, took out his knife, and peel off some bark.

"Now Sam old boy, if you can gather together some small sticks and get a fire going, you can pour water from this canteen in the coffee pot and brew up some willow bark tea. That's if you don't pass out first." As the water started to boil, he added chunks of the willow bark. He then poured in the salt. Soon had a brew that he hoped would help deaden the pain and ward off shock. He told himself, "You know what? That doesn't taste too bad. I wish old Juan was here. I'd give him some of it."

That leg throbbed something awful. "What you better do is get a splint on that leg; the last thing you want is for that bone to break through the skin." He took out his bowie knife and was able to chop some of the lower limbs off the tree. The exertion almost took his breath away. "Sit still a minute and, when the pain settles down, take a pigging string and tie some splints on each side of your thigh — that'll hold the bone in place."

By now his breath came in gasps, the pain was so severe. He leaned back against the tree trunk and sipped his brew. Covered with his slicker, he soon slept. In his sleep, he dreamed of Mattie Ann and the church filled with people all dressed up in their finest. In his dream, he stood by the preacher when Mattie Ann came in wearing a beautiful white gown that flowed behind her. It was made from miles and miles of white lace and silk ribbons. She looked like an angel.

All at once, his eyes popped open. The pain woke him, and at first he was still half-asleep and confused. He looked around. It was dark and he was in pain.

"Oh, that's right. Buck got bit by a rattlesnake, and my leg is busted." Now wide-awake, he said, "My fire has died down—I better do somethin' about that." He used a long stick to drag other dead limbs lying on the ground up to the fire. Soon he had the fire blazing up again. He could feel his fever rising, and the pain was agonizing.

Sam sloshed his canteen and said, "Sam old boy, you have just enough water left to make one more willow bark brew, and that's all." He poured the rest of the water into the coffee pot. He scraped off some more bark, added the rest of his salt, and put it back on the fire.

Sam looked over at Buck and said, "Buck old buddy, I sure am sorry I had to shoot you, because if you had run home with an empty saddle, somebody would've back-tracked ya and found me."

He thought, *Now I'm really in trouble. I just poured in the last of my water. When this is gone, I have no more and no way to get anymore. A man might survive a few days without food, but he won't last long without any water. That leg is in no condition to go anywhere.*

Another thought came to him: Poor Mattie Ann. She was so set on this wedding and fixing up that house. If I hadn't had to shoot Buck, he might have gone home and we might have had a chance. No, the venom was killing him—I had no choice. It for sure looks like this is the end of the trail. Mattie Ann, I'm sorry.

* * *

Juan stepped out of the house when the buckboard pulled into the yard. Mr. Carville spoke first: "Hello Juan, is Sam around?"

"No senõr, he went to look at the cows this morning. I have not seen him since he left."

Mr. Carville helped Mattie Ann down from the buckboard and said, "Mattie Ann brought some things for the house. While she putters around, do you have any coffee on?"

"Si, senõr, come into the kitchen. Miss Mattie Ann, can Juan help you?"

"No Juan, you and Daddy go drink your coffee."

Mattie Ann puttered around while the men drank coffee and talked about the ranch. The sun slowly moved across the sky and dipped down in the west.

Mattie Ann came in and said, "Do you think something is wrong? Shouldn't Sam be back by now?"

"Si, I was thinkin' the same thing. His horse has not come back with an empty saddle. That is a good thing."

"Daddy, shouldn't we go out and look for him?"

"Honey, I wouldn't know where to start. Juan, do you know where he was going?"

"No senōr, he told me to train some of the new horses. He was goin' to go check on the cows, now that they are scattered all back in the hills and canyons."

* * *

When Sam woke up, the sun was setting. It was evening time. The first thing he saw was a bunch of buzzards circled over the downed horse. "That might not be a good thing. If anybody is hunting me, they might see those buzzards." One of the big buzzards with a wingspan of six feet landed near old Buck. Sam picked up a rock and threw it at the buzzard. "Get out-ah here. I don't want you flying around up there, but I ain't gonna sit here and watch you eat my horse. Now get."

The buzzard hopped about three feet and started back to the downed horse. Sam picked up his rifle and shot the head right off that buzzard.

He shook his canteen. It was empty. Between the shock and the salt, he had drunk to keep the shock down he was very thirsty. He knew that if he couldn't find a way to get water pretty soon, he was going to be in real trouble. He reminded himself, *A man can go days without food, but not water.*

He had another problem—the pain was getting worse and he couldn't make anymore of the broth. Maybe he could scrape off the inner side of the willow bark and chew the pulp. It might help keep down the fever and dull the pain.

He slept fitfully. All at once, he was wide-awake. Judging by the moon, it was past midnight. At first, he couldn't figure out what had woken him. He couldn't see anything, and his ears strained for any sound.

Then he heard it: timber wolves. The first thing he did was throw some more wood onto the fire. As the fire blazed up, he could see their glassy eyes in the dark.

He grabbed up his rifle and shot two of the wolves. The rest of the wolves snapped and snarled and tore into the carcasses of the two he had just shot. Sam was terrified. All he could do was lay there on the ground and listen to those beasts snap and tear at the flesh of the two wolves they were eating. It was the most horrible sound he had ever listened to.

Without any warning, the night sky split with lightning and the rain came pouring down. Sam huddled under his slicker beneath the tree. Between the pain in his leg, the rain, and the fear of the wolves, Sam didn't sleep anymore. Finally, at light the rain let up. He realized that the wolves had eaten most of the two wolves he had shot and slunk away.

Sam chewed some more pulp from the bark of the willow tree and finally dosed again. Some inner warning caused his eyes to suddenly pop open. Three Indians stood in a semicircle around him.

He gripped the handle of his six-shooter, then realized they were not wearing war paint. One of the Indians pointed to his dead horse and then to the remains of the two dead wolves. The Indians then came closer and looked at the splints he had put on his leg. The Indian spoke something in Apache, which Sam did not understand.

Seeing the water bag hung on the Apache's horse, Sam said, "Water."

The Apache looked at him, not understanding.

Sam pointed at his mouth. "Water."

One of the Apache said something. The warrior Sam had been trying to communicate with reached up and took down the water bag. He was careful to give Sam only a few drops at a time until Sam had drunk enough to satisfy his raging thirst.

Then they lifted Sam onto one of the horses. It was all he could do to keep from crying out, but he managed to grit his teeth and hang on. Sam thought, *I don't know what they plan to do with me. I hope they take me back to the village of Running Deer. This time I'll be coming in as a prisoner. I have no idea what that could mean.*

Just as they rode away, the sky burst open and another deluge of rain poured down.

CHAPTER FORTY-SEVEN
Searching for Sam

The party mounted up at first light and moved out. Joe Carville and Juan had drawn a crude map of the ranch. They assigned two riders to search each section. Joe Carville said, "When anyone finds Sam, fire three rifle shots in the air as a signal. Unfortunately, a hard rain fell during the night and wiped out any tracks Sam might have left."

Mr. Carville and Juan rode out together. Mattie Ann insisted that they allow her to ride along and help search. They had searched for about two hours when they stopped at a stream to water their horses.

"Juan, I never realized there are so many draws and creeks. Sam could be anywhere."

Juan shook his head sadly. "Senōr Carville, I think we are very close." His right hand pointed at the sky above the next ridge. He turned and glanced at Mattie Ann.

Joe Carville immediately recognized the thing Juan pointed at. The sky appeared to be filled with black buzzards.

"Mattie Ann, honey, why don't you rest here for a few minutes?"

"No Daddy. What are you talking about?" Then she spotted the vultures too. Without another word, she slammed the spurs to her horse and raced across the creek and up the hill.

All three horses topped the rise at the same time. At once, they saw that a horse was down. Juan whipped out his Winchester and started to shoot buzzards. After he had killed six, the rest of them flew up and started to circle overhead. Everybody recognized Buck at a glance.

Mattie Ann said, "Where's Sam?"

"Honey, I don't know, but the good news is he ain't here. When they rode up closer to the dead horse, Mr. Carville said, "I can tell you what happened. A rattler struck Sam's horse. Sam killed the snake and then shot his horse."

A COLLISION OF DREAMS

Mattie Ann said, "Then he may be alright, he is just on foot."

Juan sat studying the ground all around. He said, "I wish we had some tracks. Sam spent the night here. There are the ashes from his fire."

"Might have been late when the rattlesnake struck his horse and he didn't want to walk in the dark."

"Si senōr, over there I see what's left of two dead wolves. Sam was awake during the night. He must not be hurt too bad."

Mattie Ann took out her rifle. "Do I fire the three shots?"

"Not yet, honey. We have not found Sam. Let's let the rest of them keep looking—he might run into one of them."

"If he is walking back to the ranch, he would walk that way," Juan said, pointing to a peak off in the distance.

Each rider constantly searched for any sign of a man walking or any fresh tracks on the ground since the rain. Their ears strained to hear three rifle shots from one of the other teams. Mattie Ann thought, *We have to find him—in three days we are getting married.*

When they rode back into the ranch yard, three of the search teams were already there. Joe Carville said, "We found his horse. A rattlesnake struck the horse. Sam killed the snake but had to shoot the horse. We didn't find hide nor hair of Sam. Did you boys see any tracks at all?"

"We saw a bunch of cow tracks and a few deer, but that's all."

There were two more pairs of riders still out. Mattie Ann said, "Maybe they found Sam."

"Did you hear any rifle shots?"

"No."

"Slim, I want you to ride into town and see if we can get some more people to help us search. That boy is down out there somewhere and we've got to find him."

Spring was here. The days were balmy, with spring colors everywhere. Baby calves and colts showed up around the ranch. It

GEORGE DALTON

would have been a beautiful time if everyone wasn't so anxious to find Sam. How could a man just disappear without a trace? Juan rode the ridge line every day looking to the sky, watching for buzzards.

* * *

Sam. opened his eyes and looked around. He was lying on a bearskin. A young squaw spooned a strong-tasting broth into his mouth. When she saw his eyes open, she sat back and looked at him, then turned and said something in Apache over her shoulder. A large Indian dressed as a medicine man pulled back the flap on the tee-pee and entered. He reached down, put his hand on Sam's for head, and grunted. "Huh." Then he reached down and placed his palm on Sam's leg. He left it there for several seconds.

The medicine man took the bowl the young squaw had left there and fed the rest of the broth to Sam. "You are better. You sleep now. More sleep, then you ride again."

The next time Sam opened his eyes a fire burned in the lodge. He listened to the sounds and determined it was night. He was dying for a drink of water. He looked around and spotted a water bag hung near his head. He lifted himself up on one elbow to reach the bag and pull it to him.

When he lay back down, he was wide-awake. His mind was in a whirl. He remembered falling off his horse. Then tears filled his eyes as he remembered having to kill Buck. When he shifted to lie back down, severe pain exploded in his left thigh. The pain caused him to gasp. The sound brought a large brave armed with a war club to jerk back the flap and step into the lodge. He stood there a moment, then backed out. When the flap closed, Sam was alone again. He started to wonder, *What are they going to do next? Are they treating me so they can torture me later? You never know about Indians.*

Three weeks later he rode bareback on an Indian pony. He had lost a lot of weight, had long hair, and needed a shave. Sam rode into the yard at the Tumbling C. Mattie Ann saw him first and the door slammed open as she flew out. Tears streamed down her face as she leaped into his arms. "Where have you been? We looked everywhere for you."

She sobbed so hard he could hardly understand what she said. Sam held her close and said, "I'm sorry I'm late for the wedding." By then the yard was full of people.

Loco said, "Man, you walk slow. It took you over a month to get back here."

Sam had a hard time as he tried to shake everybody's hand because Mattie Ann didn't want to turn him loose. Rosa insisted that he come in and let her feed him.

Over lunch, Sam said, "I was daydreaming and a rattlesnake struck Buck. He bolted and threw me off. When I landed, I broke the big bone in my left leg. I was able to build a fire. I made some broth using bark I stripped form a willow tree and water from my canteen. During the night, wolves came and the next morning Indians picked me up at daylight. They took me back to the village and the medicine man set my leg. He cared for me until I could ride. Chief Running Deer gave me a pony and sent me home."

Mattie Ann and Rosa began the next morning, and got the wedding rescheduled. Sam and Juan spent each day trying to catch up on things at the ranch. Sam still favored his left leg, but overall it felt good to be working.

He rode over to the Tumbling C almost every evening. One day Mattie Ann said, "Sam, we are going to have the grandest wedding ever. I even have a cousin coming all the way from Denver City."

Two weeks later, Sam still walked with a slight limp. The couple was married. The wedding turned out to be better than the dream he'd had. Mattie Ann did look like an angel in her white gown. At the reception she said, "Sam, you've got to meet my cousin, she just came in on the stage last night."

"Sally Jo, let me introduce you to Sam."

When the young woman turned around Sam couldn't believe what he was seeing.

GEORGE DALTON

Sally Jo smiled and said, "Mattie Ann, I know your Sam. Do you remember the gallant brave cowboy I wrote to you about?" She reached out her gloved hand and said, "Hello Sam."

"You're the girl I met on the train?"

"One and the same. Now we are members of the same family."

"Well, you must have made the stage to Denver City alright."

"Yes, thanks to you. Oh, Mattie Ann, you should've seen your Sam, he was so gallant. He loaned me the money for a stage ticket on to Denver City. And Sam, while I'm here I want to repay the hundred dollars."

"Aw, you don't owe me anything. If I had known you and Mattie Ann were cousins, I would've brought you home with me."

"My aunt hired a lawyer and he found mother had left a will leaving all of Daddy's estate to me. He's selling the land, but I own five hundred head of the finest whiteface stock in the country. I would like to partner with a young rancher and bring them out here."

Sam and Mattie Ann finally arrived back to the Wild Horse Ranch as the sun slid below the hills on the west side of their valley. He carried her over the threshold into their new home. He didn't even limp.

Two days later, they met Sally Jo at a lawyer's office in Cactus Tree and signed a partnership agreement. They waited with her until it was time to board the stage back to Denver City. Before she boarded, she hugged Mattie Ann and Sam. She held him tightly for a moment then stepped onto the stage.

Mattie Ann slid across the buggy seat, wrapped her arms around his right arm, and said, "She likes you a lot, you know. I'm glad I found you first."

Three weeks later, Mattie Ann decided they needed to go into town because she wanted a few things. Sam harnessed the team to the buckboard her daddy had given them as a wedding present. They were singing as they road into Cactus Tree City. Out of habit, Sam slipped the thong off his six-shooter. She went into Mr. Barlow's store and Sam walked over to pay a visit to his friend the marshal.

He was almost to the marshal's office when a voice behind him said, "Turn around. So you can see who killed you. That pretty young wife of yours is fixin' to be a widow."

When Sam glanced up at the reflection in the window glass on the building in front of him, he recognized the young Taggert boy he had seen in Ma Taggert's kitchen the morning they ate breakfast there. He might have been just a kid, but the gun he held in his right hand with the hammer pulled back was full-grown.

Sam thought, I can't turn and draw quick enough to beat a cocked gun. I'm in trouble because there is no way I can turn and fire before he kills me. His next thought was, Poor Mattie Ann.

CHAPTER FORTY-EIGHT
The Rescue

He heard a loud thump followed by a rattle—it sounded like silverware in a kitchen drawer. He glanced back up in time to see Mattie Ann strike the boy over the head with her umbrella. The kid was so surprised he dropped the gun he held.

She said, "Now you get out of here. Don't you ever try to shoot my husband again. If you ever try anything like that again, I'll come out and visit your mama. Now get on your horse and go home."

She reached up, grabbed Sam's arm, and said, "Let's go home."

As he turned the buggy into his valley, Sam's chest swelled with pride. He looked at his ranch house set upon the knoll, his cows grazing in the valley, the tall corn he and Juan had planted. "Mattie Ann, I believe I'm the happiest man in the world. I've got you here beside me and we have our ranch. What a wonderful feeling."

"Don't you wish Father O'Sullivan from the boys' ranch could see you now?"

"Yes I do."

"When are you going after those cows of Sally Jo's?"

"I thought we would leave day after tomorrow."

"Where are you going to get wranglers to help with a herd that size? You and Juan can't drive a herd that large by yourselves."

"Well, I thought about that. There is a fort near where we are goin'. I wrote to the commander and some troops are mustering out next week. If we leave tomorrow or the next day, we should be able to get all the experienced horsemen we want right there at the fort. A lot of them will probably be comin' west anyway."

"Mr. Samuel McClanton, just when were you planning to tell me that you needed to ride off for a month?"

"Honey, I just picked up the letter from the commander today while we were in town."

Wrinkling up her nose, Mattie Ann said, "Let me look at the date on that letter."

Sam handed her the letter.

"Okay, it is dated last week. So you are off the hook."

"Well—I've been thinking. I want you to stay over at the Tumbling C while I'm gone. It'll take two days to get there on the train and three to four weeks to drive the herd. I don't want to leave you here while I'm gone. It'll be a lot safer for you at your daddy's place."

CHAPTER FORTY-NINE
Going for the Herd

Two days later, Sam and Juan dropped Mattie Ann at the Tumbling C. Mattie Ann had tears in her eyes when she said good-bye. "Sam, please don't let anything bad happen to you, I couldn't stand it."

When they left the ranch, they headed east to catch the train. They each brought two extra horses for the drive back.

"Senõr, how far to the train rails?"

"About two days east the tracks bend around the base of Skull Mountain and there's a watering tank there. Somebody has built a loading ramp by the water tank, so we can load the horses there if they have room for us."

"Do you still have the letter from the commander?"

"Yes."

"What day is the mustering out ceremony for the troops?"

"It is on the twenty-sixth."

"What day is today, senõr?"

"Twenty-first."

"Oh, mama-mia, that is only five days from now."

"Barring any trouble, we should be alright. We should reach the rails by tomorrow afternoon. Then the train travels over 700 miles in a day."

"Senõr, did you say 700 miles in one day?"

"Yes Juan. Remember, the train doesn't stop at night. It doesn't need rest like a horse."

Juan was quiet for a long time, and then he said, "Senõr, I am so happy we are herding the cows back. Juan would rather be riding a horse."

"I just hope we don't have any trouble out of that old man. Remember, he's the same one I whipped on the train that time."

A COLLISION OF DREAMS

* * *

Mattie Ann and Rosa were in the kitchen. Breakfast was done and they had a few minutes to kill before they started lunch. "Rosa, let's get a cup of coffee and just sit for a while."

Rosa said, "You sit. I've got a surprise for you." Mattie Ann sat on the porch and Rosa disappeared back into the kitchen. When she returned, she had a whole plate full of donuts."

"Oh my gosh, Rosa, if those cowhands see these bear signs you'll start a riot."

"I know, that's why I waited until they were all gone before I brought them out. After supper tonight they can have some."

"Rosa, I wonder who started calling donuts bear signs?"

"I don't know, but that's what the cowhands always call them. It don't matter what you call them, the boys sure wolf 'em down in a hurry." Rosa turned and looked at Mattie Ann, and asked, "Mattie Ann, are you happy?"

"Oh Rosa, Sam is wonderful, he is so strong and yet so gentle. We had a young heifer that was having a hard time delivering her first calf and Sam sat up with her all night. He wouldn't leave her side, kept talking to her, and trying to help pull the calf. Along toward daylight she finally delivered the calf. Now they are both doing fine."

"I knew Sam was a good man the first time I laid eyes on him, just like I knew your daddy was a good man the first time I ever saw him and your momma."

"He has only been gone for one day and already I miss him," Mattie Ann said. "I'll pray for him every single day until he gets back. I wonder where they're camping tonight?"

"Honey, there's no tellin'. They'll make camp somewhere over around five points, I would guess. Okay girl, we've been lolly-gaggin' long enough. I've got lunch to fix for a bunch of hungry cowhands who'll be coming back soon."

"Yes, but after lunch I have something to tell you."

***

After they broke camp and started east to the rails, they crossed a tree-covered ridge. Sam pulled up quickly. Before Juan could ask what was wrong, Sam pointed down the hill. "Those look like Blackfoot."

"They're wearing war paint."

"Juan, I wonder what they're doing this far from their hunting grounds?"

"Senõr, they're probably stealing horses, and we have six of the finest ones around."

Sam and Juan sat back under the tree line. The Indians rode single file from north to south about two hundred yards below. They had not spotted Sam and Juan back under the trees above. Both men slipped their rifles from their scabbards.

Sam spoke softly and said, "Juan, we can't make a run for it—they're between us and the rail. I count seventeen—that would be a handful for you and me to fight."

Juan whispered and said, "Senõr Sam, maybe they'll ride on by and not see us?"

"Let's hope. I would hate to see Mattie Anna become a widow this soon." Just as Sam said that, one of the lead horses whinnied.

Seventeen hard fighting men spun their heads in their direction at the same time.

Sam shouted, "Quick, get into those rocks over there."

The rocks backed up to a rocky cliff. An earthquake long ago had broken off part of the ridge, created a cluster of boulders, and left a sheer cliff thirty or forty feet high behind them. As the horses raced into the rocks, Sam slipped from the saddle and rolled over behind a large boulder with his rifle pointed back down the hill. Sure enough, seventeen mounted fighting men charged up the hill, in a perfect cavalry charge.

Some people might sit in their comfortable homes back east and lament the poor redskin, but they had never faced them in a pitched battle. The Indians were the best light cavalry the world had ever known. The sight on Sam's rifle centered on the big broad, muscular chest of an Indian in the middle of the charge. When he squeezed off a shot, the Indian flew off the back of his horse. Sam then moved his gun sight to the rider on the right and squeezed off another shot. A second Indian flew off his mount. At the same instant, Juan's rifle barked and a third Indian flew off his horse. Like magic, all of the horses suddenly ran with no riders on their backs, straight toward Sam and Juan.

"Juan, get ready. Don't look for an Indian where you saw one fall. They'll roll and come up somewhere else."

"We got three of 'em"

"That just means that there are fourteen left."

Sam and Juan were in a good position to defend. They had a downhill shot on an open field of fire. Out in front of the rocks the grass was short and didn't appear to offer a good place for the attackers to hide. Both men knew an Indian can hide where there is nothing to hide him. His brown skin and breechcloth can appear to melt right into the ground. You can't see him until he moves. All at once, the Indians charged. When they leaped up, they were much closer than when they went to ground.

When the first Indian came up off the ground, Sam had his sights right at that spot and drilled him dead center before he got off the ground good. Juan's rifle barked twice and then there was nothing to shoot at.

Both men reloaded their rifles and waited. Sweat trickled into their eyes and the salt stung. Sam took a small drink of water to replace what he was sweating out and waited. The sun was so hot the barrel of his rifle burned his hand when he touched it. Searching for targets, he saw a foot. He aimed just up from the foot and squeezed of another shot. An Indian screamed. The foot disappeared.

A shadow passed over him. He looked up and saw that buzzards were already circling. Sam wondered how those things always knew where and when a fight was going on. The buzzard knows that, no matter who wins the fight, in the long run he is going to win.

"Juan here they come." Indians just seemed to materialize right out of the ground. They were much closer to the rocks than before. Sam and Juan both opened fire at the same time. The Indians had changed tactics. Rather than all charge, some simply rose up and fired right into the rocks from where they were. Bullets ricocheted off the rocks around them. This disrupted Sam and Juan's ability to fire at the Indians who charged them.

"Senõr Sam that worked. We didn't get a single one of them. They'll do that again."

Juan saw a small bush move just a little and fired into it. An Indian straightened up and fell forward. All was quiet for a long time, then they saw three braves mount up on ponies and race away.

"Senõr Sam, are they leaving?"

"I don't think so. That's an old trick—three ride away while the rest lie in wait."

"Are they riding to get more help?"

"It could be."

All was quiet except for a sniper shot from time to time by the Indians. Rarely did Sam or Juan get a chance to return fire. There was just nothing to shoot at. Just before sundown, they charged again. Again, three or four sat back and racked the rocks with bullets when the rest came up out of the ground and raced toward the rocks where Sam and Juan were holed up. The chargers raced toward them and yelled at the top of their lungs. Their yells were designed to put fear in the defenders.

Sam had switched to his six-gun and opened fire at closer range with a barrage of pistol shot that stopped two Indians before they could get going. Juan was working his rifle as fast as he could work the lever. The attack broke off and there were no Indians to be seen. Sam slipped back to his saddlebag and dug out his extra six-shooter. He knew the next charge would be at close quarters.

CHAPTER FIFTY
A Scary Sound

Mattie Ann said, "Daddy, I have this awful feeling that Sam is in trouble. Can you pray for him again?"

"What makes you think he is in trouble? They have only been gone two days."

"I don't know—it's just a feeling that I have, but it's real."

Joe Carville got out of his chair and kneeled down beside her, placing his hand on her shoulder. He said, "Lord, we don't know where Sam is tonight, or what his needs are, but we lift him up to you. Lord, protect Sam and Juan from any harm that might befall them out there on the plains and in the hills tonight. Amen."

Mattie Ann hugged her daddy and said, "Thank you, Daddy. I love you and Sam so much; I couldn't bear it if something happened to either one of you."

"Mattie Ann, honey, he is just going to bring back a herd of cattle. The outlaw gang is locked up in prison so they can't bother him anymore for a long time, so I don't think you need to worry. I think it's time we went to bed. You look a little peaked, are you tired?"

"Yes a little, but I can't sleep as long as this feeling is so strong in me."

"Honey, remember when you were a little girl, how your momma would tuck you into bed and then have you say your prayers? Try that and I'll bet you will be asleep before you know it."

* * *

Sam wiped sweat from his palms on the front of his shirt. "Juan, soon it will be dark. Gather up all the wood you can find. I want to build a fire right here in front of these rocks. That way they'll have to come through the firelight to get to us. We'll move back out of the firelight."

While Sam kept a close eye out for the Indian's to charge again, or for a single brave who might try to creep up on him, Juan gathered up firewood and handed it to Sam. He started a pile right in front of the rocks. When they had a large pile of wood, Juan handed Sam a large handful of dried leaves. He threw them on the pile. Then Juan handed him a branch with dried leaves still attached. Sam pulled out his matches and lighted the leaves. Then he shoved the burning branch into the pile. The dried leaves burst into flames.

The evening erupted in gunfire. The Indians fired into the flames, hoping to scatter the fire. The sun slid down behind the hills in the west. In this part of the country, when the sun set it was dark. Light was created by the fire burning in front of the rocks. The bad news was that Sam and Juan couldn't see anything beyond the fire. They moved far back into the rocks so the Indians couldn't see them, but they couldn't see the Indians either.

"Senõr, Juan would sure like a cup of coffee right now."

"Yeah, that would be good. You better find some more wood for that fire because if we let it burn out, we may lose our hair." Juan scrambled back along the face of the cliff and returned with an armload of wood. Sam thought, *It's going to be a long night. The Indians probably won't attack during the night, but the advantage is with them. We have to stay awake and be on watch. They can lie out there and sleep, then they'll be refreshed and ready to attack at dawn. Without any sleep, we will not be as alert as we need to be. Then again, they might just slip away during the night. We have hit them pretty hard. They have taken some casualties. Maybe they'll decide the prize is not worth the cost.*

"Senõr, look what I found."

Sam looked and Juan carried a section of hollow log. "I have some rawhide in my saddlebags, and a pigging string." It took a few minutes to stretch the rawhide over the end of the hollow log and rosin up a pigging string.

"Senõr Sam, you better hold onto our horses. We don't want to walk out of here if this works."

Sam crept back to where their horses stood ground, hitched against the cliff face. He gathered up all of the bridles and lead ropes, and waited. All at once, the most bloodcurdling sound a man will ever hear started coming from the rocks in front of him. It was a good thing he held tight to those horses, because even then he almost lost them.

It was quiet for a few moments, them Juan cut loose again. When he stopped this time, they could hear several ponies race away down the hill.

"Juan, save that rawhide thing. That is twice you've saved my bacon with it. I swear, if you ever come upon me unexpected with it, I will shoot you."

"Do you think they are gone?"

"Yes, and so are we. I'm not goin' to wait around and see if they come back. Let's get mounted and find another camp somewhere else."

They left the fire burning because it was in the rocks and not likely to burn anything else. They made a dry camp a few miles farther east with no fire, hoping the Indians didn't trail them. With six horses, they left a trail a blind man could follow.

CHAPTER FIFTY-ONE
Juan's First Train Ride

Sam judged by the position of the sun that it was about three in the afternoon when they came to the water tower.

"Senōr Sam, I don't see any train."

"Stick your ear down on the rail—you can hear one if he's coming."

Juan jumped off his horse, kneeled down, and touched his left ear to the rail. He jerked back like he had been stung by a bee. Then he fanned his left ear, danced around, and cussed a blue streak in Spanish.

Sam only understood a few words, but it was enough to know that Juan was cussing him. Sam laughed so hard he almost dropped the lead rope he held. At that same time, a train whistle sounded in the distance.

As the big black steaming engine huffed to a stop, the engineer yelled down, "Where you boys heading?"

"To Illinois."

"Let us get some water and I'll pull up. Load your horses. You pay the conductor. He jerked his thumb toward the back of the train. It only took a few minutes for the brakeman to fill the water tank. The wheels creaked and groaned as the train inched forward until the stock car lined up with the loading shoot.

Juan's eyes darted everywhere at the same time as they walked into to riding train car. "Maybe Juan should ride with the horses. To make sure they are okay."

"No, you Mexican bandit. Sit down, you're going to be fine." Juan's face was glued to the window. His hands gripped the back of the seat in front of him until his knuckles started to turn white. After a few minutes of listening to the rhythm of the clickity-clack of the wheels on the rails and the gentle rocking motion of the swaying train car, he started to relax.

Soon they sped into a forest area. Juan said, "Senōr, I can't see the trees. They go by so fast they are like one tree."

"Juan, you count 'em. I'm goin' to take a nap."

They pulled into St. Louis as the sun peeked over the eastern horizon. The conductor came into the car. "Well fellas, this is as close as I can get you."

"Much obliged. We appreciate the ride."

They mounted up and headed for the lawyer's office. Sam needed to present the letter from Sally Joe.

A young, pretty secretary greeted them and said, "Can I help you?"

"Yes ma'am, we're here to see Mr. Harry Goodson."

"Is he expecting you?"

"He should have a letter telling him that we were coming."

"Your name, sir?"

"Sam McClanton."

"One moment, please."

As she walked away, Juan said, "Senōr Sam, the lady, she needs to listen to some of Juan's love songs."

"Okay, Don Juan. We came to get a herd of cattle. You ain't got time to do no singing. When a woman is pretty as she is, she's heard 'em all before anyway."

She returned in a moment, followed by a large man with blonde hair. He appeared to be about fifty. "Good morning, gentlemen. I did receive a letter from Sally Jo telling me to expect you. How is she'?'

"She's fine, sir. I'm Sam McClanton and this is my assistant, Juan Alvered."

"Won't you gentlemen come in?" He indicated an office in the back. After they had been seated, he handed an envelope to Sam, saying, "Here's the documents from me authorizing you to move the herd. I must warn you to expect trouble from her old stepfather. He can be a bit cantankerous."

"I've met him before," Sam replied.

A big smile crossed the lawyer's face. "Yes, I understand you have." He pulled out a hand-drawn map showing them how to get to the ranch were the cattle were being kept. "Anything else I can do for you gentlemen?"

"Well sir, if you could be so kind as to recommend a place to stay and tell us where to get a good steak tonight, we'd appreciate it. We plan to hire some soldiers who are mustering out at the fort. We need to spend the night here in town. We've got an appointment with the commander in the morning. It'll be the next day before we pick up the herd."

"I was wondering how you planned to move so many cows with only two of you. You show up with a group of ex-cavalrymen, he may not make any trouble. The old man is mean, but he's not stupid. He won't likely tackle a seasoned bunch of soldiers. Of course, you never know."

* * *

Joe Carville sent over a couple of hands to check on the ranch for Sam. They rode into the yard and the first thing they found was a mare struggling to give birth to a foal. The colt was trying to come out breach.

Loco said, "We've got to turn the colt if we can. Otherwise, it will die, and maybe the mother too."

"Aw man—I can't deliver any baby horse."

"Take your rope and tie it around the mare's head and then loop her front feet. Pull her down. As long as she is tied this way, she can't kick me."

Soon they had the young mare hobbled down. After a while, Loco said, "Man, we need to get her on the ground. I'm going to lay her down."

He moved to the opposite side of the struggling horse and, as gently as possible, laid her over on her side. After several more minutes he said, "All right—we've got us a little stud. Look at this guy."

A tall, gangly legged buckskin colt stood on wobbly legs and stared wild-eyed at them. "Now let the mother up. Slowly release the rope you've got looped to her feet."

"Loco, where did you learn to do all that?"

"We had to deliver all of the colts when I was growing up. We couldn't afford to lose even one."

The rest of the time they scouted around and found no other problems. Loco said, "They've got a great ranch here. Plenty of water, lots of shade and good grass. Look at that view of the valley. It is beautiful, so lush, and green with that stream winding through and trees all along the banks. With the wildflowers, the whole place is like a ten-mile-long garden."

"Sam must have 100 acres fenced off for feed, and the corn is as high as the bit in a horse's mouth. He'll have plenty of grain for the winter. I sure hope a prairie fire doesn't come along and wipe him out."

"Loco, I heard he's got water runnin' right into the house. They don't even need to walk outside to get a drink."

"You want to find out if that is true or not?"

"Yeah, man, I want see that." Each touched spurs to his horse and, side by side, they galloped to the stone house. Stopping next to the spring, they found the simplest yet most amazing thing. Loco pointed and said, "Would you look at that. Sam and Juan have rigged a wooden barrel to catch spring water as it comes out of the rocks. It fills up and they use copper tubing to form a pipe, which goes through the rock wall."

Loco kicked his boots out of the stirrups and jumped off his horse.

"Where're you goin'?"

"I got to find out where that thing comes out." He eased open the door and stepped into the kitchen. They found the copper tube sticking out of the wall over a dishpan. In the end of the pipe was a wooden plug. "Well, if those don't beat all. When you pull out the stopper, will the water run out?"

Loco said, "I don't know, let's try it."

The cowhand grabbed the piece of wood and jerked. A powerful stream shot out and hit him right in the face. He was so startled he stumbled backwards and fell in the middle of the floor. The water continued to spray on his chest and in his nose and eyes. Lying flat of his back, coughing and sputtering, he flopped around like a fish. He would've been cussing too, except he couldn't get his breath. He was drowning, or at least he thought he was.

Loco snatched up the plug the cowhand had dropped and plugged it back in to shut off the water. He said, "Look here—there is a hole drilled in the bottom of the pipe. You don't need to take the plug all the way out. Pull it out just a little and the water runs right into the pan."

The other cowhand had regained his ability to talk and was sheepishly getting up. He said, "Loco, I swear if you ever tell anybody about this I will skin you."

"What—do you think I would spread the word about how you took a bath in Sam's kitchen and it ain't even Saturday night?"

CHAPTER FIFTY-TWO
Sally Jo's Stepfather

On a warm spring day, a guard escorted the Taggert gang into the warden's office. When the gang was all standing at attention around his desk, the warden said, "Men, my prison is getting crowded. Far as I can tell, you didn't rob any banks or kill anybody. None of you has caused any trouble since you've been here. I made a recommendation to the governor for ya'll to be paroled."

This statement was followed by a few moments of confused silence. Randolph Taggert finally said, "What do you mean?"

"I'm gonna let you and your boys out of prison today." He pointed his finger at Randolph and said, "Here is the deal. For the next nine years, you will be on parole. You can go home, work the farm, and take care of your families. If you get into any trouble with the law, you're gonna end up right back here in prison for nine more years."

"You mean we can walk out of here today?"

"Soon as you sign or put your mark on these pledges. You hereby pledge to obey all laws at all times. You further promise not to rustle any more cattle in this territory. Should you violate this parole in any way, I'll slap you right back in here, and you won't get out for any reason before the nine years are up. Am I making myself clear?"

Every Taggert man nodded his heads energetically, especially the younger ones. Each made his mark on the paper. They were given their personal things, and then a guard ushered them out of the prison as free men. As soon as they were on the outside, Randolph said, "Now we're gonna go kill us a sidewinder."

One of the younger boys said, "Pa, didn't you understand what the warden said? He told us if we broke any more laws, they would put us back in prison for a long time."

"Hush your mouth boy. We got a debt of honor to settle. All of our troubles started when Sam McClanton rode up on Joe Bob while he was re-branding a steer and shot him dead. We was doing just fine rustling a few head here and there from the big outfits before that. I've been sittin' in a cage like an animal for nigh on to a year and I figured out a plan. We're gonna kill him and then move on to Californy. Here's how it's gonna work."

* * *

Two days later, Sam and Juan rode out from the fort with four seasoned troopers who had hired on for the drive. Sam told them, "Now guys, if we run into any trouble when we get there to get the cows, let me handle it. You keep 'em off my back."

It was mid-morning when they rode into the yard at the ranch where they had been instructed to gather up the cattle. An old man and three tough-looking hombres were standing there. "You boys can just turn around and get. You got no business here." He leaned forward and spit a large brown stream of tobacco juice onto the ground.

All of Sam's party stayed in the saddle except Sam. He stepped down and said, "Sir, I have a letter from the court authorizing me to pick up five hundred and twenty-three head of whiteface cattle and deliver them to my ranch." He held the letter in his left hand.

"I don't care what you've got, all you're gonna get is a belly full of lead if you don't climb back on that horse and get out right now."

"No sir, I can't do that. I was sent by Sally Jo, and this letter signed by the judge and her attorney authorizes me to get five hundred and twenty-three whiteface cows. I will not leave without them."

The old man's eyes narrowed and he said, "I know you, you are the smart aleck from the train." He spit another big stream of tobacco juice. His hand flashed down for a gun as he spit another stream of tobacco juice. Sam expected him to do something like that. Sam slapped the butt of his forty-four and the pistol sprang into action before the tobacco stream actually landed on the ground. Two bullet holes appeared in the center of the man's chest.

Turning with the still-smoking gun in his hand, he asked, "Do any more of you boys want to argue with our claim?"

All of the guys standing in front of Sam looked at their hole card and didn't like what they were holding. They had seen this man palm a six-shooter and put two bullets in the center of a shirt pocket before a stream of tobacco juice could hit the ground. Four salty-looking troopers and one tough little Mexican backed him.

One of the men standing next to the dead body lying in the dust said, "No sir, if'n you've got the papers, we ain't got no argument. Indicating the old man on the ground, one of them said, "He told us he had a no-count step-daughter gonna send some guys to steal his herd. I recon he orta examined them papers a little closer. If you gents got no objection, I got business somewhere else."

Sam nodded and all of the men mounted up and rode off at a good clip. One of the troopers turned to the rest and said, "Did you see what I saw? He palmed a forty-four and put two bullets in a space no bigger than a silver dollar. Before the old man's tobacco juice hit the ground."

One of the other troopers said, "I think we've got ourselves a boss we can work for. Let's get to rounding up the dogies."

As the sun slid behind the western horizon, they made camp about twelve miles west on good grass near a stream. They passed north of the town of St. Louis. Sam rode in and met with the lawyer. Sam gave him what little money the old man had on him and asked if it could be forwarded on to his next of kin.

The lawyer said, "Well, the funny thing is, Sally Jo may legally be his only beneficiary."

"If that's the case, give the money to one of the churches here in town. She doesn't need anything from him."

"Sam, I think you're right. I'll check and, if she is his next of kin, I'll give it to Saint Luke's. That's where Dr. Ackerman was a deacon."

Every day turned out to be a grind, from sunup until dark. Sam had picked up some extra horses and an Indian boy to look after them. They ended up with a pretty good remuda, but each day was grueling, with dust covering the backs of the cattle and their clothing—it even got into the pot of beans they cooked.

After a few days, the cattle got broken to the trail and the physical stress was a little easier. At least now trying to keep the herd bunched was not killing the horses. On the third day, an old mossy horned steer stepped out and took the lead. Sam rode point, the others taking turns riding drag because the person behind the herd had to eat a lot of dust.

Sam glanced at the old steer and said, "Okay big fellow, take us home."

One of the troopers turned out to be a pretty good cook. After two days on the trail, they crossed over into Oklahoma territory. Sam told Juan, "Move up to point. I'm going to get us some fresh meat. I saw a bunch of antelope back on the ridge."

Sam had been gone about two hours. A group of hard cases charged up out of a draw. Juan pulled up and stopped. "Hey Mexican, we're going to cut your herd. You came through our land back there. We think you've got some of our stock mixed in with yours."

"No senõr, these cows all belong to Mr. Sam McClanton. These are all whiteface. We got no longhorn cows in the bunch."

"Listen, you little greaser, we didn't say we had longhorn cows. We said you've gathered up some of our cows. I didn't say what kind of cows, now did I boys?"

One of the troopers was an ex-sergeant. He had been working the right flank when he recognized what was happening. He spurred his horse around a little knoll and rode up behind them on their left. In all of the noise of the bawling cattle and their concentration on Juan, they didn't notice him ride up. They couldn't miss the unmistakable sound of a hammer being pulled back on a rifle.

"Now boys, seems to me there's been a slight mistake. This ain't the herd you're looking for. That Mexican fellow is slicker than greased lightning with a six-shooter and I will empty at least two saddles before you can turn around. So here's what we're going to do. Real easy like, each one of you drop those gun belts down on the ground. Now be real careful when you drop 'em 'cause this old Sharp's got a touchy trigger. Should I get nervous, somebody's breakfast is going to get splattered all over half the Oklahoma territory."

Observing the confrontation, two other troopers spurred their horses and rode up on the left and right corners of the herd with rifles drawn. The would-be cow thieves in front of Juan caught the sound of hammers being clicked back on those other two rifles. Juan reached down, took the thong off his six-shooter, and said, "What we have here is a Mexican stand off. You better do what the sergeant said."

One of the hotheads said, "I'll be damned if I'll give up my gun," and reached for his gun.

CHAPTER FIFTY-THREE
The Shoot-Out

Juan slapped his palm on the butt of his six-shooter and fired at the same instant the troopers cut lose. A wild melee ensued with guns firing, and in a few seconds all four outlaws lay on the ground.

"Sergeant, do you want to take time to bury 'em?"

"No, they don't deserve a Christian burial. Throw them over in the gulley they came out of and let the buzzards have them. Take their guns and turn the horses in with the rest of the remuda." He turned to Juan. "Juan, you shook that iron out pretty fast yourself. Have you and the boss been practicing?"

"Last winter me and Senõr Sam, we had a competition every day to break the monotony. He usually won."

* * *

Sam tied the haunch of meat behind his saddle and started to mount up. He thought he heard gunshots off in the distance. The wind was flowing toward the herd so he was not sure if he heard gunshots or not. He thought, *I'd better get mounted and go check it out.* Topping the rise about a mile further down the trail, he could see a bunch of buzzards.

His horse dipped down into a small canyon and he lost sight of the circling birds. Climbing out the other side, he could see the dust from the herd hanging like smoke in the air.

An hour later, Sam rode in with the haunch of an antelope over the rump of his horse. "About two miles back I saw some buzzards circling close to the trail of the herd. I rode over to find out what they were circling and I found four rough-looking characters shot up like the rag dolls in a shooting gallery, down in a gulley. What happened?"

One of the troopers spoke up. "Boss, those four tried to cut the herd. Juan here stood up to them. The sergeant flanked them and told

A COLLISION OF DREAMS

them to drop their gun belts and ride on somewhere else. Me and McKinsey both realized there was trouble. So we rode up to the front of the herd, him on one corner and me on the other. We both shucked our rifles. One of them fools tried to draw on Juan. Everybody started shooting, and when it was over, there wasn't any of them left. We did keep their guns and turned their horses in with the remuda."

"Well, I'd say you fellows handled the situation well. Let's broil us an antelope steak."

For the next three weeks, all day everyday they ate dust, rode half-broke horses, swam rivers, and kept pushing west by southwest. On the twenty-third day, Sam recognized the mountains on the horizon. He rode back to where Juan was working and pointed to the mountains. "We'll be home by tomorrow night. There's a stream about a mile ahead of us. Let's cross the stream before we camp for tonight. No reason to push the herd today since we're this close to home."

With the cattle broken to the trail, the drive was easier, except for the dust. Now they only needed one rider circling the herd at night, so the rest of the guys sat around the campfire and yarned. One of the troopers pulled out a harmonica and they sang off-key cowboy songs. Once someone said, "Listen."

They got quiet, and then they heard the trooper singing to the cows. "He's singing along with us."

The laughed when one of them said, "Yeah, but he sounds better from out there."

The stories started again, about the toughest broncos, the worst storms, the meanest steers. Finally, one by one they turned in. Sam added some more logs on the fire to make sure there would still be coals in the morning. He stretched out on his bedroll and thought of Mattie Ann. *Just a few more days, if nothing else happens, and I'll see my Mattie Ann.* He lay there a little longer and thought, *It sure seems a lot longer than a month since we left her. I sure hope she's all right.*

Finally, he drifted off to sleep and dreamed of his wife. In his dream, they had two little kids—a little boy and a beautiful little girl who seemed to be just like her mother. He woke with a start. *What is the matter with me? I shouldn't be dreaming about kids.*

The next morning, Sam said, "Juan, can you and the boys bring the herd on in without me? I've got a feeling something ain't right. I want to ride on up to the Tumbling C and make sure Mattie Ann's alright. You bring 'em on in, will ya?"

"Si senõr, no problem, the men are good at their jobs and the cows are getting gentle. We'll bring 'em home."

After breakfast, they climbed into the saddle and got the cattle lined out, with the old mossy horned steer leading the way. Sam cantered off toward the ranch. He had to force himself not to run the horse. The distance was a good ten miles, and running it would kill a mustang.

The suspense was killing him. He sang songs to get his mind on something else. His mood lightened a little when he rode near a big old cottonwood tree and listened to a lone robin singing in clean, sweet tones, complimenting the neighborhood.

The sun indicated the time to be about noon when he stopped at a stream and watered the horse. He moved a little way upstream and lay down on the bank and drank some of the coldest, clearest, best-tasting water he had ever tasted. He thought, *The spring this comes from must be close by.*

Mounting up, he started up a rise to the south, thinking, *I'm closer to my place than the Tumbling C. Maybe I need to swing by there first and make sure everything is okay before I go get Mattie Ann. I can't be more than a couple of miles from the ranch house now.*

He topped the hill near his ranch, and his breath stopped. What he witnessed sent cold chills through his system. Trees were uprooted and scattered around like a child's toys. The barn was gone...the bunkhouse was gone...the roof of the house was gone...the windows were gone.

A COLLISION OF DREAMS

"What happened?" All at once, it hit him—a twister had come through.

The stonewalls were the only thing still standing. He sat in the saddle, pressed his fingers to his temples, and moaned. "This is the last straw. I can't take anymore. All of my work is gone. All of my hopes and dreams for a home and family are gone. I can't take care of Mattie Ann. I have nothing left."

Even though the temperature hovered around ninety degrees, he felt incredibly cold sitting there looking at the devastation. Finally, he said, "I'm going to touch spurs to this horse and run away and just keep riding."

All at once, he spotted an old man standing by the side of his destroyed home. He appeared to be a prospector. The man spoke up and said, "Sam, you can't run away. Juan will be here before sundown with almost six hundred head of cattle. You are responsible for another hundred in the bowl, when you count the calves. You not only gave your word to take care of Mattie Ann, you signed a contract with another beautiful young lady who is counting on you."

Sam stared at him and said, "Mister, do I know you?"

"Well I kept your fire going all night in a cave behind the waterfall. I showed you how to find your way home in a snowstorm. I had a jaybird watch over you one night so you could get some sleep. I sent three young braves to take you to their village so their medicine man could fix your leg. I also arranged for all of them." He pointed to the trail.

Sam turned and looked to the east and didn't believe his eyes. Over the hill came a long line of wagons. Sam looked and saw that Joe Carville drove the lead wagon. Mattie Ann sat beside him. There must have been a hundred people in the wagons and on horses. They pulled up and Joe said, "Sam, some old man came and told us what had happened to your place." He swung his right arm back and pointed toward the others. "We're here to do an old-fashioned barn raising."

Mattie Ann held out her hand to him and Sam lifted her off the wagon. He put his arm around her and stared as his neighbors jumped down from their wagons with axes, saws and all kinds of tools.

One of the men walked up to him and said, "I'm Pastor Jacobs. These are your neighbors. Once they knew what happened to your home, they came here to help you rebuild."

Soon the ladies had one of the doors off of his barn lying across two sawhorses the men had hastily made for them. They spread food on the make-shift table. The atmosphere had the feel of a carnival. Work was quickly in full swing everywhere. You could hear axes ringing all down the valley.

Sam glanced at the women putting food on the table. He couldn't believe it. The Taggert women were there. Mattie Ann kissed him on the cheek and left him.

The rest of the day, she was everywhere working and supervising. She smiled at him several times, and he caught himself grinning back. He thought, *She is beautiful. But something about her looks different.*

By late afternoon, the barn had been raised and the roof was on the house. There was no glass in the windows yet—that would need to be ordered. They did put shutters back on the windows.

One by one, the neighbors said goodbye and loaded their tools onto the wagons. The last one to load up was Pastor Jacobs. He walked over and shook Sam's hand. "God bless you, Sam. I hope we can see you in church soon."

"Yes sir, you will."

Sam looked up and there was the herd coming over the ridge. Mattie Ann had walked over and stood beside him. She reached down and took his hand in hers. Sam put his arm around her shoulders and said, "Mattie Ann that is a beautiful sight."

She tilted her head to look him in the eye and said, "Prettier than me?" Before he could answer, she said, "Sam, that's not all. Look at the new colt in the corral."

He turned toward the corral and thought, *My eyes must be deceiving me.* Standing with his head though the bars was a young stud with a black mane and black tail—a perfect buckskin horse with the same markings as Buck. She snuggled against him and said, "Well, it appears old Buck left you a present."

Sam remembered the old man. He looked for him, but he was nowhere insight. He thought, *It seems he is always around when I really need him.*

CHAPTER FIFTY-FOUR
Revenge is Sweet

Randolph said, "Now that we are out of prison, first we're gonna steal some horses. Then we are goin' to hold up a couple of stagecoaches and get us some travelin' money. After we get home, one of you boys is gonna watch his place. Sooner or later, he'll go to town for supplies. When he does, we're gonna catch him on the way to town and get the drop on him and take them guns of his. After that, I'm gonna take this old Arkansas toothpick and cut him up. He killed some of ours so I'm gonna see he dies real slow."

"Pa, I don't want to go back to no prison. Let's just let him be."

"You shut up, boy. We've got us an honor debt and it hast'a be paid."

Ma spoke up and said, "Pa, listen to the boy. Half of that hillside is covered with the graves of our kin. I don't want to bury any more of my boys on that hill. If you succeeded in killin' him—and that's for sure not certain—everybody in the territory will know you did it. The marshal will be back out here quick, only this time they'll hang you."

"No, here is my plan. The territorial border is only twenty miles away. We'll load up everything we want to take with us and camp out here until we get him. It'll take the marshal a while to round up a posse and ride out here. By the time they get here, we'll be gone and they can't touch us once we get out of their territory."

"Pa, this ain't right. Let me tell you what he did while you were in prison. We had a big blizzard, and we ran out of food. Me the kids was starvin'. He killed one of his own steers, loaded the meat onto a sled, and brought it all the way out here, to feed your grandkids. He wrapped the beef in burlap and hung it up in the barn away from the varmints. We had food all winter by eating his beef."

"Ma, can't you see nothin'? That was just a bribe. He's trying to butter us up so I won't kill 'im. It ain't gonna work. I'm gonna kill 'im."

A week later, the oldest Taggert son raced his horse into the yard at a full gallop. He leaped down and dashed through the back door. "Pa, he and his missus just got in the buckboard and headed for town."

Randolph sat and stared at the fireplace for a moment before he said, "If'n he's got the lady with him, we'll wait until he gets to there. She'll go do the shoppin' and he'll go get a drink at the Silver Spur. We ain't killin' no woman. Folks would trail us all the way to Californy if we did."

* * *

Sam halted the team in front of the mercantile, then jumped down and lifted his wife out of the carriage.

"Sam, you go on over and have a drink. I'll tell Mr. Barlow what we need. I'll walk over to Aunt Millie's shop and check on her. Don't get into any trouble." She reached up and lightly kissed him.

She gave her order to Mr. Barlow. Rather than walking directly over to the millinery store, she went to see the doctor. He examined her and said, "Yes Mattie Ann, you are definitely pregnant." He sat and chewed on the leg of his glasses for a moment, then said, "Does Sam know?"

"Not yet."

"Mattie Ann, your heart is a lot stronger than last time I saw you. Be careful and get plenty of sunshine and rest. I don't think you will have any problems. Do you have a milk cow?"

"Yes."

"Drink lots of milk and come see me every month."

* * *

Sam's spurs jangled as he walked into the Silver Spur. A long time ago, he had developed the habit of stopping before entering any saloon. He slipped the thong off the hammer on his six-gun with his right thumb. With his left hand, he eased open the bat wing doors. The first thing he noticed was how dark and cool the room was. He stepped through and paused inside the door to allow his eyesight to adjust to the difference in light. After his sight had adjusted, he observed three men standing at the bar and eight more cowhands lounging at tables scattered around the room. In six long strides, he bellied up to the polished wood bar.

The bartender said, "Morning. What'll it be?"

"How about a beer? That's all I need."

A foamy mug swished down the length of the polished bar top, sliding expertly to a stop right in front of him.

Sam took a sip of the warm and sudsy but tasty beer as he listened to the slightly out of tune piano and the buzz of conversation around him. The room had the peaceful, relaxed, and comfortable manly smell of a western bar. He recognized the smell of spilt beer, cigarette smoke, and working men. It was a place to relax and listen to the latest news from around the territory.

All at once, Sam heard the bat wing doors fly open, and felt tension fill the air. The sound level noticeably dropped. He glanced up at the big mirror behind the bar and was startled to find a familiar group of men staring at him. He counted five salty looking characters. Randolph Taggert stood in the center of the gang.

Sam said, "Hello, Mr. Taggert. I thought you were still in prison. You rustled any more cattle lately?"

"Well, we're not in no prison," Randolph Taggert said, "and we've come to give you what you've got ah comin'."

Sam sensed the men on each side of him moving away as he slowly turned his back to the bar and faced them.

Taggert said, "We're gonna kill you. I'm gonna do it with this knife." His hand held a long knife that looked razor-sharp. "So you die real slow."

A COLLISION OF DREAMS

Sam still held the beer mug in his right hand. He threw the mug overhand like a baseball and hit old man Taggert right in the face, then kicked the bar stool on his right in front of the two men that tried to grab him from the right. Slipping inside the perilous right thrown by the closest man on his left, Sam smashed a right into the outlaw's ribs, and then threw a beautifully timed punch that landed solidly. Sam rolled and hooked a left into the face of another gang member that came at him from the other side. For a brief violent moment, Sam was swinging both fists with all his might into the two men in front of him until a powerful blow hit him in the back of the neck and flashes of light shot through his head.

Sam jerked back his right elbow and connected with somebody right before two powerful hands grabbed both of his arms and shoulders and pinned him to the bar. As the light flashes cleared in Sam's head, he was able to see old man Taggert with a wicked grin on his face and the knife in his hand.

"You boys hold him a minute. I'm gonna gut him like a hog."

Sam lifted his right foot and kicked Taggert in the stomach, pushing him back and knocking the breath out of him. One of Taggert's men slammed a wicked blow to Sam's midsection. Another man grabbed a chair and pinned Sam's feet and legs to the bar as Sam tried desperately to kick the chair away.

Old man Taggert had regained his breath now, and he was roaring mad.

"Now, by gawd, I'm gonna kill you." Taggert reached up and cut Sam on the shoulder, drawing blood.

As Sam looked down at his own blood running down the front of his shirt, he thought, *I have always known my life would end like this.* His mind then turned to thoughts of Mattie Ann and the life they had planned. With one final effort, he tried to jerk free. When he tried, they slammed him back against the bar. Sam could see was the sunlight reflecting off that gleaming knife blade. He saw the swirling dust particles in the light from the window. He knew fear for the first time in his life.

All at once, a gunshot exploded in the room. Sam felt pain in his ears from the concussion. Old man Taggert spun around and found he was staring right down the barrel of a smoking .44.

The gun was held in his wife's right hand. She looked him right in the eye and said, "Me and the womenfolk have got the wagons right outside. You turn that man loose and get in the wagon. We're leavin' this territory."

Taggert, still in a rage, said, "Woman, you get the hell out of here, this's man's business. I'll deal with you later. Right now, I'm fixin' to kill him."

Everybody in the room recognized the unmistakable metallic click of the cocking of the hammer on a pistol. "Randolph Taggert, you're not gonna make my boys hang for a murder you did. I've got this forty-four aimed right at your head, and if you don't turn him lose your brains are gonna be painting that wall on the bar behind you. You know I can shoot because you taught me. I'll kill you before I let you get my boys hung. Now you turn him lose and get in the wagon or by all that's holy I'm gonna kill you."

Tears were streaming down the face of Taggert's wife as she held the gun in her hand, which trembled slightly. No one could mistake the look in her eyes. The ticking of the grandfather clock filled the room and the men were not even breathing.

The big clock ticked—tick-tock, tick-tock. Finally, one of the boys said, "Pa, she ain't bluffin'."

Sam watched as Taggert slowly lowered the knife. The four men who held him released and backed away. Taggert and four men with hangdog looks on their faces slowly eased out the front door as a stern-faced old lady stood there with a cocked .44 aimed their way.

As Ma Taggert turned and looked at Sam, he thought, *Now she's gonna shoot me.* She slowly lowered the gun and said, "Mister, you done a good thing feedin' my babies last winter. We won't be botherin' you anymore. Would you do one thing for me?"

"Yes ma'am, if I can."

"Go by every spring and put flowers on my babies' graves for me."

"Yes ma'am, I'll see it gets done."

She lowered the hammer on the pistol and, head held high like a grand lady, she walked out to the lead wagon and climbed aboard. Would she have shot her husband? Yeah, Sam thought she would.

A few minutes later, Sam had all the supplies loaded in the buckboard when Mattie Ann walked up. She noticed the blood on his shoulder. "What happened? You have blood on your shirt."

He glanced at his shoulder and said, "Must have scratched myself while I loaded the supplies. Are you ready to go? You find anything interesting?"

"Sam, let's go. I do have a surprise for you. I'll tell you all about it on the way home."

ACKNOWLEDGMENTS

I want to thank some special people with which this story could never have been told.

Thank you to Shirley Smith, my most encouraging reader, Frank Ball my teacher, Jan my loving critic, and all of the members of the North Texas Christian Writers Association for your encouragement.

My kids, grand kids who are my cheerleaders.

And to God, who puts a book in all of us.

CPSIA information can be obtained
at www.ICGtesting.com
Printed in the USA
FSOW02n0646120416
19103FS